HOW DO YOU CHOOSE BETWEEN
THE LOVE OF YOUR LIFE
AND THE PASSION OF A LIFETIME?

He is an art history professor. She is a translator. He is married to a woman who sleeps with his best friend and jogs everyday to outrun her fears. She is married to a man who is obsessed with success. They both have children.

Slowly, sensuously, something wonderful and dangerous slips into the space between them. Call it passion. Call it infidelity. But with rare storytelling grace, Ellen Schwamm makes their reckless clandestine affair into an intensely moving experience of vitalizing love.

ADJACENT LIVES is being married, having children, and leading a double life. It is the bright New York world of arts and letters, with all its romantic perils. It is the struggle between secret adjacent lives and the deep pull of separate family lives. And it is having to choose between the love of your life and the passion of a lifetime.

"A LOVELY WORK OF ART. . . . Beautifully written, ADJACENT LIVES is an impressive first novel, a contemporary love story brimming with generosity and wisdom."

Library Journal

"TREMENDOUS EMOTIONAL INTENSITY. . . . She describes lovemaking poetically, even romantically . . . a book of extraordinary depth and accomplishment."

Women's Wear Daily

ADJACENT LIVES

ELLEN SCHWAMM

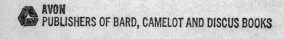
AVON
PUBLISHERS OF BARD, CAMELOT AND DISCUS BOOKS

Grateful acknowledgment is made to the following for permission to reprint previously published material:

Doubleday & Company, Inc.: Excerpt from "The Longing," Copyright © 1962 by Beatrice Roethke, Administratrix for the Estate of Theodore Roethke, from *Collected Poems of Theodore Roethke*. Used by permission of Doubleday & Company, Inc.

Farrar, Straus & Giroux, Inc.: Excerpt from "Message" from *Love & Fame* by John Berryman, Copyright © 1970 by John Berryman. Reprinted with the permission of Farrar, Straus & Giroux.

The New Yorker: Excerpt from the poem "Mr. T. S. Eliot Cooking Pasta" by József Tornai (Translated, from the Hungarian, by Richard Wilbur.) in *The New Yorker*.

AVON BOOKS
A division of
The Hearst Corporation
959 Eighth Avenue
New York, New York 10019
Copyright © 1978 by Ellen Schwamm
Published by arrangement with Alfred A. Knopf, Inc.
Library of Congress Catalog Card Number: 77-19317
ISBN: 0-380-45211-1

First Avon Printing, September, 1979

AVON TRADEMARK REG. U.S. PAT. OFF. AND IN
OTHER COUNTRIES, MARCA REGISTRADA,
HECHO EN U.S.A.

Printed in the U.S.A.

FOR JAY

Adjacent may or may not imply contact but always implies absence of anything of the same kind in between.

Webster's Collegiate Dictionary, 1961

CHAPTER

1

HER INTENTION IS TO ARRIVE EARLY TO AVOID CONFUSION, but a detail detains her at home. There is the usual human disorder connected with a first day. The crowd is thick, sluggish, noisy. She senses, however, a feebleness in the uproar. They are massed for individual purposes only. This gives her courage. She joins them, arms pinned to her sides, and allows herself to be carried toward the bank of elevators.

She is late. She has never been late before. Six years of being on time. The lecture has already begun. She moves to her seat, the seat she has occupied for all these years, the particular seat that has assumed the contour and shape of a home. After so many years her spine has molded to its curve. From her point of view the seat is well located. She chose it for its location. From it she can see and remain unseen. He will never raise his eyes, has never raised them to the extreme rear of the room. She can repeat the course for the next decade and never arouse his attention. Hers is one of a hundred changing faces each semester.

She squeezes her way along a narrow corridor of legs, whispering excuse me as she goes. Only when she arrives at her seat does she see that it is already taken. That every seat in the row is taken. That every seat in the hall is taken. She is trapped in the middle of a nightmare. Her legs churn but she remains in place. An intense localized whispering erupts around her. She understands what is being asked but she is unable to move from the worn

9

flooring in front of her rightful place. There is nowhere to go.

After a moment, she realizes she is being offered an alternative. "Please come down to the front," he says and beckons her with a hand. "There are a few seats in the front row. Dead center, in the eye of the storm." His hand assumes the shape of an arrow.

She backs out of the row, her row, and begins the long humiliating descent. With each step she takes, he grows larger. When, finally, she arrives at her new place he is fully life-size. She narrows her eyes and tries shrinking him in order to see him again as he has appeared to her for the past six years. A brilliant, irreverent, doll-sized presence. It doesn't work. The perspective is all wrong. She is too close. Perspective is supposed to increase one's sense of reality, not diminish it. A lecture of his, many years ago, on Dürer's contribution to civilization. A lecture that caused, still causes her to suffer. Dürer is to be admired, yes, but with restraint, because essentially his curiosity did not extend beyond appearances to causes, in contrast, say, to Leonardo, who was interested in both. Though she is of a lesser order of human beings she knows that this distinction applies equally to her, and she is left feeling hopelessly limited.

She looks up. There is a stranger in front of her. For years she has been deceived by distance and a flattened retina. The light which emanated from him she took to be him. From the back row he appeared dark and featureless. In the large white space he looked to be quite small. She widens her eyes and forces herself to see him. She sees that he is quite tall, pleasantly thin, loosely jointed, appropriately rumpled, blue-eyed hawk-faced, restless, energetic and confident. The brain has acquired bone and flesh, that is all. Still, she cannot quite make the adjustment required of her under his tutelage: To move toward the new image, to go with it all the way in order to remove the strangeness and, hence, the threat.

He looks dead ahead. He lectures as usual without seeing, his audience a blur. Gradually his eyes are drawn to her. Her total attention to him rivets him. The intensity of her concentration breaks his. Her hair is jet black and crenulated. She has narrow brown eyes and cheekbones that curve back on themselves like scimitars. A Russian cza-rina. He is given to descriptive excesses. Her face is un-usual. Not to everyone's taste. Not young but girlish. Familiar. Why familiar? He stores faces along with paint-ings in the file of his mind to pull them out when he needs them, a gift which rarely fails. He is interested in the process of visualization. A close friend, a physicist, is un-able to visualize at all, which intrigues them both and has started him off on an investigation. She is not in his file but he knows the face. It nudges at him all through the lecture.

"Have you taken this course before?" he asks later as she struggles into her coat. He reaches forward to help her with a dangling sleeve. He is still trying to place her.

"Yes," she answers, backing off.

He sees a red flush seep under her skin. "May I ask your name?"

"My name?" She sounds incredulous.

"Yes," he says. "Your name." He is now so close to her that she is pressing back against her chair. He is afraid that her knees will buckle and that she will tumble. He can see that dignity is important to her. It brings out the clown in him.

"Mrs. Barnes." She throws the name up in front of her like a shield.

"Do you have a first name, Mrs. Barnes?" There is a trace of mockery in his voice. Her skin flames again, her chin tilts at a vulnerable angle and he is instantly sorry for having taken advantage of her.

"Natalie," she answers so softly that he is not sure he has actually heard it. If he has, he would change the end-ing. She looks like a Natalia.

"I promise I won't use it." He laughs and sees that he has only made things worse.

"Thank you." She flees up the stairs.

"Thank you?"

But she has mingled with the hundred others and is gone.

Natalie notes with relief that she is the first to arrive. She claims her old seat in the last row, covers its back with her coat, places her pocketbook squarely across its desk arm and tries not to think of the last class. She has not allowed herself to think about it. She has kept herself busy all week with her ailing grandmother. She lowers herself into her seat with economy and care. She tries never to take more than her share of space, and resents those who do. In this she is a crank. When her family teases her about it, she is disturbed. She cannot understand why anyone who objects to the trespasses of modern life in the name of a better life should be maligned, even in fun. She is not swayed by fun or by teasing. She goes on objecting.

He thinks about her occasionally during the week. He arrives fifteen minutes early which is unusual. Normally he is late, not late enough to give offense but late in the way of otherwise sensitive people whose lives are somewhat beyond their control, people who are always rushing from one important moment to another. He does not feel important. He cultivates not feeling important. He tries hard not to be ponderous or even serious in his life apart from his work.

There are hardly any men in the hall at eleven o'clock on a weekday morning. He will not lecture in the evenings as the university has urged him to do. He writes in the evenings. He will not lecture for credit out of a kind of pride. He wants only those who are pure, interested in the subject and not the payoff. Even so, he feels he has not achieved his true audience. There are mostly older women listening to his words. Some scribble the full hour. A few knit or do needlepoint. Some look puzzled. He has often thought of giving it up but he does not dare. He lectures because he has no self-discipline. Talking forces him to written conclusions. He invests all his passion in these conclusions. His verbs are action verbs, his adjectives are sensuous. The gorgeous rumpled silks of a Titian inspire lust in him but only for the fabric itself. For the woman he feels nothing, while the skin tones he could swallow whole. In the guise of these lectures he has written several books and established his credentials.

He flings his briefcase on the desk and pulls off his coat, tossing it at the chair. It misses and falls to the floor but he is already pacing in quick erratic strides, his hands clasped together and pressed against his lips. His physical analogue for thinking. His lecture today is to be on experimental music. From the concert hall to the loft. He is scrapping his prepared text. He moves to the chair, ignores the fallen coat and sits down abruptly, long legs shooting out straight. The room is empty. Almost empty. He sees Natalie. She is sitting alone and painfully erect in the center of the last row.

"Mrs. Barnes," he says. Her reply is inaudible. He gets up, cups his hands to his mouth and says, "Please come down to the front." It's the wrong thing to say. He sees her stiffen further. She strikes him as quintessentially private and resistant. Quaker-like in her silence. His curiosity is aroused. He is used to responsiveness, to being liked. People like him immediately. They are happy in his presence. His wit is sharp and encouraging. Others are wittier in his presence. They like themselves better. For a man in his position he has few enemies. Critics but no enemies. He doesn't count his wife.

Natalie descends. Her face is closed. Her mouth is taut and her head has that slight tilt he noticed the week before. There is cadence to her walk. She is almost marching. Her eyes are hooded. She slips into her assigned seat before he can speak. He stands over her, looks down onto her head, down onto a snug cap of hair gathered into a severe knot. The neck curls which have managed to escape are soft and fine as a baby's. He feels an urge to untie the knot and plunge his hands into her hair. He has never touched such hair. But instead he sits down in the next chair and leans toward her, chin on hand, determined to be earnest and businesslike. He can see that she doesn't like jocularity.

"You said you'd taken this course before. Was it last semester or some time ago?"

She turns and looks at him. He is already infatuated with the oddity of her face. She doesn't look like anyone else.

"Both," she answers.

"How long ago?" he rushes on. He doesn't want to give her time to blush, to stiffen, withdraw. "I ask because, well, I'd like to know whether there's enough. If it bears repeating." Why is he asking? He knows it bears repeating. And perhaps she is one of those who knits, who comes because she has nothing else to do, because she is a perpetual student.

"You don't repeat yourself. Your topic is so vast. And so far you've been equal to it."

He doesn't expect this. He's not sure what he expected. Her cool verdict gives him a sharp interior jolt.

"How long ago?" he asks again.

"I can't answer it that way," she says. She takes a deep breath. "I've been coming ever since you started."

"Six years?"

"Do I have to defend myself?"

He hears fiber in her voice. "No, of course not. I'm sorry if I gave you that impression." Now he is flustered. He sees that the room has filled up. "We'll talk later," he tells her. "Wait for me." He retreats to his large safe white space in the front of the room. He addresses the crowd. "Today," he says, rubbing his hands together to release some of his energy, "we're going to talk about a new development in art, one that incorporates music. I think you'll find it very promising."

A sigh escapes her. He hears it. Her sigh as she sinks into the contemplation of civilization reminds him of the sigh of a woman sinking into a warm bath. He knows then with certainty that she is not one of the needle-pointers, not one of the dutiful. He knows also that she is not puzzled by what he offers, his gift. He feels brilliant, unusually persuasive and lectures forcefully for a full hour to an audience of one.

She waits because he has asked her to. She should be on her way uptown to visit her grandmother. She waits because these lectures are central to her life. She waits because he is surrounded by eager women. They are like schoolgirls waving their hands for attention. She wonders what kind of exchange it can be when one party has nothing to offer but homage. While she waits she smooths her hair. This smoothing amounts to a tic. It drives her husband mad. It is the thing about herself she most dislikes, this hair of hers with a life of its own. Gregory loves it as he loves everything about her. He tells her she is too critical, that she lives up to and surpasses her own high standards. He worships her in the way that his Germanic forebears worshipped the land. In all other areas Gregory is a pragmatist. Yesterday and tomorrow are his boundaries.

The room is emptying. Slowly the knot of women loosens.

"Look," he says, taking her arm, "let's have a cup of coffee somewhere in the neighborhood. We can't talk here."

He doesn't wait for an answer, propels her up the aisle. She feels dwarfed. He is so much taller than anyone with whom she is used to walking. She has to take short hurried steps to keep up.

"Today's lecture was unusually dynamic," she volunteers. The instant the words are spoken she hates herself. A neat prim dry declaration. A textbook declaration. She isn't herself. She has been displaced by an awkward girl. Her legs are trembling. Her voice is trembling. She is not used to strangers, particularly such animated strangers. She mistrusts vivacity.

"Thank you," he says. "Do you have time for lunch?" He is holding the restaurant door for her. "A quick lunch?"

"All right." She wants to leave. She wants to stay. This has never happened to her before.

"I'm very curious about you," he says.

"There's nothing to be curious about, Dr. Rilling."

She feels they are proceeding sideways and doesn't know how to change the direction. The best thing about her marriage to Gregory is the simple straightforwardness of it, the lack of guile. When she was nineteen he cut his way into her tight family circle and snatched her from their hysterical midst.

"Please call me Tom."

He smiles and tips back in his chair. The angle is precarious. She watches him, studies him. She is certain he will fall.

"Do you work?" he asks.

Do you have a husband, children, a mother, a father? What are your interests, your desires, your deepest fears? She can hear an avalanche of questions threatening in his voice. She puts down the menu the waitress has given her.

"Please forgive me," she says, "but I can't stay. My grandmother is very ill and I promised to be there to feed her. She won't allow the nurses to do it."

"Of course," he says. He looks stunned. "Perhaps we

can do it next week." He jumps up and his chair crashes to the floor behind him.

They are both red faced.

He is aware of his growing obsession with Natalie. The state of tension in which she holds the opposing elements of her personality renders her a work of art. He would like to take a bite out of her. Purely an aesthetic consumption. He begins to write his lectures for her. He studies her for a response but she is difficult to read. Her facial muscles barely move. Her eyes blink occasionally, alert but neutral. After a few weeks, weeks in which she has consistently refused to lunch with him, he discovers that it is a question of becoming sensitized, something he has learned from a musician friend who experiments with long, sustained drone tones. For the first few minutes the tone sounds simply like a prolonged sonority. But then your ears become sensitized, allowing you to become aware of wonderfully subtle changes going on within the single tone. He applies what he has learned to Natalie. As a style, minimalism appeals to him. He can be relied on to supply what is omitted.

There are other problems. While he lectures he feels dry, feverish and chapped. He shudders, feels chills and shivers. He wants to put his arms around Natalie to stabilize himself. He wants her to come across, to fork it over, to give him herself, the part, that is, which no one else has. The part she is guarding. He feels he needs it. But she will not see him after class. He wonders if the grandmother exists.

She does not tell Gregory about him. There is nothing to tell. She is determined not to let Dr. Rilling drive her from class. Her resistance, she feels, is being met by an equal force. She feels he is pushing at her all the time. She thinks about relenting. She would like to be intimate with his mind. What she means is that she would like to take affectionate tender liberties with it the way she does with her children's bodies. Tender squeezes and rumplings, affectionate handfuls. A sort of taken-for-granted everyday access is what she would like. But she knows the way to that is physical, and the physical part is out of the question.

After class one day he invites her to a private "evening." He describes it as a mixed-media event which may nevertheless prove interesting. The expression "mixed-media" offends her and she prays that he is being ironic.

He knows her so well by now that he has predicted even her hesitation before accepting. He also knows that he has made a clever move and his mood swings wildly up.

An hour before their appointment the phone rings. On the other end her uncle, Laszlo, screams. She hears panic and exasperation in his voice.

"She's turning blue! Yes, the ambulance is on the way. No, the nurse is not here. Yes, she's late again! Blue! You must come immediately to the hospital!"

Though Laszlo can vault the abstract with room to spare, he is easily felled by the actual, reduced in midair to a witless spill of arms and legs and crossbar.

Her grandmother, on the other hand, meets whatever comes with a rigid stoicism. Natalie knows that these frantic rushes to the hospital are practice runs for the real thing although, secretly, she believes that her grandmother will live forever, has, in fact, already done so and will continue to do so in a condition of permanent pain. She also believes that in Hermine's overwhelming desire for something to be sure of, she has settled for pain. She can picture the scene. In the emergency room there is eternally Laszlo in his worn blue suit waving his arms around like an upholstered windmill. "It's the end of an era," he shouts each time they gather. There is eternally herself, white faced and tight lipped, feeling put upon and then abysmally guilty for feeling put upon, and there is eternally Gregory taking charge, using his natural gifts, his natural muscle to get them preferred treatment over Hermine's objections.

She hangs up with a sigh. She collects her handbag and umbrella and leaves the apartment. The loft is on Murray Street, south of SoHo. She will have to hurry.

He is not there when she arrives. The crowd is intimidating. They all seem to know one another. She takes refuge in the bathroom. In other circumstances she would never use such a bathroom. There is a length of green-gray mold growing along the high-water mark in the open shower. The plumbing fixtures are crusted with grime and rust and years of neglect. But artists are different or her standards for them are different (just as Gregory's standards for her are different) which amounts to the same thing. She does not dare use the toilet. Apart from the odor, the waste material of cats and humans in an unappetizing mix, the door is secured by nothing more than a flimsy hook and eye. One good pull would remove it from the wall.

After a few minutes someone knocks. She closes her compact and opens the door. She sees that he has arrived. Tom. She must try to get used to his name which he now insists upon. He is being greeted affectionately by the other guests. Laughter explodes around him. The loft is filled with people. From where she stands alone and uncertain, from this unfamiliar vantage point, he looks like an old and valued friend. She greets him with relief. She allows him to take her hand so that he can lead her through the room.

The performance emerges rather than begins. The participants move from one place to another and mill about with the audience. Occasionally they sit down. The room quiets gradually. A television screen drops from the ceiling on ropes. At least it looks to Natalie like a television screen. Words appear on it written in light. After a while the audience joins the actors in the recitation of these words. She hears Tom's voice raised. She cannot raise her own. No amount of encouragement from Tom can induce her to open her mouth.

When the communal sound recedes it is replaced by an individual sound. A small bald rosy man walks through the crowd. His eyes are closed. He is singing short tones, pausing, singing again, pausing, and singing. He is fiercely, unilaterally concentrated.

Natalie is bewildered. She is more than bewildered. She is annoyed. The man's ego annoys her. He is taking up too much room.

"What is he doing?" she asks Tom.

"Listening to his echo."

He puts his arm around her during the last pause. She freezes.

The performance interests Tom. The Turk is an old friend. He doesn't give the performance his usual attention, though, because he is absorbed by Natalie. Beside him he can feel her quivering. He is sure it is with pleasure. It is this certainty which prompts him to put his arm around her. She doesn't move away. He feels that at last he has found her pulse. At this moment with his arm around her he has all but forgotten his wife. They share a name and little else. His wife gave up on him years ago. Even his achievements don't move her. He feels that though she expected it and even married him for the promise of it, she has never quite forgiven him his success.

The Turk is distributing large white squares of paper. "Tear into it," he demands.

Natalie is angered by the demand. It is some kind of test for which there was no warning and for which she is therefore unprepared. It is also an invasion of privacy. There is simply no choice but to comply. She watches Tom for a clue. Without any hesitation he punches his fist through the center of the square and rips back triangular wedges from the large hole he has made. It reminds her of the sun. She thinks of his lecture on Erasmus and knows that Erasmus would have approved of Tom's sun. While he is busy folding back the ragged triangles, she makes one vengeful, microscopic tear in each of the four corners of her page.

Tom looks up from his finished work. She hands him her sheet. He can feel her eyes on him as he studies it. After he sees the four discreet tears he smiles at her. She returns his smile. Her smile releases her face. It is a mischievous smile. Perhaps he doesn't know her as well as he believes. Is she capable of mischief? He asks her.

"No," she replies, laughing. "I've been accused of other things but nothing as much fun as mischief. I wish it were true. I think I'm a rather grave person."

He feels very clearheaded, like a man whose fever has suddenly broken. He hands their efforts over to the Turk and pulls her into a corner.

"I," he announces, "am a mischief maker. And a joke

teller. Dialects are my specialty. My best is Italian. Then Russian. I'm not bad at German or Spanish."

"Tell me a joke," she says. Where is it coming from, this movie script she is using tonight and which has no connection to her real self?

"Now?" he asks.

"Now."

"Wait. Give me a minute to think of one. Damn it. I'm a blank."

"Can you do Hungarian?"

"I doubt it. I don't know what Hungarian sounds like."

"I'll teach you. I'm Hungarian. Better still, I'll introduce you to my Uncle Laszlo. You can imitate him." She bursts out laughing.

"But you have no accent," he protests.

"My mother was half-English. We spoke it at home." She is still laughing.

"Is your Uncle Laszlo funny?" he asks. He wants to laugh with her.

"No," she gasps, "not really. I don't know why I'm laughing."

"What is he like?"

"It would take too long to explain."

"Does he have a beard?" Tom asks in his best Russian accent.

"*Da*," she answers, giggling.

"Is there really a grandmother?" he chances.

"*Da*," she replies.

"Do you really speak Russian?" he asks in Russian.

"*Da*. And French and Hungarian. I'm a translator."

"Amazing," he says and shakes his head.

"Not really," she says. "All European refugees speak several languages. And for a Hungarian it's a necessity. No one speaks Hungarian."

He doesn't dare say a word. He might stop the flow.

"I've been married a long time," she continues. "I have two children." She is rushing headlong. "I collect Chinese porcelain." Her eyes are closed. "I don't know what's happening anymore."

She looks as though she may collapse. He puts his arms around her just in case. To his astonishment, there is no resistance. "I have a wife," he whispers into her hair. "And a daughter. What period?"

She looks up at him.

"The porcelain. What period?"

She hesitates a moment and then, with a trembling smile, she says, "Damn it. I'm a blank."

He raises his hands from her shoulders and carefully, tentatively, touches her hair. The soft damp neck curls.

She sighs and sinks against him.

All about them are sounds of ripping and tearing. Over her shoulder he can see that though most of the guests are using their hands one man, the man closest to them, is improvising with his teeth. Tom is certain he knows exactly how the fellow feels.

CHAPTER

2

THE SITUATION IS IMPOSSIBLE. THIS MUCH IS OBVIOUS TO everyone. Everyone is Laszlo and herself. The nuns would not agree. Natalie knows that her grandmother cannot possibly share a room. Natalie knows that at her age she can barely share the world. She also knows that Hermine would argue with her on both counts. Through the lightly draped hospital sheet Natalie can see how stiff her grandmother has become. She suffers from arthritis. She has been suffering for years. The parts of her body are no longer comfortably related to one another. The transitions between them have become awkward and abrupt. She is separating at the seams. Still, in spite of the arthritis and the stroke which robbed her of her voice, she is alert and self-contained. Only the nuns in their starched coifs hovering over her bed disturb her. She signals Natalie to get rid of them. She moves her fingers. Her knuckles are swollen and tuberous. They are almost as large as she is. Once she was a fair-sized woman. Now she is bird bony. A sharp beak, fiery shocked eyes. Wherever she looks, she sees pain.

Hermine wiggles her fingers a second time. Natalie is slow to understand this morning. She has Tom on her mind. Hermine rolls her eyes in the direction of the nuns. The Church frightens her. Saints and martyrs make her uneasy. "Do you realize," she used to tell Natalie when she was a child, "there were actually saints who approved of the Crusades and the Inquisition." And later: "Even if I believed in God I would certainly never have allowed a political thing like the Church to come between us. " Natalie is living proof that no one has ever come between her grandmother and the object of her grandmother's interest. Natalie's own mother, Hermine's daughter-in-law, was forced to move aside. The nuns, however, do not. They continue to fuss. Their pace is fixed and they will not be hurried. They have a cosmic timetable. Natalie enjoys watching them. They move with the same slow luminous assurance of the women in Vermeer's paintings. Their smallest actions have weight.

Laszlo is pacing. This is his usual response to crisis. The more serious the crisis the faster he paces. Even in moments of relative calm there is drama to his stride and to his appearance. His hair is parted melodramatically in the center from which point it flanges out into two black wings. The wings are streaked with silver. The wings and the frantic pacing confer on him the look of a grounded, demented bird. Laszlo is pacing because Hermine's condition is serious and because he knows that she should have a private room. Private rooms are against his principles. They should be against Natalie's principles too, he tells her, but Natalie is married to a bourgeois and her principles have softened.

"Where is the doctor?" he is asking. "He should have been here an hour ago." He spreads his arms for emphasis. His jacket pulls wide and Natalie sees that his fly is open. The nuns see it too. They are gone in an instant. Laszlo is raging against the doctor. He notices nothing. *"C'est pas possible,"* he says. Natalie hates it when he drops into other languages. She thinks it's affected. Laszlo would argue with her; in fact, he does argue. They argue about most things. Laszlo is an arguer with life in several languages. His accent in all of them is irritating to Natalie whose ear demands perfection. She knows that for Laszlo accent and grammar are of trifling importance, that is, important only to people like herself. For him, in this as in everything else, it is the vernacular that counts.

"Uncle Laszlo," she says, "you haven't quite finished dressing."

"Thank you, dear girl," he says. He reaches for his zipper without looking down. He zips while he paces.

Looking down, Natalie sees that his blue serge pants are bare and shiny at the knees. "You're going through at the

knees like a little boy, Uncle Laszlo. Have you been playing baseball or is it possible that you've taken up praying?"

"*Tu es bien ce matin, Natalie. Décontractée.*" He grins.
The grin is a slow one. The beard and moustache split,
showing a slice of dingy teeth, worn-down nubs overhung
with facial hair. Natalie cannot get him to the dentist.

There is a sound. A throat clearing. They both jump.
The other occupant of the room is awake and squinting
fiercely at them. Hermine signals again. Now that there is
an audience she is demanding to be straightened in the
bed. Natalie and Laszlo adjust her fractionally. It is
enough. Lifting her, Natalie is stunned by the thinness of
Hermine's upper arms. It seems like an eternity since she
last sat on Hermine's lap and held the loose satiny skin of
her grandmother's underarm between her two small hands.
All the softness in the world seemed to have been collected there just for her. What she feels now is bark.

Hermine's roommate is staring at them. She is a ravaged
old lady. She wears a terrible auburn wig, far too abun-
dant for her shrunken face. As they watch she pulls her
teeth from a glass and snaps them into place. She smiles,
a slow proud smile, a child's smile. "I also am doing the
best with what I got," she announces to them. "How do
you do. My name is Rebecca Miller. Some people are
lucky and grow old gracefully. Not me. In this competition I'm doing bad. My chief trouble is with the eyes. The
back end of your eyes are like mirrors, in case you didn't
know it. When the quicksilver wears off, this is what im-
pairs your vision. I'm going blind."

"I'm so sorry," Natalie murmurs. They must get Hermine out of here. She and Laszlo exchange looks.

"It's all right, honey," Mrs. Miller assures her. "I've seen
everything I ever wanted to see and, thank God, my hearing is excellent."

They check Hermine for a reaction. Hermine doesn't
approve of chattering. It is one of the few things she will
not endure. She has closed her eyes. Natalie looks down at
her lap. Laszlo ruffles his newspaper. Mrs. Miller will meet
a united front.

When Natalie thinks it's safe, she looks up. Both women
are dozing. The side rails of their beds are up, turning
them into steel cribs. Natalie closes her own eyes. Her

head aches. She is trying to forget the previous evening. Impossible. She is saturated with the memory. In spite of her resistance some absorption is taking place. Over the sound of her grandmother's breathing, over the sound of Rebecca Miller's breathing, over the sound of Laszlo's sighing, she can hear Tom asking when they are going to see one another again. Over the sound of paper tearing she hears him ask WHEN. She feels his lips brush along her ear. The hairs rise on her arms. A chill rises along her skin.

"I don't know," she said. "But I have to leave now."

"What?" he whispered. "Leave for where?"

She told him where, spared him what she was thinking, thinking that at the very moment she and the others were making meaningless, egotistical tears in poor-quality paper, her grandmother might well be dying. What was she doing there? Even with Hermine in the best of health she didn't belong.

"Okay," Tom said. He took her hand (she loves his hands) and led her along the living room wall to the bedroom. On the floor, several large pyramids of coats. In her hand, a useless stub. No system was apparent. The Turk's children had taken her coat at the door and given her a homemade check. At the time she had been amused and touched. Now she was merely frantic. She would never find her coat. A few cats lay curled among the pyramids. She started digging, dislodged the cats. She was angry enough to mew and spit back. When she found her coat, it felt damp around the neck.

"I'll call you tomorrow morning," Tom told her as he put her into a cab. She nodded, hardly heard his parting words. After nodding, she sniffed. An odd smell in the cab. It took a few minutes for her to make the connection. The dampness in her collar derived from the cats not the rain. This she would not forgive the Turk.

At the hospital everything was under control. Hermine had been admitted, a bed found, her breathing normalized. And Laszlo had managed it all without her. "Where were you?" he demanded, his hair rumpled, his beard wild. "What took you so long?"

"I'm sorry," she answered. "I had to make a stop first."

If Tom has called she is unaware of it. She has been at the hospital since early morning waiting to speak with

Hermine's doctor. Hermine demands to go home. She is convinced that the hospital will kill her. Though Natalie argues soundlessly with her, it is without conviction. Hermine is probably right. Laszlo agrees. He has told Natalie that recently he read an article in the paper in which some 30 to 40 percent of all nurses surveyed reported that they would not want to be patients in the hospitals in which they worked. Natalie wants to believe that the nuns are different but she cannot. Hermine has raised her to believe that the nuns are not different, that in many ways they are worse for consenting to be part of the religious power structure, an unpaid part. Sometimes Natalie wishes that Hermine had not blackened the idea of faith quite so assiduously. Sometimes Natalie yearns for the power of faith. She yearns for it most when she contemplates the death of her grandmother.

Laszlo has finished reading the paper. He is now paring his nails. This is unusual. He is not normally attentive to his appearance. He needs as much supervision as a child. She wonders what has inspired this excursion into good grooming. He is trimming his nails but his mind is elsewhere. When his mind is elsewhere, which happens often, his eyeballs drift up. He can make them disappear completely. This habit used to frighten her when she was a child. He disappeared along with his iris, leaving only a blank white orb behind.

"What are you thinking about?" she asks him.

His eyes return. When his eyes are present they are a soft amber color. Liquid, soulful and very tender. "Well," he answers, "since you ask so earnestly, I assume you really want to know." He finishes off his last nail with a theatrical flourish. "Somewhere between thoughts of mother's illness," he looks at Hermine with concern, something he permits himself only when she is asleep since she hates any display of love, "the contract for my book, and a forecast of C. P. Snow's on world famine, I was thinking of my new secretary. She is, as the French say, '*extra*.'"

"I thought the French weren't given to hyperbole."

"You're right. They don't make use of it to compliment anyone but themselves."

"What's she like?"

"Oh, the usual. Young, beautiful, smart, romantic."

"I thought the young weren't romantic anymore."

"Nonsense. They're just romantic about something else. Today they believe in the possibility of being true, complete and authentic. And they work for it with as much moral rectitude as their parents worked for a decent home and a car and an education for their children. They will eventually be sucked up, poor fools. They will assimilate. All of them but you, Natalie. You're the one holdout."

"So, she's in her twenties," Natalie says. "It's inappropriate."

He bursts out laughing. "Inappropriate? Can I help it if I like them psychologically virginal, before they've been compromised?"

Natalie tilts up her chin and smooths her hair. Battle signs. "What can you possibly have in common with her? With any of them?"

"Very little. But surely you don't consider that an obstacle. Look at you and Gregory." He has a toothpick out and is digging at a molar.

"Laszlo, that's going too far."

"Nonsense, Natalie. We always go this far. No farther. Or is it further? You're the grammarian. We always end up here no matter where we start out." He makes a chirping sound and switches the toothpick to the other side of his mouth.

"Are you going to move in with this one too?"

"With Mother so ill? Don't be an idiot."

A nun glides in heralding the Divinity of Medicine. They are all thralls of the system. Even Laszlo forgets his principles and jumps to his Marxist feet.

"Ah, the King," he says to Natalie under his breath as if this will redeem him. Natalie will never forget it. She doesn't let go what she has learned. In bad times her memory is a prison. She flashes Laszlo a warning look. A bright smile for the doctor.

"We'd like to talk to you after you've had a chance to examine Grandmother," she says.

"Of course," says the doctor, returning her smile.

"We are lucky," Laszlo sputters in the hall. "The Almighty will deign to talk with us. He will grant us the favor of an audience. This is what passes for compassion in the medical profession today."

"Stop it, Laszlo. Why are you always so angry?"

"Sorry," he says. "You know how I like to growl. Pay no attention."

A few minutes later the doctor joins them in the hall. He is a small man with a weary boy's face. His gray hair is short and wavy, his cheeks are pink, his glasses rimmed in steel. He looks very clean. He has a mild manner, a mild mouth. "Well, from the look of it," he tells them, "she's had another series of small strokes." He pats Natalie's hand. The pat is automatic. "There isn't much we can do but keep her as comfortable as possible."

"She'd like to go home," Natalie says.

"We'll see in a few days."

"Can you be a little more definite? She's very agitated about staying here."

"Well, I'd rather not rush things. It's easier on everybody else if she's here, isn't it?"

"That's not the point, Doctor," Laszlo breaks in.

"Yes, I think it is," the doctor says. "Actually, it's the largest part of the point, Mr. Várády. I also am agitated. I'm a very busy man, an overworked man. I had a heart attack six months ago. As I said, as long as I'm your mother's doctor we'll wait and see how things go. I'm sure you can explain to the patient." He delivers this ultimatum in a tranquil voice. He moves off down the hall without waiting for their response, his swan boat a pair of coifs. He has healing to do in the world to which he is returning. No time to waste.

Laszlo is muttering in Hungarian. He speaks the language of his birth only when he is angry. "These doctors won't tell you anything." He takes a large calico bandanna from his breast pocket and mops his face. "It's useless to question them. They keep you in the dark because they know that information is power. What they do is feed you just enough to prevent wild speculation but not enough to let you make an informed decision." He is moving rapidly back and forth in front of Natalie. "And that is how we come to be so dependent."

Natalie catches him by the back of his jacket. "Laszlo, stop whining. Remember what you always say? Life is politics and politics is power. Or is it the other way around? If you believe that then tell me why you get angry when you see this principle in action. It seems to me that you're being naïve. I'm against changing doctors again. At least this one tolerates old people. And I don't think we should irritate him any farther. Or is it further?"

They both laugh. Natalie knows that where Hermine's needs are concerned, or her own, Laszlo will permit his principles to soften. Hermine will stay in the hospital and she will have a private room. When they reenter the room Hermine is awake and looking into space. She doesn't hear them. A few large tears are sliding down her face. Laszlo rushes to her side, looks at her closely. The tears have caused a short circuit. Her eyes are dead, the glint gone. He is overcome. To his certain knowledge, his mother has never in her life cried. Not at the death of her husband, not at the death of her eldest son, Natalie's father. He glances at Natalie. She is pale and uncertain, her chin quivering. She, too, may cry. Another first. He picks up his mother's hand. Hermine turns to look at him. She tries to stem the tears with her other hand but she cannot lift it from her side. In desperation, Laszlo kisses the hand he is holding. His kiss is not styptic enough. Tears continue to fall. He trembles. Hermine's throat trembles. Natalie moves closer. He will be rescued. No. She is merely pulling the curtain around the bed to hide them from Mrs. Miller. What is he to do with these two women? This niece who sees herself as his mother and this mother who never wanted the job. Natalie moves to the other side of the bed, pats at Hermine's face with a tissue. He puts down the hand he is holding. Hermine turns away, stares straight ahead. Natalie stares straight ahead. They are a pair of bookends. They have kept him upright all his life.

"I'm going to see what I can do about a room," he says.

There is not much he can do about the room and he knows it, but he needs to walk around. In confining situations he gets the jitters. The jitters are his strongest link with the past. They remind him of his borders, of his trade-offs. Long ago he reached a concord of sorts with his adopted country. He bartered uncertainty and fear for mobility. At this stage of life, he prefers to describe himself as mobile. Approaching sixty, he finds freedom a grandiose notion. He is mobile and lonely, his loneliness final and unrelieved. But how lucky if this should prove to be the worst! His mobility makes the loneliness tolerable. In the past, whenever he mentioned freedom, someone or other, Natalie, his mother, various women, nagged at him to surrender it, whereas no one troubles him about his mobility. Vivianne, his present companion, "secretary," for Natalie's sake, has so far troubled him about nothing. She is one of the few who has ever respected his distance. She doesn't empty herself trying to fill him. She understands that a part of him is closed to all such traffic. Thinking of her, he smiles, rubs at his beard with his knuckles.

"You may move in, if you like," she told him. "We can wait together." There was an unhurried smile on her face.

"Wait for what?"

"Perhaps we'll find out once you are here."

He moved in with her weeks ago. Of course, he hasn't told Natalie nor will he, nor will he disillusion her about his "girls." He hasn't been with a twenty-year-old in twenty years. Vivianne is nearing forty, her skin lightly tarnished, her hair beginning to gray. But her eyes, her eyes. They pour with light. And with a disturbing depth of shadow.

"I have no patience for romance," she warned him as he unpacked, her prose contradicted by her appearance. Long, loose hair, a flowing gauzy dress. "It always ends in abuse."

"No romance, then," he agreed, amused. "What shall we have instead?"

"I would be satisfied with sex and friendship."

"Are you sure I'm worth the trouble?" He laughed at her seriousness. "Friendship is so difficult."

"I hope you are," she answered. "I respect your ambition. You have some remarkable qualities."

"You're being romantic already," he said as he passed her with an armload of clothes.

"It's a hard habit to break," she said, pulling open a drawer for him. "But worth trying, *non?*"

He shrugged, smiled, took her in his arms.

There is a line at Admitting. Everyone on it has a complaint. He waits to join his voice with the others.

Natalie would like to run after him. She cannot watch Hermine cry. It is an invasion of privacy, an act of treachery. She concentrates on Laszlo's departing back,

watches him run off to plead for a private room for which
Gregory will pay. The pleading angers her, not the money. Laszlo runs off regularly to plead for causes for which
others will pay. Only the cause matters. He is engaged in
a permanent war against private money. He is energized
by, thrives on, the rivalry between wealth and learning.
He has subverted this struggle to his own purpose. He has
the intellectual's contempt for money without being an intellectual. He has a rich man's suspicion of the intellect
without being rich. (He suspects Gregory as he does any
man who has money since Gregory's learning is of a technical sort and therefore convertible to cash.) Toward those
with both wealth and knowledge he maintains an aloof
posture, as aloof as it can be considering the state of his
wardrobe and the ardency of his gestures. He takes a
wait-and-see attitude. If he waits long enough what he will
see is what he already knows to be true: Money softens a
man to the point where it ensures the sacrifice of his
morality in a tight squeeze. The same holds true for the
overdeveloped intellect. Look at the Germans. He believes
this passionately. It's no good arguing with him but she
does.

Natalie tells him he wouldn't have trusted Marx. He
tells her she is right. In his own way, Laszlo is a terrible
snob. He is, after all, a second-generation Marxist. He is
also a second-generation worker while Marx himself was
neither. Laszlo's father left the farm and became a man of
the factories. His mother worked as a milliner. Both were
labor organizers in Hungary. In spite of this pedigree,
Laszlo does deal with wealthy intellectuals. These re-
nouncers, the lapsed scions of doctors and lawyers and
industrialists, are his friends. They are in the vanguard of
revolutionary activity in the Third World and it was on
their behalf that he once traveled in South America front-
ing as a Levantine exporter of olives. This and other ad-
ventures will soon become public knowledge. He is com-
pleting his memoirs, the high point a meeting with Che.
Natalie is doing the translation. Laszlo cannot write in
English. The book is in Hungarian, the language of his
soul, of his rage.

Apparently the cool, nerveless power he ascribes to himself in his book works better in the Third World, for when
he returns from Admitting they are still without a private

room. Natalie studies him as he runs his hands through his hair, as he hitches up his pants, as he buttons and rebuttons his jacket. What is he getting ready for? He is always readying himself for something.

"Perhaps Gregory can do something," she says. "He must know some capitalist who donated a pavilion."

Laszlo also knows many capitalists who could help them out and would be grateful for the chance. It is Laszlo's self-imposed poverty which brings them to their knees. They defer to him in the largest and smallest of things as a being of a higher moral order. In his presence, they try to justify their lives. They empty their pockets readily for his latest brainchild. The International Third World Medical Research Fund. His charm lies in the fact that he spits so colorfully and good-naturedly on the very system which provides the money to finance his work. There is no doubt that the dividends of competitive enterprise make it all possible, yet it is impossible to get Laszlo to admit to this. Natalie tells him he has a fortress mentality. An occupational hazard of all revolutionaries, even peaceful ones, she tells him.

"And what you have, dear girl, is a refugee mentality. Hiding in your four walls like a mole. Buried in an intimate life. Think what sort of character develops in such limited company! If you fence out all the rottenness of life, how do you expect to get strong enough to deal with this world? You need some hair of the dog. Look, dear girl, is it really humane, you who are so obsessed with the humane, to be soft in a hard world? What is so bad about being the way I am, living the way I do? I live a political life, I admit it. But in a political life, in politics of any kind, warm human relations are misplaced. Recognize it, Natalie. The world is mad. A reasonable life like yours is an anachronism."

Natalie sees that Hermine has fallen asleep again. The tears collected in the craters under her eyes are running off slowly. There are wet spots on the pillow by her ears. Looking at Hermine's ears, she thinks of Tom's. How can she be thinking of him at a time like this?

Laszlo sighs. "We have no need of a capitalist, mine or Gregory's. Mine, of course, are better. At least they have a sense of guilt." He puts his arm around Natalie's shoulders and squeezes. "Mrs. Miller is staying only another day or two and, in the meantime, if we keep the curtain closed she won't be able to talk to Mother."

"Shh," Natalie says, struggling out of his embrace. "She can't see the curtain but her hearing is excellent. Remember?" She puts a finger to her lips.

"In that case," he whispers, leaning forward, moist eyes dancing, "we should have no further trouble."

"No further trouble," Natalie repeats, swallowing thoughtfully. The words leave a fiery aftertaste.

CHAPTER

3

BARBARA HAS LET HIM OVERSLEEP AGAIN. THOUGH THE room is still dark Tom knows that outside, beyond the blackout shades and heavy frayed drapes, outside the sun is striking the buildings of the side street on which they live in the manner of a De Chirico, that is, shedding light only to cause shadows, to imply a mystery where there is none. He dislikes this obstructed light. He dislikes De Chirico. He would like to move to the West Side, facing the park, so he can get his sunshine straight on. Barbara will not move to the West Side. She has her fears and they can be lulled only on the East Side. She is more than willing to front the park from Fifth Avenue but this they cannot afford and she knows it. She doesn't accept it quietly.

"If your father weren't so stingy," she says each time the subject of moving comes up, "he could make us very comfortable."

"My father wouldn't call it stinginess. He would call it thrift. It's what comes of a Scandinavian upbringing. You get used to living in the dark and you don't lay out extra money for light."

Light. He knows about light, about the giddiness of round-the-clock light, every summer of his childhood spent in Sweden with his grandparents. He stands up. His wrists and ankles stick out inches beyond the cuffs of his pajamas. He stretches, scratches, bends over and slides his feet into a pair of worn wooden clogs. He likes the feel of them. They have been honed by his feet. If he is attached

34

to anything material in life, it is to these clogs. They attach him to his grandparents, to his summer giddiness, to the garnet of berries, the smell of pine, to the sound of water and of flat bread being rolled out and broom dusted, his grandparents' bread, a joint effort and the thinnest in the valley, as thin as the ancient linen burial sheets of the Nile.

He opens the bedroom door and calls out, brushing a spill of lank brown hair from his eyes. It falls back down. No answer. Barbara is not home. He looks over his shoulder at the clock. 9:30. She is out jogging around the reservoir. He admires her persistence and her self-discipline. She runs every day. She is becoming a long-distance runner. He hopes she will develop enough stamina to outrun her fears. They are numerous and as stubborn as she.

Barbara was not stubborn when he met her. She had an enthusiasm that matched his own. Her exuberance won him. He fell in love with her vigor. He knocks a hardened crust of toothpaste from the tube's opening, pulls out his lower lip and begins to brush. Barbara was blond and tall, blue-eyed and bosomy, slim-hipped with narrow thighs. There was a kind of light, easy amplitude about her. And her feet. Oh, God, how he loved her feet. He loves them still. She has perfect feet. Her arch is classic. He will match her feet with the Knidian Aphrodite's. Back then she rode horses, read economic tracts for pleasure, understood why nations chose as they did. It occurs to him now that this understanding is what attracted him to her in the first place. It is also, sadly, what repels him now. Glancing at her nightgown, half-buried in the bed, he decides that repel is too strong a word. His marriage, he feels, is very much like his childhood (exclusive of the summers): a condition of not quite being able to get out from under. He pulls on a pair of corduroy pants and a wrinkled turtleneck shirt. He finds his belt on the floor near the bed. Socks are not so easy. He has never mentioned this feeling to Barbara and he never will. She would assume he was blaming her but this is not so. He is doing everything that needs to be done the best way he can do it, now as then. It's not good enough now and it wasn't then. Although, clearly, it's not good enough for Barbara or for his father, it is good enough for his daughter, Laura. He misses Laura who is at boarding school for the first time. She comes home often but he is already in mourning for the future which will bring her permanent departure. He is no fool. He is using these years to acclimate himself. He knows that if he tries to rise too quickly to the surface of his loss he may get a fatal case of the bends. He gives up searching and puts on yesterday's socks.

He is having coffee when Barbara returns. Inside her gray sweatsuit she is moist and muscular. All except her breasts. Their opulence goes unsupported even when she jogs. He has observed her jumping rope on days when the weather forbids running in circles outdoors and the activity beneath her shirt is so chaotic that it seems dangerous. He hates her for not wearing a bra. She knows it. Their one conversation on the subject went something like this: "It makes you look—I don't know." He was unable to finish the thought. There was no way to say what he felt without hurting her.

"I look unattached, predatory, threatening, SEXY? Is that what you're trying to say?"

He didn't answer.

"Okay, then I look like a women's libber, possibly a lesbian?"

"Christ, Barbara. It's not sexual or ideological. Just look at yourself. You've got large breasts and you've had a child. They're down at your waist, for godsakes."

Her face collapsed. Her voice, when she was able to get it under control, was murderous. "God, I hate you. You and your fucking aesthetics."

That was all some time ago. She has not worn a bra since. He knows Barbara and he knows that she will not wear one now even if she wants to.

He pours her some coffee.

"No, thanks," she says. "I haven't got time."

"Where are you going?"

"I've got a luncheon meeting."

"It's only ten o'clock."

"So it is."

"You forgot to reset the alarm for me."

"Sorry. It's so damn dark when I get up." She shrugs.

"How many miles did you do this morning?"

"Six." She smiles for the first time.

"Congratulations." He can see that she is exhilarated.

"Thanks. I ran with the regulars. I was the only woman to finish."

"Great. Well, you're tall. You can keep up."

"Height has very little to do with it."

"Oh? I thought the length of the leg was what determined the length of the stride, etc."

"Well, then there's something you don't know. This isn't a life-drawing class. There are things more important than height."

"Such as?"

"I don't have time to educate you now. I'm going to be late."

He can hear the shower running. She will be in there forever. He uses Laura's bathroom. He wants to get out of the house and away from Barbara so he can concentrate on Natalie. He does the morning dishes and leaves to the sound of Barbara's voice rehearsing "Calm Sea and Prosperous Voyage." She has recently joined a choral group. She has recently stopped smoking. Running was the link. When she rhapsodizes over her expanding lung capacity, he imagines a giant auditorium inside her chest. When she brags that her lungs now operate like a bellows, he sees them pleat and unpleat like the center of an accordion. He is a visualizer, a concretizer. As a result of all her activity the house is filled with singing. He loves it. It is one of her few charms these days. All her phoniness is erased when she sings. He loves her when she sings. Her voice is not exceptional. She has no expectations for it, no illusions about it. She sings for herself and not to prove anything. Her singing is a worthy defense against what she is becoming.

Once he is out of the house he can think about Natalie. If he had to, he would guess that Natalie does everything for herself and nothing to prove anything. He wants to know her. She is so goddamned oblique. He wants some time alone with her. He wants to take her to lunch before he takes her to bed. Bed may be a problem. He wants her to know him first. To know him well. Lunch. He is a lunatic for food, though looking at him no one would believe it. He is a thin man and a passionate cook. Barbara isn't interested in food but his daughter is. He has taught her everything he knows.

By the time he reaches his office he is in a frenzy to talk
to Natalie. The voice that answers her phone offers him
"Barnes residence" when what he wants is to hear her say
Yes Tom Yes. He hangs up. His disappointment is serious.
He cannot seem to get hold of her any which way. He
can't even daydream about her. There isn't enough to go
on. He settles into an ancient mold-brown chair and goes
on anyway. As an aid to thinking, he plucks wads of stuf-
fing from the armrests, rolls them into pellets and tosses
them across the room at the wastebasket. A small pile
builds up on the floor.

He starts with the things about her appearance that he
doesn't like. He will get rid of those first. She polishes
her nails. She is carefully groomed, conventionally fashion-
able. His father is a champion of good grooming. Tom
gets up. Thoughts of his father always bring him to his
feet. He jams his hands into his pockets. One pocket rips
through. His change rolls down his leg, out of the bottom
of his trousers and onto the floor. He gets down on his
hands and knees. His glasses slip. They need tightening,
have needed it for months. He shoves his glasses back up
on the bridge of his nose. His father is also a champion of
conventionality and God. He believes that the three are
inseparable. His kind of trinity. Rilling, Sr. has not given
up on his son's tailoring or on the other two. Lately, he
has been most outspoken on the tailoring. Tom retrieves
two nickels, a dime and a quarter. He has vivid childhood
memories of his father standing in front of a mirror turning neat knots in his dark ties. The final deft elevation of
the knot into place under the collar always brought a
smile to Senior's lips. But what Tom remembers best is the
sight of those same lips in front of that same mirror, those
same lips straining hours on end to move in the American
manner. After years of practice Senior destroyed all but
the slightest trace of his Swedish accent. He never got rid
of the shame. Tom locates a few more coins and stands up.

Natalie wears the wrong kind of jewelry. He would or-
nament her with jewels that have a history. Egyptian jade.
Indian ivory. No fussy modern trinkets. She is not a modern woman. He cannot imagine her without a bra. He
cannot imagine her holding a tennis racquet, wearing jeans,
running laps. Is there any girl in her? What he does like is

her hair. He wishes she would wear it loose. Her hair is like Cleopatra's. He drops into his desk chair, letting himself down fast. Too fast. He jumps up and rubs at his bony seat.

Natalie is smaller than Barbara. Her proportoins are better. He is sure of this even though his only experience of nudes, except for Barbara, has been with the marble and plaster variety. He has an insatiable appetite for the man-made nude. Poor Barbara. He remembers persuading her to let him test out on her the one classical canon of proportion on which all art historians agreed, the canon dictating that the distance between the breasts must be of the same unit as the distance from the lower breast to the navel and again from the navel to the division of the legs. Straight from Sir Kenneth Clark. (He felt he knew her well enough to ask. They had been going out for a few months.) Barbara failed. Her naval was almost twice as far down her body as the classical scheme allowed. When he told her she had a Gothic rather than a Greek body she was so devastated that he never asked to measure on to the next division. It took all his skill to woo her back to serenity and into marriage but he managed it with a quote from Francis Bacon: "There is no excellent beauty that hath not some strangeness in the proportion."

In recent years the quotes have gotten pretty thin. But then, he thinks, so has the criticism. The truth is that some time ago their enthusiasm for each other dried up and nothing came along to replace it. Since they have not mellowed into a state of devotion, a feat which some of their friends have pulled off and which he envies, they are left with disinterest. Fortunately, it's mutual. They have mutually agreed upon, although unspoken, separate lives. In his separate life he works hard and mingles harmlessly. He doesn't know what Barbara does in hers, apart from the meetings, the endless rounds of them. He suspects but would rather not know.

Natalie's proportions may be classical but her body has a curious archaic flatness. She is not quite three dimensional. She holds her body too stiffly to permit a unification of all its parts. He thinks of her as being in transit to the Ideal. It wouldn't take much. He picks up a pencil and begins to doodle. He jiggles in his seat. He wishes he knew what hospital her grandmother is in. He consoles himself with the worst that can happen. He will have to wait until the next lecture to see her. He prays that the grandmother won't die and force her to miss the next class. Another week.

Real work is impossible but there is a letter he has been meaning to write for some time. He pulls open a few drawers. Where the hell is his paper? The typist never puts it back in the same place twice. He hopes that *The New York Times* will print his letter. In it he will attack one of the city's major art museums for going heavily into the retail business with its sale of "authentic" reproductions to replace what is not replaceable. He will charge that museum-sponsored reproductions (a fancy word for fakes), in the name of budget deficits, are undermining the originals and lowering the level of public taste. He is certain his letter will be published since his father is a member of the museum's board of directors, and the spectacle of a son killing off his father in public print, a kind of Akhenaton chiseling the name of his father, Amenhotep, out of the cartouches where it had been inscribed, makes for exciting news. Now that he has decided to write the letter his anger alone will fuel him until dinner time. He settles in. He takes pains with his handwriting so that the typist won't nag him for every third word. He hates neat, constricted hands. He wonders what Natalie's handwriting is like. He imagines it as an old-fashioned, calligraphic sort. That would suit her.

At lunch time he decides to take another risk and call her again. If her husband answers he can always tell him that the call concerns a change in the class schedule. This is not what he is afraid of. He is afraid that Natalie will resent this intrusion into her homelife and will cut him off permanently. He suspects that whatever develops between them will have to be played out in a vacuum. He suspects that if she could she would prevent him from learning even her husband's first name. But he knows it already. It's there in the phone book in front of him. Gregory. He cannot imagine the sort of man she is married to. The name by itself is loaded. It conjures up for him nothing less than the entire history of Christianity. He has no way to countervail the name's historic weight for he doesn't know any Gregorys personally. Now that he is started on these Gregorys he can't stop. He pulls down a reference book. My God, there are pages of them! There is Saint Gregory the Illuminator, the Apostle of Armenia, who died as a hermit; Saint Gregory of Nazianzus, champion of orthodoxy, one of the four great doctors of the East; Saint Gregory of Nyssa, philosophic theologian and one of the Cappadocian Fathers; Saint Gregory of Tours, who wrote the *Historia Francorum;* and, finally, there is Gregory, name of popes, sixteen of them plus one antipope into the bargain. This stockpile of Gregorys sticks in his throat, blocking his voice, so that when a man does indeed answer, Tom is so unnerved he hangs up without a word. "Hello? Hello?" he hears as he puts down the receiver. The voice is worried and insistent. He hates it.

He tries to focus on something else. Further work is impossible. Food. The contemplation of a good meal always soothes him. He puts his letter next to the typewriter. He and Barbara are giving a dinner party tonight. They will start with escarole soup, he decides, move on to *pàglia e fièno*, continue with veal chops sautéed in butter and sage and finish with fresh figs and a creamy Gorgonzola. He will market on Ninth Avenue since he has the time. Ninth Avenue offers some additional consolation, at least those few blocks along it which have been sealed in a time warp. Here he pretends that he is not a denizen of the country which is responsible for introducing shelf life and nursing homes into the history of civilization. Here, in the small markets, there is color, texture, odor. Saran Wrap has not yet been invented. Nude rabbits with white fur anklets hang in shop windows. Grainy brown sausages are stacked like logs, pasta is made by hand, saffron threads and cardamom pods sit in open barrels, ropes of garlic hang from rafters. He can taste it all. He grabs his coat and briefcase and heads for the door. He will sit in the back of his favorite store and breathe. He will sip a capuccino with the owner while he makes out his marketing list. He must cook for Natalie and soon. He cannot wait to cook for her, to create something splendid which will force her to see his uniqueness.

It will be easily nine o'clock before their first guests arrive. Since she has started to run Barbara hates these late parties. No one goes home before two. Recently, she has taken to excusing herself, going to bed before coffee, which she no longer drinks. Tom doesn't notice. She is superfluous. Was she ever not? He prepares the food and collects the compliments. He and his friends talk shop about which, privately, she doesn't give a damn. There is one thing she does on these evenings. Tom has charged her to serve and clear. It is the only thing he allows her that has any connection with food. She is certain that he begrudges her even the taste of his cooking. He would deny it, she knows, but she is certain that, privately, he feels she doesn't deserve his cooking. Her palate isn't subtle enough. He is turned on by those fine distinctions which are not of much interest to most eaters, i.e., the difference in water content from one butter to another. FOOD is not her religion, neither is ART or CIVILIZATION. She has failed on three essential counts.

It is nearly nine. She smudges her eyelids with African Mauve, colors her cheekbones Grape. A dab of Luscious Creamy Red on her lips, a run of the comb through her heavy blond mane, a dusting of powder to cover the rumble of panic and she is ready to face the evening.

She used to be certain that being a human being and treating other human beings with respect was enough. Not anymore. Not for Tom. His unspoken judgments make her feel crass. They incite her to vulgarity. In the course of their eighteen years of marriage he has discredited her taste, her mind and her body. All bases covered. The best that can be said of their sex life is that it is intermittent. And incomplete. For years she assumed it was her fault. Classic! Then one day, some eight or nine years into her marriage, an attractive stranger approached her at a party and said, "I believe in being direct. I'd like to get to know you." She wasn't sure she'd heard him correctly over the roar of the music. She just smiled. That was safe. Her hearing proved excellent. And he was as direct as he had promised. The first time they were together he told her: "I'm not going to marry you. You have to go into this with your eyes wide open." She lost more than her breath. She missed a fold in the bedspread they were turning down, forcing them to start again. By the time he embraced her nude Gothic (she never forgot) body, she was weeping with the strain. It took her three years to give him up. In all that time he never said I love you. In the years that followed, there were others who did but she counted only the ones who didn't.

In the living room she fluffs a few tired pillows. Hopeless. The room will never come to life. She puts out some cocktail napkins. They never have cocktails. Tom serves only wine. The doorbell rings. She brightens at the thought of Eric. Eric is an architect, a friend of Tom's and her present lover. Tom yells for her from the kitchen. The master chef cannot leave his domain. She opens the door to find them all assembled. The entire pack. They stick together. She sits among them at the dinner table. Eric is next to her. He grins at her and looks down at his lap. She follows his gaze, sees his erection, smiles back. She watches Tom from a great distance, his friends from a greater distance, the greatest possible one, the distance of not belonging.

They are golden, these dinner partners of hers. They are brimming with Life. They are the Makers, untouchable in their natural superiority. Her husband is their Spokesman, the one who explains to the world why they deserve to be called Artists. Without him they would not exist. The public would never get it on its own. They need him. Unlike the Impressionists, they are not resigned to public ridicule. Unlike the Impressionists, they are impatient; they want their understanding and immortality NOW. Her husband is serving a dinner fit for these valuable, these precious folk. Theirs is the best possible world, after all. In between sips of escarole soup and munches of bread this is the message that is being sent and received. Unfortunately, the agreement is unanimous. After years of indoctrination, she believes it too.

She clears the soup plates. Tom is watching over the pasta, testing one strand and shaking his head. Five minutes until she is needed, he tells her. In five minutes she will be dead of rage. She signals Eric discreetly from the kitchen doorway. She goes the back way. They meet in the powder room. She drops to her knees. He drops his trousers. They return separately. She clears the pasta. She clears the veal. She clears the salad. Tom pronounces the Gorgonzola ripe. They are all peeling figs. By now she is exhausted. She excuses herself from the table. Tom will have to manage the coffee alone.

CHAPTER

4

HE DOESN'T MAKE A THIRD ATTEMPT TO REACH HER. HE decides to wait it out. The week passes. Drags. When he arrives at class, early, she is already seated in her customary place in the first row.

"How is your grandmother?" he asks.

"Holding her own," she says. "Thank you for asking."

"What hospital is she in?" He slips this question in as he turns away from her to throw his coat at his chair.

"A good one," she answers.

He hasn't gotten away with it. He looks at her and they both smile. Her smile is friendly. He feels hopeful. "Can we have lunch today?" he asks. He knows she will say yes. She does. He is in high gear. His voice wants to fly. He will have to control it for his lecture. He plunges in.

"The video-art movement has been around for a decade or so now. Long enough and promising enough to interest even those halls of reverence, the museums. Experimental workshops have been established by a few television stations. These video artists don't work with paint and brushes but with capacitors, resistors and semiconductors."

Natalie is startled. It is as though Gregory, sensing danger, has materialized in front of her. Gregory lives on semiconductors. Capacitors are in his blood. Tom is striding back and forth across the front of the room, banging his fist against his open palm for emphasis. His energy is not lost on her but the thread of his lecture is. Radical software. Signal manipulation. Her ears pick up familiar terms. Video synthesizers. Interrupted circuitry. Cathode

45

rays. Horizontal input. Negative images. She could be at her own dinner table ladling out soup to a group of executives and their wives. The faces change with the seasons. The survival rate is low. One year's crop of rising young men is next year's harvest of crack-ups and dropouts. They haven't done much entertaining lately. Gregory hasn't been sleeping well lately. She gives up trying to follow Tom, the first lecture in six years on which she has been unable to concentrate.

The silent intensity that he has come to expect of Natalie is simply not on her face today. This disturbs him, throws him off his mark. It must be all the technical details. He is winging it as far as the technical aspects go, parroting what others have written on the subject. This movement interests him for other reasons. He is sure that the art of the future will have as its chief function the transfer of information and that, in the process of this transfer, the artist's individuality will have to be submerged into the general whole. If this should happen, the modern concept of "art" as beauty isolated from its function would atrophy, returning us to the days of the medieval cathedral builders. He is saving this speculation for his next lecture but he is tempted to throw it in now just to see some enthusiasm on Natalie's face. Video art affects me like a sleeping pill, he would confide. He would risk saying it aloud to everyone if he could be sure she would come to life.

"Did you know," he asks her as he seats her, "that the Vikings were considered great hosts?"

"No, I didn't," she answers, off balance again. An ingenue. A silly flirt. Where is her intelligence, her gravity? She is sorry she accepted his invitation. She doesn't know why she took this step which will now give him the opportunity to clarify his intentions. She is aware of his general feeling for her and this is all she can take for the moment. Any further specificity is unthinkable. But she is thinking of it. And she has said yes. To retreat from him now, after six years, means to face a void. A void in the sense of suddenly nothing outside of herself against which to press the tensions of her mind. What she would like is to have things stay where they are and go no further. She is not inclined toward the kind of relationship he wants.

"The Vikings were legendary hosts. The conditions for entertaining were laid down by the god Odin in a poem called 'Hávamál, the Viking's Code': Fire, food and clothes, water and towels and a welcoming speech should he find who comes to the feast. Badly paraphrased, of course."

"Is there some connection?"

"Connection?"

"Between you and the Vikings?"

"Well, if I can believe my father, something I'm not usually inclined to do, we're descended from a long line of Vikings. Do you know, my grandmother always kept a basketful of flatbread and cured meat under the roof of her storehouse in case anyone dropped by unexpectedly?"

Grandmother. She thinks of Hermine and doesn't know what to say. She feels she is expected to carry her share of the conversational burden and grandmothers seem a safe enough subject. "My grandmother never cooked," she offers. "She believes that most wives are mistresses reduced to slavery."

"Who did the cooking?"

"From the time I can remember until I took it over, Uncle Laszlo was our cook." She laughs.

"We always seem to laugh when we talk about Laszlo." He feels they are old friends and Laszlo is their history.

"Well, to be fair, Laszlo does strike me as amusing but everyone else takes him very seriously. He takes himself seriously."

"Does he resent that?"

"I don't think so. We understand each other."

"Oh." The subject is exhausted. There is something drastic about the silences between them. "In my parents' house," Tom says, rushing in, "every Thursday night, all through the winter, we had the same supper. Yellow pea soup called *ärter med fläsk*, pancakes and lingonberry jam. It's a Swedish custom. My father is ashamed of his background but for some reason he hangs onto a few of the old rituals."

Just as she begins to wonder why he is chattering about pea soup, he says, "I'd like to make it for you sometime soon." He says it so earnestly that it changes the entire tone of their conversation. Just when she was getting comfortable. There must be safer ground somewhere.

"I had a little trouble with your lecture today," she says.

"Trouble?"

Now she has done it. She will have to bring up Gregory. "Well," she says with a sigh, "my husband is in the semi-conductor-components business. It seems that the equipment I've been hearing about all my life is vital to the 'new art.' It was a shock."

"It is a difficult subject," he reassures her. "So much highly technical stuff. I don't understand it myself. Film I understand. Film is chemical. But video is electronic. I've been told its possibilities are infinite. Would you like to meet a few video artists?" In his mind he is arranging a long, an endless, series of meetings. He has hundreds of people he can introduce her to. Thousands. Christ! Will they ever get past this stage? Do you like me? he wants to ask. How much? Is it safe? He chances it.

There's a deadly moment when she looks as though she can't breathe. Then she says "yes." It floats out to him on her exhaled breath, almost inaudible. He waits for the qualifier. There is none. Strange, but he feels all her pent-up energy in the yes. He perceives a lifetime of waiting for a moment like this. Her energy is coming at him with the speed of a train. They are both silent. They've stunned themselves into silence.

The food arrives. They eat. He can't tell if the food is good or bad. It looks beautiful. The smell is laudable. His taste buds must have died under the assault of his passion. And for years he thought it was his passion that had died. Finally, he can share Barbara's indifference to food. He can take it or leave it, in her words. He decides they will leave it.

"Let's go," he tells Natalie. He gets up. He gets the check. He gets the taxi. As he takes her arm to help her into it, he feels the slam of her presence against his chest. In the taxi he is senseless.

Natalie is trembling so violently that she has to press her hands hard against her thighs to stop them from bucking. She sits next to him burning and ice cold. Her skin feels raw. Now that he has gotten them this far he is staring straight ahead like a man in a trance, incapable of any further movement. She has no control left over her body, feels it is being automated from somewhere outside. A shaft of intense heat shoots through her, then a blast of deadening cold. Let them get this over with quickly, she prays, so they can get on with the business of knowing each other. As far as she is concerned, their bodies are the main impediment.

His office is a shabby one-room apartment located in the Corridor, that unpleasant, unaesthetic, statistically dangerous zone between Columbus and Amsterdam Avenues on the Upper West Side. His office is here because the rent is cheap but since the second break-in, last month, the one in which his door was ripped from its hinges because the "perpetrators" couldn't cut through the new steel panel with their blowtorch, he has been thinking of moving. He would like to relocate in SoHo but the rents there are prohibitive. Then there is SoSo, the area below SoHo, SoHo being the area south of Houston Street. Knowing the origin of words and place names comforts him. The world is less random. He likes to think that at a given point in time and space, not given to him to know, everything in the world interlocks. It puts him in a good humor to think this.

He wants to move out but he doesn't want to give Barbara the satisfaction of being right. She did warn him about the neighborhood and she will remind him of this every chance she gets. "It's sheer insanity," she said. He hasn't told her of the robberies. When he does move out he will tell her it's because of the noise. That's a fair compromise and half of the truth. Acid rock, punk rock, country and western, folk, R & B, soul and disco. He has survived all the trends. In return, he plans to introduce his neighborhood to a classic. He plans to put *Götterdämmerung* on at top volume with the knob at full treble and then leave the place. This will give him a few hours of revenge for all the years of torment. He thinks about it and plans to do it one day soon but knows he never will. In the meantime, it makes a good story.

He is so nervous that it takes him a while to get the key into the lock. Once it's in it turns easily enough but then he has to hurl his full weight against the door to get it to open. This is a recent development. According to his superintendent, the new hinges don't fit like the original ones and can't be made to. He is stuck with a snug door.

After the second unsuccessful hurl, he turns to Natalie and says, "I can't think who right now but someone famous once said: 'Everything in life is resistant to man and his wishes starting with gravity.' The moral is you just have to keep on pushing." He puts his shoulder to it a third time. In between shoves he gasps, "I think it was Rilke."

Though she smiles at his remark Natalie seems to be disappearing into her coat. He is sweating inside his. A few more shoves and the door accedes. It's almost worse once they are inside. What is he going to do with her here? He takes her coat and throws it over his desk. He rips off his own and piles it on top. He motions her to the one armchair but she doesn't appear to notice and goes instead to his bookshelves.

"It's dark enough in here to grow mushrooms," he says, going for the light.

"Yes," she says when it comes on, "and there's enough dirt too. I'm sure you could." They both laugh.

"Do you have a system?" she asks.

"For what?"

"For arranging your books. They're not alphabetical and it doesn't look as if they're by subject."

"No. I don't really have a system."

"How do you find what you want?"

"I usually remember where they are and if I forget, well, it's torture."

"Oh." She sounds disapproving. "I keep everything alphabetically but broken down by subject first. The nonfiction, that is."

"Do you keep your books separate from your husband's?"

"No."

"I do but that's my only system. Can I fix you some coffee?"

"Yes, please. May I help?"

"No. It'll take only a minute."

As he waits for the coffee to drip through, he watches her browsing among his books. Her head is angled sharply to one side so that she can read the titles. She runs a fingernail, a polished one, across the spines as she works her way along the wall. It's smooth going until she comes to a pile of spilled books. Before continuing, she rights these on the shelf. He knew it! Christ! He likes disorder, cultivates it. He equates neatness with sterility. At least Barbara isn't neat and doesn't nag him the way his father does. Natalie has taken a book down and is smiling tenderly at it. He forgives her the straightening. With that face, he will forgive her anything.

When she enters Tom's office she is overwhelmed with fear, frozen with it. She feels him take her coat away, sees him throw it onto his desk, throw his on top. The room is very dim. Through the dimness and her fear she can see the dirt. It bothers her less than the disorder. She is not prepared for the disorder. Clutter wherever she looks. No free space. None. This puzzles her, disappoints her. She knows from Tom's lectures that Dürer's engraving of Erasmus's room sends him into raptures. To think she had imagined him living in an Erasmian room. Sun. Order. Clarity. And this room is positively feral in its darkness and disorder.

She clings to the walls of books. He must have thousands. The room is alive with books. She feels calmer and less disappointed looking at them. Surely they are organized even though the rest of his things are a shambles. She needs to know. Perhaps he has an esoteric system. He tells her he has no system at all. And then he asks her a curious question. It seems disloyal to Gregory to admit to Tom that she keeps her books separate from her husband's so she lies to him. Disloyal? My God, she is here!

Her books are her own. She has never shared them with anyone. She makes lame excuses to avoid lending them out. She doesn't want anyone else's hands on them. She suffers over her lack of generosity in this matter, hates herself for it.

The coffee is delicious. Her knees are still unsteady so she puts the saucer carefully at her feet. He sits at her feet on a beautiful small carpet which glows even in the gloom. He tells her it is a prize, an antique prayer rug he found on a trip to the Middle East. They exchange enthusiasms for the art of dyeing, the lost art of the vegetable dye. When that subject runs dry he retrieves the porcelains. "Tell me about them," he asks. She tells him, her eyes shining as she describes the glazes. Creamy white, celadon green, pale blue, the blue of certain winter skies,

blue with a glazing of ice. She has the almond eyes one
sees in Byzantine mosaic frescoes. He will put her together
piece by splendid colored piece. At the heart of the puzzle
she is, is an ardent coolness. He wants to get to the bottom
of this paradox and he doesn't care if it takes forever.

Natalie knows her porcelains and she is a good teacher.
Even her passion has poise. Is there no crack anywhere?
The Sung monochromes are her favorites. And the celadons
of all periods. As she talks, her hands mimic their shapes.
Tom has no depth in Chinese porcelains but he does know
that the Chinese artist, whatever his medium, was most
often a man with a message. It is fitting that Natalie collects these porcelains. The hell with Chinese porcelains.
He wants to know more about her. He doubts that her
answers will satisfy him. Her responses so far have been
pared too thin to satisfy anything.

"Are your parents alive?" he asks.

"No." She is surprised by the question.

"When did they die?" He will be a bulldog if he must.

"My father died during the Second World War. My
mother, let's see, about eight or nine years ago."

"My father is still alive. My mother, too, although at
times it's hard to tell."

"What does that mean?"

"My mother is a very submissive person. Forty-five years
of marriage and she still believes in the miracle of my
father."

"What's he like?"

"Very difficult. Dogmatic. Rigid. A tyrant, actually. But,
of course, he sees himself as heroic. He prides himself on
being a leader. De Gaulle was his idol."

"Have you always been so bitter?"

"No. Do I sound bitter? When I was a kid I wasn't
bitter, just terrified. I couldn't even look him in the face.
In my dreams he used to turn into a lion and come after
me. You might say my bitterness is retrospective."

Her silence is a rebuke. He has said too much, been
too casual about his hatred. "Did you all live together? I
mean you told me Laszlo was your cook."

"I did?"

"What about your mother?"

"My mother married again after we came to this country. Then she moved to South America."

She has mastered the grammar of evasion. He will never find out anything this way.

"How did you ever manage with such a father?" she asks.

"I guess I didn't."

"But you did. Look at you!"

The compliment is so unexpected, so spontaneous, that he fumbles his response. "My summers must have saved me, the summers I spent in Sweden with my grandparents."

She asks him for another cup of coffee. After a period of great distance she feels reality coming closer. Everything is closer, space swallowed up, the walls pressing in, the field narrowing. She is being run to ground.

He returns with the coffee. As she takes the cup from him the walls begin to quake. Music. Loud, ravening. It pours through the walls and into the apartment like water through a collapsing dam, flooding the last bit of space, taking her last bit of strength. She falls back against the chair, limp.

"My God! What is it?"

"I'm sorry," he says and throws up his hands.

"Can you do something about it?"

"No. The neighbors don't appreciate my sensitivity. I've tried."

"You mean this goes on all the time? How can you work?"

"Once I'm really absorbed I can block it out."

"You're very lucky."

"Noise bothers you that much?"

"Yes. I wish it didn't." She squints against the glittering sound of the marimbas. "The best in Salsa," croons the disc jockey. "Tito Puente, the King of Latin music. Carlos Santana. 'Oye Como Va.' 'Para los Rumberos.'" The music is forcing a party on them but one look at Natalie's tense face tells him that there will be no dancing here. She is pressing her fingers delicately to her temples. He prepares himself for her departure. In a way it's a relief. His chronic failures with Barbara have left him a little uncertain. He doesn't like to dwell on the subject. It gets him nowhere. Barbara's reluctance is okay with him. One less responsibility. He can't stand her cool critical posturing, her little surprised gasps of pain, her removal of his hand from some place on her that he has been stroking, her let's-get-it-over-with attitude. All of this makes him feel clumsier than he is. He knows he's clumsy. He doesn't know how to be less clumsy. Objects come to life under his hands but when he touches anything animate his fingers lose their way. Perhaps it's because he has had so little practice. Glacial governesses, remote parents and then boarding school where cruelty was added to coldness. Poor imprinting for a would-be lover.

"Is there a book you'd like to borrow before we go?" The idea of a book of his in her house pleases him.

"I don't know. Do you have something in mind?"

"Yes," he says and goes right to it. He gives her Ponge. *The Voice of Things.* "Can we have lunch again next week?" he asks as he hands her the book. "I'd like to cook for you."

"Do you think we'll have this musical accompaniment?"

"I'll work it out." He strokes the side of her cheek and then removes his hand. He will need both of them to pull the front door closed.

CHAPTER

5

"AREN'T WE GOING TO YOUR OFFICE?" NATALIE ASKS AS the taxi turns south instead of north.

"Yes. But not my old office. I've moved."

"Since last week?"

"Yes."

"Why?"

"The truth?"

"Yes. Why not?"

"For you."

"For me? That's insane."

"Well, for me too. The rush part was for you. I've been ready to move for months. For years. I was ready to move out the day after I moved in. Wait until you see the new place. It's terrific."

It is. Brick walls, fireplace, windows, light, garden, plants, prayer rug.

"How did you furnish it so quickly?" she asks, pointing to the brown corduroy couch, the butcherblock table, the oak-and-steel chairs.

"I bought everything from the previous tenants."

"Where are your books?"

"In storage until I get some shelves. How long can you stay?"

"For the afternoon."

"Hungry?"

"Nervous."

"Can you eat?"

She shakes her head. She can't even speak. Then he's

across the room, his arms around her. She reaches up for his neck. Their clothes are undone, a soft fall of fabric grazing her ankles. Under them the prayer rug is silken. His body is silken, long, lean and silken. He has long silken flanks. She wonders what flanks are. She is not certain but he has them, of that she is certain. She wonders what his body looks like. Her eyes are closed. She wonders if his are. She looks. They are. She closes hers again. She feels warm and liquid. Along the length of their bodies their skin has joined. She is covered completely by his skin. They are lightly joined, skin to skin. She wants never to be separated. He has joined even the skin of his mind to hers. Their minds are joined. Now she is warmer and more liquid. Now she is porous. Now she can empty herself, drop by drop, through this single skin of theirs into him. She wants to. She will. She does. Drop by drop. When the transfer is complete she weeps.

He strokes her hair. He says over and over "IloveyouIloveyouIloveyou." It's like a lullaby, soothing. She is still liquid. His face is drowning in her hair, his hands tangled in it. Her uncovered mouth is liquefying. He covers it with his own.

They are in the shower. The water wakes her and who is this stranger looking at her? Soaping her breasts? Her breasts. One is larger than the other. They are both too small, the nipples too dark. He lathers her stomach. She has a childhood scar there, fat as a leech. Oh, God. Her thighs, the backs are striated. Her body is absurd. It has betrayed her. She is too short, her arms too thin, her legs bowed. One kneecap is off center. Her feet are too long. Her feet are too narrow. Her head is filled to bursting with the small noises of her mind. He may not look! She will not allow it.

"You're beautiful," she hears him say. "You're perfect."

He is a liar. She will never believe him again. He puts his arms around her and pulls her to him. Their soapy skins glide apart. She backs off, wide awake. She can't meet his eyes. She looks at the rest of him, sees that his wet hair is thinning, that his shoulders are narrower than they look in clothes, that there are no muscles in his upper arms, that he has a small slack belly, that his legs are long and beautiful, that he has two deeply webbed toes on each foot. Looking at his feet, she feels better about her own.

She rushes out of the shower first. She hardly dries herself. He may walk in on her. Her clothes stick as she pulls them on her damp body. Her hair drips onto her shoulders. Her mascara runs into her eyes and burn. She tries to cope.

He stays in the shower a long time. He feels like singing but he restrains himself. He has a terrible voice. When he joins in song he causes other voices to miscarry. She cried! No, she wept! Weeping is deeper. He has her. Nothing went wrong. He has read that some women weep. Barbara has never wept. He has never made her weep. He could pound his chest and roar like Tarzan as he used to do for Laura. Now he could do it for himself. He feels silly, giddy. Christ, he feels good! He gets out of the shower and goes to the kitchen to serve her the best damn meal she has ever eaten.

The menu is deceptively simple. He hopes she will understand that it took him the entire morning to prepare this meal. He has decided not to fix *ärter med fläsk,* steering clear of anything Swedish. He doesn't want to be reminded of his father today. They will start with a fish soup, go on to *Spanakopitta,* the dough homemade, the spinach fresh. He has washed it six times and removed all the stems. The feta cheese comes from a Greek store on Twenty-ninth Street. For dessert he has made a hazelnut cheesecake. Toasted hazelnuts cost six dollars a pound! He pays no attention to prices. For these precious hazelnuts he ran from Twenty-ninth to Seventy-first Street. Barbara would kill him if she knew the price. She will kill him when she discovers what he is paying for this studio. She doesn't understand why he can't work at home now that Laura's room is empty.

He pours the wine. The color is glorious. "How do you like the soup?" he asks after she has taken the first taste. Stupid. An overeager boy.

"It's delicious. The fish is done perfectly. How long? Not more than three or four minutes, I would guess."

"Yes, that's right." His heart stirs. This woman KNOWS. "Do you like to cook?"

"Oh, yes. It's one of my greatest pleasures."

Now who else would say it that way? Others would say, "I love to cook." "I adore cooking." They discuss fish soups with warm enthusiasm. They share recipes, hints, techniques. They discuss fish soups of all genders, of all races, of all nations. They spend an hour on fish soups alone. If that takes an hour, imagine how long it will take to cover everything! Food is a better subject than grandmothers, the best subject, clean, clear and bracing, the sea air of conversation.

"*Spanakopitta*," he announces. "Spinach pie. I'm showing off."

"Marvelous," she says. "You've made the dough yourself."

"How can you tell?"

"I make it myself. I learned from my mother. By the way, whatever happened to the pea soup we were supposed to have?"

"Another time," he promises. "It's too heavy for lunch. It'll have to be for supper one day. And on a Thursday."

"Supper would be impossible, I'm afraid. It's late," she says, looking at her watch. "I really have to go."

"You can't go yet," he tells her. "Your hair is still wet."

"You sound like a mother."

"I am."

"I'm sure you're a wonderful father."

"I am. I was. My daughter is away at boarding school."

"Why?" Her intonation leaves no doubt about her disapproval.

"It wasn't my idea. I hate it. She wanted to go and my wife wanted it too. It's her Alma Mater."

"I'll never allow that," she says and shakes her damp curls. They bounce like small springs. She rakes them with her fingers, then binds them with an elastic. "My boys are going to have to live at home while they're at college."

"Are you serious?"

"No, of course not. It's not permissible to be serious about such things."

"Are they nice kids?" He raises a hand to stop himself. "Don't answer that. It was a stupid question. Of course they're nice kids. My daughter is a nice kid too. She's a fabulous kid. What are yours like?"

"Well, they're poles apart. The oldest one, Adam, is very quiet, very private, almost antisocial. He's very gentle and equally sensitive. He has a talent for drawing but he's a terrible athlete. The younger one, Stephan, is outgoing, funny, noisy, bright, athletic and highly competitive."

"Does the athletic part matter to you?"

"Why do you ask?"

"Well, you mentioned it twice."

"It matters to their father, not to me. He's a believer in team sports for children. He thinks they build character and spirit."

"They mattered to my father too. I'm a terrible athlete, much worse than Adam, I'm sure. The only sport I ever attempted was riding and then only because I was less afraid of the horse than of my father. Is Adam afraid of his father?"

"I don't think so but he does want to please him. I suppose that amounts to the same thing for Adam. I really do have to leave."

She gets up and he sees there's no holding her. He tries anyway. "Are you enjoying the book I gave you?" he asks.

"No, but it's not the book. The book is good. It's my mood."

"I've just finished reading this one," he says, taking a book from his desk. "You might like it."

"I've read it," she says. "It's a fine book."

What a fool he is. Of course she's read it. She's probably read it in Russian. He has fallen into the stance he normally takes toward his wife, toward the world, a kindly, instructive, faintly patronizing stoop.

He helps her on with her coat. Their goodbyes are awkward, clumsy, separating them before they are actually apart. They don't know each other any longer. They revert to formulas. The formulas get them through this sticky time. "Lovely lunch." Pause. "I'm glad you liked it." Pause. "Well." Pause.

"I'll drop you off in a cab. I'm going right by your block," he tells her.

"No, thank you anyway but I prefer to go alone. You might like to know," she tells him at the door, "that you can save fifty cents a pound by toasting your own hazelnuts."

What if this inclination to thrift runs as deep as her earnestness? What if she saves bits of string, old rubber bands? What if she washes off wax paper and reuses it? If she saves old envelopes and makes marketing lists on their backs? If she uses one-inch pencil stubs, jars for drinking glasses? If, in an age of plastic bags, she still lines her pail with newspaper? What if? What if she is a squirrel like his mother? He sees her straightening his books. My God, what if she is obsessed like his father?

It won't matter, any of it. He will still love her.

She is disturbed and exhausted and exhilarated. She wants to be alone, to be quiet and to think. A subway ride is the last thing she wants but it can't be helped. It's rush hour. At the token booth she asks for directions to her stop. She can't hear over the noise. People are shoving at her. They want their tokens and the train that has just pulled in. She is pushed aside, boards the wrong train but she is in Queens before she realizes her error. There is no logic to this train. It leapfrogs the city in a random way. In Queens there is no one to help her. She climbs up several flights of stairs, down several others, traveling against the prevailing tide. When her train does finally arrive it is almost empty. She jumps out at the first stop in Manhattan. Who knows where it will go next? She takes two buses to get home.

Both boys are sitting at the kitchen table, waiting.

"It's very late," Adam says. "You should have called."

"It's dark out," Stephan adds. "You're always warning us."

"Dad tried the hospital. You weren't there," Adam says.

"I took the wrong train. I wound up in Queens," she says.

"Queens! Did you get as far as Shea Stadium?" Stephan asks.

"Where is Dad?" she asks.

"He won't be home till very late. He said to tell you something important came up."

She sits with the boys while they eat. She cannot eat, may never eat again. Spasms of heat and cold alternate. In between these spasms she talks to the children. She is in no way connected to her words, in no way connected to her children. It is all a dream which will pass. It must pass. A potentate once asked a wise man to devise a single sentence whose meaning would hold true forever. The wise man answered without hesitation. "And this, too, shall pass away." Hermine. She can hear her grandmother's high nasal voice.

She clears the table in a trance, does the dishes. She wants a bath and some music. She installs the boys in their rooms. Homework is begun. Aid is needed, given. Doors are closed, finally. Water is running, music begins, at last. She exhales and sinks into the tub. How can she feel she has fallen from Grace when she doesn't believe in Grace? The water isn't hot enough. She opens the faucet a crack and lets in a steady trickle of heat. Steam is rising all around her. She sinks lower into the tub. Water laps at her chin line. She is weak from the steam. Away from him, in her own home, at this moment, she would choose to undo what they have done. At this very moment, she has the strength not to do more. This thought makes her feel heavy. The heaviness persists. The bath water feels like hot lead. It weighs on her. She cannot rise out of the tub. She is weighted down. Only the steam is rising. She knows they will do more, much more. The deception will grow. She is growing toward him. Tom. She feels more connected to him than she does to her children. There isn't room for all her connections.

The pressure is on now. She knows how much he wants her, to what degree and in what way. He will not be satisfied until she bursts through the skin of her reserve, bursts through it the way an acrobat hurtles through a paper hoop, bravely, blind-folded and at high speed. Just the thought of such a performance causes her heart to thud. The thudding and pounding and knocking are unbearable. She drags herself upright and hangs over the side of the tub.

She pretends to be asleep when Gregory comes home. She should be asleep. It's past one o'clock. She hears him in the bathroom, hears the click as he replaces the cap on his bottle of vitamins. She has given up stealing the Valium out of this bottle in which he hides them, mixing them in with the ascorbic acid. His doctor just refills the prescription for him. Hermine's doctor, the same doctor who is recovering from a heart attack. He probably takes them too.

Gregory gets into bed next to her carefully, so carefully. His consideration makes her feel even worse.

CHAPTER

6

TOM DOESN'T WANT TO LEAVE THE STUDIO. THE RUG IS still damp with Natalie's thawing. Why abandon its moist warmth for a cold pillow at home? And the couch can be instantly transformed into a bed by a five-year-old using two fingers. An adult can speed the metamorphosis with one politely crooked pinkie. He had planned to open the couch, to turn it into a bed for Natalie and himself, but the prayer rug was there, already unfolded. He found the prayer rug in a shop in Jerusalem long ago, sandwiched between some indifferent local rugs. On the very top was a pile of Arab bridal dresses smelling of goat. He wishes he had bought one of those caftans so that now he could take it out, smelling of mothballs and goat, and give it to Natalie. He would love to see her in one. With her dark hair and precise bones and delicate sway to the small of her back she would look like Scheherazade. He wants to give her a present. Tomorrow he will go shopping for something, something vivid and loose and soft, not at all like her own clothes which vary from gray to beige to brown to black and are so neat. Red. Red would be a detonation.

Barbara isn't home when he arrives. He is in the kitchen reheating some leftovers for their dinner when she walks in.

"What are you doing?" she asks. "Don't tell me you've forgotten it's your mother's birthday? We're expected there for dinner tonight."

He knows how Barbara loves going to his parents'

home. It means dinner dresses, jewels, perfumes, hairdos, silver, crystal, candles, servants. Barbara loves his parents. She is more devoted to his mother than to her own. She is frightened of his father though filled with admiration. She has turned herself inside out and yet she cannot seem to win him over. She doesn't feel secure in his affections. But then who does? Tom's poor vaporous gray mother has been at it forever and she doesn't. No one who works for his father ever has. Tom himself feels menaced.

His tuxedo is a mess. He will have to ask Barbara to press it for him. He hates asking her for favors. He has become as self-sufficient as possible to avoid asking. He does the marketing and the cooking. He takes his shirts to the laundry, his suits to the dry cleaner. If he had a separate bed he would wash his own sheets. But he has never learned to iron. This gap in his education will now cost him.

"Yes, I'll do it but Christ it's so late," Barbara grumbles. "And I'm dead. I wanted to take a short nap before we left. I don't know why everything with you has to be at the last minute."

Barbara is wearing a close-fitting black dress to the floor. Over it she has thrown a printed chiffon sack. Her hair is tied up in a smaller triangle of the same material. Blond gypsies are a contradiction, he wants to tell her. My father will be put off by your appearance. There is a slackness about Barbara that irritates Senior. Tom has watched his father observe Barbara's breasts as they gyrate under her clothes. He could apprise her of his father's objections but she wouldn't believe him, would accuse him of foisting off on his innocent father the things he holds against her himself. She would be bitter and ice-cold and if they were going out with other people she would be more seductive than usual. It's a pity. His mother is too timid to register an objection and his father never will. Senior likes to have just cause for dislike.

A butler opens the door. There are servants everywhere, white servants. Senior has been slow to hire blacks in his empire as well as his home. There have been a few court cases to speed things up. It's not racism, Senior maintains. He believes in Merit, the first and best of which, and actually the only one that counts, is the merit of having been born white.

Tom greets his mother.

"Hello, dear," she says and smiles vacantly at him.

She is muffled to the neck in pale gray chiffon. Her hair is blue-gray, her eyes the color and texture of fog. A few grains of caviar are caught in her teeth, her breath fish-smelly when he kisses her.

"Get some champagne, dear," she says. She has a glass in her hand, this floating gray lady who passes herself off as his mother. On an impulse he looks down at her hands. Her fingers are lax around the cut-glass stem. If he blows on the glass it will fall from her grasp. Her free hand twists a lace handkerchief, the only hand left in America still clutching one.

"Happy birthday, Mother," he says.

"Thank you, dear," she whispers behind her handker-chief as if she has no rights to his wish for her.

His mother has no sheen at all, no light-reflecting possi-bility. Even standing under the Waterford crystal chan-delier, itself a gray-blue, with all the candles burning, 164 of them, she is opaque as bisque. He loves the chandelier, loves the candlelight. There are no electric lights in the formal living room of his parents' townhouse. It is his mother's only idiosyncrasy. She has settled for this, her first and last ditch. Well, at least everything looks better in this light so perhaps she is right to have taken a stand here. Privately, his father rails against the high cost of candles. Publicly, he takes the credit.

Barbara is mingling. She has a gift for it. She hits her summit in such social gatherings. In this light she looks softer. This light blurs the edges. Her chiffon sack has ac-quired a conquerer's grace. Her generous lips are parted. She is breathless with excitement, hot, the heat rising steams her blue eyes. She is moist all over, working as hard as if she were running. Barbara brings a furious energy to seduction. She is trying to charm Senior. It takes all the muscle and endurance she has built up. He might as well greet his father now and get it over with. He throws back his shoulders and propels the long bones of his legs forward to cross the distance between them. He is tired before he begins his journey.

"Son," Senior says, extending a hand.

Tom takes it. They shake. Son. The word smarts on his cheek. Son followed by a nod, a slight inclination of the handsome, magisterial, snow-white head. Not Hello, How are you, Glad to see you. Just SON and the NOD. There is no more forthcoming and there never will be though he woos his father more ardently than Barbara has ever dared to do. He doesn't know what he wants from his father. Yes, he does. He wants to be taken seriously. He wants respect, acknowledgment. The hell with love. He wants this bastard's respect. By now he is so angry, has worked himself into such a state, that he can barely manage a smile.

"Dad," he says and trades nod for nod. With this nod I designate you father. He wishes he could designate Senior right out of existence. He makes a slight formal bow. Then he takes Barbara by the elbow and moves her away from his father's side. She resists but he keeps a cold presure on her arm. He needs an ally. Even an enemy will do. "By the way," he says over his shoulder, "you might want to watch for a letter of mine to the *Times* in the next few weeks."

"On what subject?" Senior asks.

"Reproductions from the museum's assembly line."

"Oh?" Senior arches one snow eyebrow. "In that case," he laughs, "I'll skip it. I'm familiar with your opinion on that matter."

"Are you two fighting again?" Barbara asks.

"No," he says. "Just the usual mine-sweeping. Who's here tonight? Anyone interesting?"

"No," she says. "Just the same old boring heads of government, business, finance, communications. No one you'd find interesting."

He laughs. "Sometimes you're very funny."

She smiles back. "I'm glad you notice occasionally. It's good for my morale."

He squeezes her arm affectionately. The afternoon with Natalie has made him feel charitable toward Barbara, that is, until she joins in a conversation whose principal subject is the columnist, James Reston. "Scotty," Barbara says, "Scotty told me the last time I saw him . . ." He skids away from her. She doesn't know James Reston. She met him once, shook his hand on a receiving line, stood in an adoring circle of admirers as he gave his views on current affairs. Then why try to convey the impression of long-standing intimacy? Why the boastful, mundane deception? The empty roving? She is not a stupid woman. He doesn't want to hear any more of what she is saying. He would like to put his fist in her mouth.

Dinner is the usual tasteless fare served in the usual ornate silver vessels. He is seated between his parents. In the presence of his father he grows cold. He knows he is superior to the crowd that is assembled but his brain is chilled, an incapacitating freeze that turns him as witless as the rest. He might as well be a dead man for the interval. What has he done to prove he is alive? In his father's eyes, nothing. In his father's eyes, his kind of knowledge doesn't count. His credentials are feminine. His father groups him with the professions that wear skirts, the priests, teachers, poets of life, the men who don't count in any sensible scheme. Certainly he is still treated like a child, the spindly, sulky child he was, the child so frightened that even the dogs, that pair of sleek greyhounds on whom his father lavished so much love and tenderness, could smell his fear.

He sits through dinner hearing the sounds of silver against china, the hum of well-modulated voices, the short bursts of laughter, hearing the whisper and swish of nylon uniforms as the servants appear and disappear, hearing it all through closed ears. Inconsolable.

The evening is interminable. At the earliest decent moment he grabs Barbara and announces that they are leaving.

"No," she says. "I'm having fun. If you're so anxious to leave then go without me. I don't mind."

He considers this a betrayal. Barbara knows he won't leave his father's house without her. The evening drags on. There is fevered chattering. The city's latest crisis. The guests exchange information they have received from the same newspapers, television networks, circle of friends. An endless duplication of swill. No one knows anything! There is no hard knowledge, no grip on history. Incompetence at every level. Yet these are the captains whose decisions mold history. It bleeds the mind. Crime. The talk turns to the subject of security systems for the home, sophisticated burglar alarms, private patrolmen, bodyguards.

"The crime today is to have anything worth stealing." Tom says this to one of his mother's oldest friends, a woman who affects great regality. Mrs. Rilling is one of her ladies-in-waiting. Tom's mother floats him a worried look. She doesn't want anything to mar her birthday. Tom returns her smile. His face is cracking. When he lets go of the smile the pieces of his face will crumble and fall to the floor. His mother's worried looks are killing him. Barbara's high-wire, death-defying social climb is killing him. This house is killing him. But since he's dead already he can hold out a while longer. He keeps the smile going.

Barbara rolls over to him in bed. She hasn't done this in a very long time, rarely crossing the buffer zone of cold sheet which separates them. He is grateful to her for this. He cannot stand her attitude toward him in bed. She is sexually exasperated with him all the time. He doesn't blame her. He has always been a reluctant partner. If there are other men who feel as he does about sex he has yet to know one. All information in the public domain is to the contrary. What's bruited about is that all men have strong drives, unrelenting ones, and if they don't it is because they are impotent. Impotence is a condition which results when fear kills off normal lust. The idea here is that lust is normal. If it is true that lust is normal then he prefers the fear, as would anyone who bothered to look at the consequences of accepting lust as normal human behavior. He can't explain his lust for Natalie.

What he hates about sex is the power it gives people over each other. At least this is what happened between Barbara and him. He's afraid that it will happen with Natalie too. Barbara has a certain hold over him because he doesn't come through for her sexually. In the end, it doesn't do her much good because she would rather have the sex than the hold. She is next to him now, pressing her breasts against his back. He knows he will have to respond. There are times when he doesn't have a choice. He turns to put his arms around her. He is thinking of Natalie. He smooths Barbara's hair, his thoughts lingering on Natalie. Barbara's face is unexpectedly wet, which frightens him. Her vulnerability is frightening enough when she is acting to hide it but when she lets go and delivers it nakedly like this, well, it's numbing. She begins to sob. He tries to comfort her, kissing her hot forehead, covering it with quick, cold kisses.

"Oh, God, oh, God," she cries over and over. "I have nothing of my own. Nothing. I'm nobody. I'll never be anybody. I'll never have anything."

Eventually her sobs taper off. She removes her night-gown and presses herself to his chest. He knows that for the moment he is all that stands between Barbara and her agony. The responsibility shrivels him. He is a slug and she cannot bring him to life. Thoughts of Natalie cannot bring him to life. Barbara is frantic.

"Oh, God," she breathes. "Nothing in my life ever goes right."

"I'm sorry," he whispers, and he is. "Would you like me to do it some other way?"

"No," she says, and the contempt in her voice makes him hate her again. "That's hardly the point."

Tom is not trustworthy. Barbara will never trust him again with her feelings. It is so humiliating to be turned down. Tom turns her down in different ways. There is outright refusal, or worse, passive resistance, or the worst, unwilling consent. Tonight it was unwilling consent. He made it clear long ago that she should take care of her needs on her own. He certainly wasn't going to participate. He makes her feel unnatural. Christ, she's not a sex maniac. It's he who is celibate. She wants to get out of this life they have together. Her present therapist tells her to stay until she has some options. Life, after all, is a business. What, he asks, will she do with herself alone in a small dark apartment? He answers for her. She will wait to be invited out of it by friends. She will have exchanged one dependency for another. She must work to make herself independent and then she can decide if she wants to go or to stay. It sounds good, she tells him, but there is a problem with his logic.

"I have no skills. And how can I take a job that's on a lower social level than my life?"

"You can't. Press your friends. Use your influence. Use your husband's, your in-laws'."

"They won't help me."

"Then you have to help yourself."

"My husband says I'm my own worst enemy."

"Do you think you are?"

"No." She laughs. "I think he is."

"Then work on his guilt."

"He has none. I have all the guilt."

"Then go back to school and get some skills."

"In what?"

"Law. Journalism. Social work. Anything. Pick something that interests you."

She can't tell him that she was turned down by a law school and two schools of journalism before coming to him.

"I'll think about it."

She can't tell him that even if she is accepted at graduate school it takes years to get a degree; that she's not young anymore; that she's frightened that if she leaves Tom she'll be old and alone for the rest of her life. Tell him that? He's a man. He's jumped all the hurdles. She's the one left limping along behind.

She vows not to cry in front of Tom ever again. Her weeping upsets him and she likes that, but lately she feels she's giving up more than she's getting. Each time he is less and less affected. Tonight he wasn't there at all, kissing her forehead like a programmed machine over and over in one spot until she screamed at him to stop. She would like to pound on his chest with a clenched fist right this minute, the way they do when a person's heart stops beating, punch it hard enough to start it up beating for her or else hard enough to kill him. She's not sure which.

"By the way," he says as she is contemplating his murder, "I moved my office yesterday."

"What do you mean, moved? You mean you found another place and you're going to move?"

"No," he says. "I actually moved yesterday."

She sits up in bed. "You're kidding! You didn't say a word. That's really crummy."

"It happened very fast. It's a sublet and I had to decide on the spot. You were so busy this week I hardly saw you."

"Is it nice? Where is it?"

"It's downtown, near SoHo. It's very nice. It's only a studio but there's a garden and a fireplace."

"A garden and a fireplace? Christ, it must cost a fortune. How much?"

"It's not too bad for what it is."

"For what it is? How much?"

"That's my business."

"That means it's an arm and a leg. How much? I'm not joking around. I want to know."

"I'm not joking around either. It's my business. I earn the money that pays for it."

"Well, goddammit, if you earn so much money why can't we move from this dump?"

"Anytime. Just find something we can afford."

"How did you get moved so fast? It takes time to move."

"I left everything but my books and the rug."

"Are you crazy? Do you mean to tell me that now you have to go out and buy new furniture? On top of the rent?"

"No. It came furnished."

"A furnished sublet?"

"Yes. No, not exactly. I had to buy the furniture from the previous tenant. It was the only way I could get the apartment. And the furniture is really nice. Almost new. All I need are bookshelves."

"I don't believe this! There's never enough money for me to get a paint job or to re-cover the furniture but somehow there is enough for you to rent a fancy apartment and buy all new things. What's going on? Is there something you've forgotten to tell me, like you're moving out?"

"Nothing is going on. You were right about the other place, that's all. It was dangerous and noisy. I couldn't work it was so noisy and I was robbed twice. I never told you. The second time they ripped the door right off the hinges. I thought I'd surprise you since you always hated the other place so much. You'll like this one, you'll see."

He knows he has smoothed it over. He can feel Barbara relaxing. He's given her what she wants which is to be right. He has said it. You were right. Barbara would rather be right than be loved. She has so much invested in being right. She is still waiting for him to agree that she was right to send Laura to boarding school. She will have to wait a long time for that. Laura belongs at home.

She doesn't believe a word Tom is telling her. She doesn't believe him capable of engineering such a move unless something drastic has happened. He doesn't make changes easily. She's frightened. What if he leaves her? She has al-

ways thought of it the other way around. What will she do
if he leaves her? What if he's found out about all her affairs? What if he's found out about Eric? Eric is his friend.
Sometimes she thinks that all her lovers hang around with
her just to get closer to Tom. This thought is with her all
the time. Her husband is so prodigiously popular. He's at
his best in public, a public man is what he is. In private
he tends to overdo it. In private he's a bit windy. All her
ex-lovers stay on to become friends of Tom's. Often she is
troubled by the thought that this was their intention in the
first place. She can never get rid of them. They are always
lurking around waiting for Tom. They offer him basketball
tickets, private boxes for hockey games, screenings of the
latest movies. They take him out for dinner, to interesting
parties. Of course she is included, but all heads are turned
to Tom. That is the order of the peck. Tom at the top,
herself at the bottom, a lot of strangers with whom she's
gone to bed, in between. Tom is more comfortable with
men than he is with women. Sometimes she wonders if he
has an unexplored preference for them. Probably not. Most
men seem to prefer other men to women for everything
but sex. She prefers men for everything! Meanwhile, as
she burrows deeper into her side of the bed, she is left
with the feeling that something dangerous has crept into
the space between them.

"I'm at the end of my rope," Barbara tells Grunewald, the
German Prince, her therapist. "Tom has taken an apartment of his own. Oh, he calls it an office but I'm prepared
for the worst."

"Well, this may prove useful. Perhaps it will force you
to take this venture more seriously. Your sense of humor
is often misplaced here." He looks at her over the top of
his glasses. He has the remote face of a man engaged in a
grand internal debate.

"How much more seriously can I take it? It's my life,
after all. I know that as well as you do. You won't be
satisfied until I weep in your office."

"Being ironic is not being serious. Neither is going to
bed with every man who asks. You are not going to work
out an authentic life with this sort of attitude."

"Dr. Grunewald, all your brilliant logic has gotten me

nowhere. I'm fed up with these games I have to play in order to have a little peace. Why can't I just be me?"

"Who are you?"

"Oh, shit. You win."

"But this isn't a competition. If you think that, then our time together is worthless."

"Okay," she sighs. "I'll try again. Where were we?"

He jiggles in his chair. His knees bounce. "The future is an attitude. What you are after is transcendence. Another matter entirely, a matter outside of time. Transcendence doesn't last when it's achieved only in the bedroom." He leans back in his chair and cracks his knuckles.

"I know how I should behave," she tells him. "The trick, the secret, is in knowing how to change. And none of you clowns is able to teach that." She pulls her hair over one ear and twists it into a rope.

"Precisely," Grunewald answers. "For a woman like yourself, transcendence occurs in moments of discovery, very rare moments. Transcendence and orgasm are not necessarily synonymous. There is some confusion over this point."

What is he saying? She has no idea what he means.

He gets up from his desk and sits down in the chair next to her. "What I mean is that it's only your perception of an affair that can alter the moment. Your fitting of it into your own life's puzzle. One piece closer to completion, to authenticity. Do you understand what I mean?"

"I'm not sure," she answers with a short laugh. "But at least I'm authentic in my unhappiness."

"Then you mistake the meaning of authentic."

"That's nothing new. I'm always mistaking something."

"No, you're mistaken only in your expectations. You're not neurotic, you know. A change in attitude is all you really need."

"Now you sound just like my husband."

He smiles. "But you will grant that there is a difference."

"Really? I hadn't noticed. What is it?"

"I'm a disinterested party."

"So is he."

The smile she expects doesn't materialize on Grunewald's face. Instead, he picks up a pencil and, pressing the eraser end to his forehead, says to her in a grave voice,

"Mrs. Rilling, your repartee is often very amusing. Unfortunately, entertaining me won't help you find what you're looking for."

"Back to that again?" Barbara sighs. "You do have a one-track mind, Dr. Grunewald."

"Your unhappiness is equally one-tracked."

Barbara tips an imaginary hat in his direction. "I'd call it a draw today. Wouldn't you agree?"

"Perhaps," he says. "But so what? For you it's still a loss."

"You're a heartless bastard," she says, as lightly as she can manage.

"Let's not waste any time on your feelings for me. Transference isn't part of the process here. It isn't allowed." He smiles at her.

"What is allowed?"

"That which helps us understand your uniqueness and your totality."

"So, you want me to suffer?"

"Not at all. I only want you to be sincere, to operate in good faith. Some humor is sincere, other humor is not." He rises. "Think about that during the week."

"I'll try," she says, "although I won't promise. I've got so many other important, pressing things to do."

"Nothing more pressing than your future, I hope," he says as he closes the door.

CHAPTER

7

NATALIE'S GRIP ON THE HOUSEHOLD IS LOOSENING. AFTER the boys leave for school she looks in their rooms. The clutter accumulating there bothers her yet she feels incapable of putting it right. She can bring no drive, no spirit to the task. Her office is a mess. The kitchen disorients her further.

She takes her coffee and goes directly to the living room, pausing in front of a small vitrine. It houses the few vases, bowls and pots that make up her collection. She views the simplicity, the order, the refinement behind the glass pane with a sigh of relief, as though she had been away from it for too long a time, as though, in her absence, things might have changed. But no, the shapes are exactly right. The glazes are still more subtly beautiful than anything in nature. If the discovery of the porcelain glaze was accidental—the ancient Chinese masters stumbling on it while looking for the philosopher's stone or the *elixir vitae*—her passion for it is decidedly not. For her it is an elixir.

She is studying a small, copper-rimmed bowl when she hears Gregory enter the kitchen. She doesn't move. The bowl reminds her of Hermine. Minutely crackled, singularly pure with a rough mouth rim and an ivory-white glaze that runs in teardrops along the outside. She opens the cabinet door, reaches in and removes it for a closer look.

Behind her another cabinet door slams. Gregory is down much earlier than usual. She's not prepared to see him yet, not certain she can behave naturally. She replaces the pot, takes a deep breath and crosses the foyer to the kitchen.

Gregory is standing over the stove waiting for the coffee to reheat. His back is to her, his head hanging forward limply. Natalie sees the familiar cowlick riding the crown of his head, his short blunt fingers spread on the counter, his wide, bare feet with their impossibly high arch pressed to the cold tile floor. He is still in his pajamas. From this angle he looks like an older brother to his sons. This is the hardest, the worst moment of her married life.

"Good morning," she says. "Sit down and let me get the coffee for you."

He turns to face her and seeing him she gasps, "What is it? Are you sick?"

She rushes over to him and puts her hands to his face. He is warm. She strokes his forehead, tests it with her lips. He submits. She senses that he would like nothing better than to lower his head to her shoulder and cry, let his wet weight sag against her. "What's wrong?" she prods. "I know something is wrong. Just look at you. You look dreadful."

"I was late last night because we got the news we've been waiting for. It's definite. SemiCo is coming out with the same chip as ours for fifteen percent less." He shrugs his shoulders in despair.

"What does that mean?"

"It means my ass is on the line."

"Isn't there anything you can do?"

"Yes. Resign now or wait to be shuffled."

"After all these years? One mistake?"

"You're a child," he tells her wearily.

"Things will work out. I know they will. There are plenty of other companies in this field. Better ones than yours. You've told me so."

In the middle of her sermon he doubles up his fists and screws them into his eyes. She has never seen him like this before. "What about leaving the business altogether?" she persists. "What about law school? You've always wanted to go to law school."

"Not now, Natalie. I'm too exhausted."

"Why don't you go upstairs and lie down."

"I'm going to."

"You can reach me at the hospital. I'm going to the library this afternoon. There are some things I have to double-check for Laszlo's book." This lie rings so loudly and so long in her head that she's certain Gregory can hear it tolling. "Are you going in to work later?" she asks.

"I don't know." He takes his cup and shuffles out of the kitchen.

She hears him sighing on the stairs. She feels sympathy and love and sadness for him but the energy, the force which sends her feelings to him, is missing. It's as though all this is happening to someone else.

When she goes up to the bedroom a few minutes later to collect her things, Gregory is fast asleep, an uncapped bottle marked Vitamin C on the night table. She bends over and kisses his forehead. There is a puzzled look on his face, a look she cannot remember seeing before. How strange. She has lived with him for so long, lived with his arching feet, his affectionate hands, his stubborn cowlick, his sober industrious energy all her adult life. Looking back, it now seems like all her life. She feels irrevocably related to him. One family's blood runs through them both. He is her family. And now, suddenly, blank. The habit remains but the force that drives it home is gone. Nothing left but the habit and her sense of duty. And she thought she knew herself, thought she knew Gregory. Who ever knows anyone? She sits down on the edge of the bed and looks at her sleeping husband, at his open bland decent safe smooth face. After so many years of queerness and foreignness with Hermine and Laszlo she was ready for Gregory, dreaming of someone like him. Here was a man who had never been in hiding, never crossed any oceans, wasn't passionate for pure truth, didn't suffer migraines. All he had done was to declare for success. A small vice. If his desire for it was at the root of his Sunday morning football games, she was all for it. If it was what gave his eyes their lazy blueness, his hair its blond lights, his body its clean muscled sheen, then she fell in love with his desire to succeed. She fell in love with his Americanness.

Thinking of their first meeting, she strokes his forehead. He takes her hand, presses it against his cheek, mumbles something. He doesn't wake up. They met at a music appreciation course. Gregory had just moved to the city from Minneapolis. He had been told he could meet all the girls in the world at adult education classes. Natalie invited him home to dinner. Hermine's revolution to feed the world began at her own table. They sat among the strange, shabby, excitable workers, the "regulars," the out-of-work and hungry who appeared nightly at dinner time. Their heads were filled with theories, their voices with rage, their souls with suffering, only their bellies empty. What charm there was in Gregory's lack of suffering. He had no anger in him, none that Natalie could see, none resembling Laszlo's floating reserve which could be mobilized in an instant and fired. Gregory was like the rest of the world, the others. He was attached, purposeful, and assertive.

After a few dismal evenings at home Gregory took her out to eat. After dinner he took her dancing. He taught her to dance. He taught her the latest songs. He introduced her to jazz, to electronics. Electronics, he told her, was the future. She believed him. She was ready to be persuaded of the beauty of technology, the romance of facts. She was ready to give up the life she shared with Hermine and Laszlo, to trade the eccentric for the ordinary.

Gregory looked like an ordinary human being, dressed like one. He wore dark suits, striped ties, white shirts. He polished his shoes to a reflecting shine and he wore socks which covered his calves and never fell down, unlike Laszlo; Laszlo who was always bending over to yank up a heap of sock; Laszlo whose hair was too long, whose clothes were too noticeable. Even if on the hanger they looked normal, once on his body a strange transformation took place. Laszlo and Gregory disliked each other on sight. For her sake they tried, still try to be cordial. Hermine refused to take Gregory seriously. No capacity for sacrifice, she told Natalie. Her attitude toward him has not changed with the years.

Natalie opens her bag and takes out lipstick and a mirror. A quick stroke of color and she is ready to leave. At the door she turns around and looks at Gregory. The blanket has slipped onto the floor. He is curled against the chill in a fetal position, his normal sleep posture, a wide confident sprawl on his back, contradicted. She walks back to the bed, picks up the blanket and spreads it over him.

The smell hits her as she steps off the elevator. The quintessential hospital smell. It leaves her weak with its immediacy, flinging open the door on another world. With the smell comes a feeling of dread. Hermine is dying. She knows it. The doctor knows it too despite his denial. Laszlo is right. Each day there is simply less of her. Her hand has no weight at all. Gorky's words of devotion to Tolstoy haunt her. "I am not an orphan on this earth so long as this man lives on it." Natalie has been carrying this sentence in the lining of her mind for years, a gold piece against a lean day. She cannot imagine the world without her grandmother. She is not comforted by the belief that those you take into your memory continue to live on in you. This is as far as Hermine's inquiry into the spirit and its harmonies has taken her. It is not far enough for Natalie.

Mrs. Miller is sitting up in a wheelchair next to Hermine's bed when Natalie enters the room. She is squinting at Hermine in an effort to catch her likeness, her eyes thick, as if a rind had grown over them.

"I'm a lot tougher than I look, Mrs. Várády," Mrs. Miller is saying. "Once when I was very young I ran away and hitchhiked to Florida all by myself. My parents didn't know what to do with me. I was crazy. A troublemaker. My husband neither. He died of nerves and a heart condition. I never could settle down."

Natalie sees Hermine smile. She can hardly believe it. Humor has always fatigued her, wit tolerated only when the incongruities of the human condition were commented on from a strict moral posture. Then she might manage a weak smile. But laughter for the sake of laughter?

She greets the two women.

"Natalie," Mrs. Miller says, "please meet my companion." She flings a fleshy arm toward the corner where a black woman sits reading a small book. The woman wets her thumb and forefinger with her tongue as she prepares to turn each page. "Wilhelmina," Mrs. Miller calls. The woman looks up. "Please meet Mrs. Várády's granddaughter."

They nod to one another. Natalie pats Hermine's hand and sits down by the side of the bed. Mrs. Miller wheels herself away. Hermine looks at Natalie for a long moment. Natalie can read nothing in her gaze. Hermine closes her eyes, hangs in a half-sleep. Every now and then her lids

lift, then close, sliding slowly down over the watery surface of her eyes.

In the corner, Mrs. Miller and Wilhelmina talk and
laugh. Bird sounds from Mrs. Miller. Snorts and guffaws
from the companion. "Willie" is enormous. She stands six
feet tall and she has the bones of an ox. Her shoes are off.
She is airing her immense spatulated feet. Natalie can see
pink hummocks at the backs of her heels. When Mrs.
Miller dozes off, Willie gets up from her chair and lumbers
to her patient's side. Then, with the straight back and
strong legs of a weight lifter she reaches down and raises
Mrs. Miller from the chair. She holds her aloft for an in-
tant, dipping her in Natalie's direction like a trophy, before placing her gently on the bed. Crooning, the only
word for what she is doing, she tucks in her blind baby.

Natalie would like to draw the curtain which separates
the two beds. Mrs. Miller takes up too much room with
her laughter and her blank eyes. Willie takes up too much
room. The air around them is charged with electricity. The
air around them is so dry that it crackles or perhaps it is
just the low incessant static of Willie talking to herself.

"Pardon me," Natalie says. "Are you talking to me?" If
only she can embarrass the woman into silence.

"No, Missus." Wilhelmina's voice rings like a bell. "I'm
talking to God, praying for these here women, these poor
lambs. Prayer is the only thing which help, Missus." Her
voice is loud and sonorous, its rhythms evangelical.

So is Natalie's book, to be accurate, Tom's book. *Le
Parti-pris des choses.* "The Voice of Things." Its author is
trying to persuade her that the act of peeling a boiled
potato of good quality is a "choice pleasure," one which
leaves the peeler with "a feeling of inexpressible satisfaction" for having accomplished something "right and proper, long foreseen and desired by nature." Who knows this
better than she? Today, though, she is impatient with such
sybaritic refinements. Today the book's thesis strikes her as
frivolous. If Hermine picks up on her thoughts—and this is
not farfetched, Hermine having always been peculiarly at-
tuned to Natalie's thoughts—she will be annoyed with
Natalie for reading such insignificant material.

When she was a child, Natalie believed that Hermine
could read her mind, a terrifying intimacy and their only

one. She learned to edit her thoughts. Years of thinning her mind to keep it pure, years of censored thinking, of mental fatigue.

Hermine's eyes open, fix themselves on Natalie. Grandmother! What can she do for this godless woman whose Franciscan passion for abstinence is all that ever sustained her? Can she pray for her? Natalie stretches out her hands and smooths the blanket. No more than that.

When Laszlo arrives Natalie gives him her usual restrained greeting. Behind it, though, he can sense a relief verging on gratitude. He drags a chair from the corner and kisses her absently.

Wilhelmina looks up from her Bible, carefully marking her place with a moistened finger. "Good day, Master," she says. Her voice resonates, undoubtedly reaching heaven. Laszlo looks at Natalie. He can tell she is scrutinizing his clothes. For Natalie, as rigid in her taste as in her privacy, everything he wears, everything he does is shocking. He has tried to describe her reactions to Vivianne but the humor of it is beyond his talent to convey.

"I've told you before, Wilhelmina, my name is Laszlo. Please don't call me master."

"Can't help it, Master Laszlo. It is the way I was learned. I be sixty years old next week, too late to learn a new way. Besides," she sniffs, "God be the only proper teacher."

He throws up his hands in disbelief.

"Where are you going, dressed that way?" Natalie asks.

"What way?"

"You're wearing a tie."

"I've been to see a lawyer."

"What for?"

"I have an appointment in Washington to discuss the fund. I'm being reviewed for tax-exempt status."

"Is this anything to worry about?"

"I don't know. That's why I went to see a lawyer."

Of course, he's worried. Without tax-exempt status the whole venture will fall apart. Donations will flow the moment he has it. This project is vastly more ambitious than his past ones. It is the prototype for others. Diseases of the Third World for which no research is done in the First and Second. Pre-industrial-age diseases with strange lyrical names. Schistosomiasis. Chagas'. He has marshaled his statistics and he presents them in a white-hot rage, pacing the living rooms of wealthy friends. He must book these opulent rooms well in advance. They are in great demand. They are the Theaters of Charity.

"There is no known cure," he says, his forehead wrinkling in dismay. "Research is done only in modern industrialized countries. It's concentrated on heart disease, cancer and the like. My people don't live long enough or well enough to get these diseases. Eight million! Think! Eight million South Americans suffer from Chagas' disease. Shall I tell you what it does? It attacks the central nervous system and causes the vital organs to malfunction and swell." His passion increases with the accumulating horror of what he has to describe. "Eight million," he says and pulls on his beard. "In Brazil alone four million have schistosomiasis. By the time most of the victims can get treatment, the medicine has to be given in great strength to kill the parasite. Unfortunately, the dose required usually kills the patient as well. And, if this isn't enough, reinfection is very common. You see the problem? Now, I'm asking you for money. Large sums. I don't want to get involved with ego. No charity balls with fancy committees. No theater party benefits. No publicity, newspaper coverage, etc. Anonymous, openhearted, generous giving is what I'm asking for. I'm appealing to your consciences, to your souls. I'm asking for mercy and help in the form of money. You'll get nothing out of it. The benefits are purely for the other guy."

At the end of the last meeting Natalie attended with him, the audience rose to its feet and applauded. He watched her trying to absorb that, to fit it in to her picture of him.

"Do you know why they've delayed you for so long?" she asks.

"Because I'm political and because they know I won't be a front for the CIA."

"Don't you think you should consult Gregory?"

"Gregory? What for? When it comes to things like this he's a baby. Like most Americans. If they're not stupid then they're naïve."

"But generous. Where else could you raise the money?"

"Yes, of course they're generous. That's part of the naïveté."

"What did the lawyer say?"

"He's putting me in touch with an associate in Washington who lobbies for special interest groups like mine." He sighs and stretches his legs, sighs again. "Why don't you go out and get some air," he says, straightening up. "It's not necessary for both of us to sit here all day."

"All right," she says, surprising him. His offer was a formality. Natalie prides herself on her endurance. "Come for dinner tonight, Laszlo."

"No, not tonight," he tells her. "I have plans already. I'll see you here tomorrow."

He has promised himself an evening with Vivianne and he is not yet ready to introduce her to Natalie. Perhaps he will never be. Vivi's imprint is nonetheless indelible. He is marked. First her eyes, then her energy. He can hardly remember his past preference for nonchalant women. Vivi's intensity is rarely lacerating the way Natalie's or Hermine's can be. Though she is wide-eyed and assertive, she never usurps. There is no grabbing. There are no scenes, frozen or passionate. He attributes this less to her sensibility than to her blessed lack of nerves. Still, he is suspicious of their tranquility and wonders occasionally how long they can maintain it.

"Not long, I would expect," she said lightly. It is not in her nature to be regretful.

"And what next?" he countered.

She shrugged, lifting her long, slippery dark hair above her head and allowing it to spill down through parted fingers. "Sometimes I envy the Italians their history, their families. Never would it be necessary for them to consider such a question." Her first husband had been a Roman.

"Are you reproaching me?" he asked.

"Yes, and myself as well. I'm as curious about it as you are."

"It?"

"Our future."

"Let's not analyze that," he said, laughing. "Look how quickly Freud destroyed the magic of our dreams. We don't dare let him near our waking hours."

"Destroyed only for the educated like you." She laughed.

"My dreams are still things that happen to me. I refuse to believe that I am their inventor."

"You're lucky," he told her.

"You think so?"

"No," he said, "not really. Continued good luck is boring, claustrophobic and, eventually, stunting."

"What isn't?" she asked only half-seriously.

"The most difficult challenge one can rise to without failing."

"Which returns us to the original question. If one should ever find such a balance, how long could it last?" She was serious, her eyes unwavering.

"I love you," he said.

"*Vraiment?*" She looked startled.

"*Oui.*"

When Natalie is gone he opens his briefcase. The facts with which he must build his argument lie crumpled inside. His scorn for neatness is equaled only by his contempt for committees.

When Laszlo suggests she get some air, Natalie's response is immediate and affirmative, she hopes not too immediate. Her airing is at Tom's. "Come for dinner tonight, Laszlo," she offers, certain he will refuse. He does. "I'll see you here tomorrow," he says.

"Tomorrow." Natalie kisses him goodbye and then goes to Hermine. Goodbyes. Unilateral goodbyes. She bends over and kisses Hermine. Her grandmother's face is losing its human symmetry. Through her skin, Natalie can see the bone thrustings of an unfamiliar gray muzzle.

Tom has set up a small party for them in the garden. The butcherblock table and two chairs are outside. He has filled straw baskets with artful tumblings of fruit and cheese and nuts. A cornucopia of his expectations. A tall carafe of red wine blooms in the sun. His longings landscaped. She is touched by the effort, this investment in atmosphere. Usually it is she who engineers such efforts. In the presence of the wine and the roses they are strangers again and so formal. Have they ever touched? For an answer he covers her fingers with his baroque hands. Dark hair on bony wrists. His eyes are unfamiliar and very grave. He has changed his glasses. That's it! These new frames are heavier and darker in color. He is more the owl. Small changes unsettle her as well as large. "Your glasses are different," she accuses him.

"Yes," he says. "I had a bad week. I broke the frames on my others. I bent over and they fell off onto the sidewalk. Do you mind these? This is my spare pair. I'm blind without them."

"I rather like them. Your eyes look more serious."

"Good."

"Everything looks beautiful," she tells him as they walk into the garden.

"Good," he says again. "As long as you approve." He holds a chair for her. She sits down. He fixes her a plate of cheese, pours her a glass of wine.

"Have you ever heard of a singer from Brittany, Alan Stivell?" he asks.

"No."

"I think you'll like him. He's very sympathetic. I'll put on one of his records for you."

He disappears. Music drifts out into the garden. The music and the wine take the cutting edge off their shyness. Tom pours each of them a second glass. He tips his chair back, balancing it on its two hind legs. By now she knows that this is part of the vocabulary of his daily movements. He tells of hearing Alan Stivell in concert in Brittany. He waves the empty carafe in the air, punctuating his sentences with it. Natalie can see the fall coming. She wants to reach forward and right the chair, jerk him impatiently as she would a child. But too late. The chair hangs weightless for an instant before it tips over. In that instant she reads the shock of self-betrayal on Tom's face. Then he is on the ground on his back. The carafe christens the flagstone, and glass showers him like confetti. There are enough shards of broken glass glinting in the sun to rebuild a dozen carafes. Tom is trapped in his stocking feet, his loafers a few yards away under the table, out of reach. The correct tone is equally out of reach. He is seriously rattled and red to the ears.

"Christ," she hears him mutter. Without looking at her, he gets to his knees and begins picking at the broken pieces around him.

"Well," she tells him, "if you were one of my sons I'd

kiss you and tell you to get up before you cut yourself.
Where's your broom?" She will mother them out of this
mess and hope he won't hate her for it.

"A broom?"

"Yes."

"I don't know if there is one."

"Never mind. Don't move." She brings him his shoes
and rights the chair. "Sit here and let me see if you're
bleeding anywhere. There's glass in your hair." She picks
out what she can see. "Now," she orders, "close your eyes
and shake your head hard, like a dog drying off." He follows directions. His color has cooled off although she can
still feel the heat of his embarrassment. "Okay," she says.
"I think it's all out now."

"There is no broom," he announces after a search. He
throws up his hands and grimaces as though he has failed
her. "I'll buy one later this afternoon, after you leave."

"Let's carry the furniture back inside," she suggests,
directing him through the narrow garden door. They get
reacquainted across a forty-two-inch diameter. "Angle it
this way first," she says, lowering her end.

He is stunned by the ease of it. "It took me the entire
morning to get the damn thing out there," he confesses.

The rest of the afternoon isn't going to be as easy. When
they sit down together a needle-fine shower of glass sprays
from his trousers onto the couch. They get up. He brushes
off the couch with the newspaper she hands him. They
stand there looking at one another. Abruptly Tom bends
over and hooks his fingers under the bumper of the sedate
brown couch.

"This will be more comfortable," he says and pulls up
and out. The cushions are caught. They stick. He removes
them, flinging them across the room, and continues pulling.
A bed emerges.

This conversion shocks her out of her mothering mood.
She does what is mandated by the intrusion of this yellow-
sheeted bed. Dutifully and with chilled fingers she begins
to unbutton her blouse. Tom rushes to the window and
draws the curtains. While his back is turned she undresses
and slips quickly under the covers. She closes her eyes
while he peels off his clothes. Good manners and the habit
of chastity die hard. Thank God for good manners. They
are crucial in her present situation, a replacement for pas-

sion and spontaneity. What a mistake, being here! She is as rigid as a plank in his arms. She wishes she knew what he was thinking, wishes she could read his mind.

He can't take in what has happened so how can he begin to make sense of it? His mind has simply stopped working, clamped off, no blood getting to it. The blood meant for his brain has been rerouted to his heart. This gush of extra pints is too much for that poor organ. He can feel the pump slowing down under the strain. He can feel the pressure building up. If his heart doesn't start pumping again and soon, he'll be dead of the pressure in his chest. To his amazement, in spite of all of this, he is still able to move around. Somehow, minus the power of thought, of recall, or of imagination and in spite of this terrifying pressure, he has managed to move a table and two chairs indoors. He has managed to remove his clothes, to sink into bed with Natalie, to put his arms around her. Her hands are doing something to his body but his poor brain is dead of starvation and the message isn't getting through. Will this miserable day ever end? This is the worst day of his adult life. This day is shit. He wishes Natalie would vanish, leaving him to his mortification. He doesn't need a witness. He will be witnessing this day's events in his head forever. If she tells him she understands and that it's all right he will kill her. Thank God she is not saying a word. Not one. The trouble is, he has to say something, the right something. And what the hell is that? In the closet is his present for her. Not today though. He can't give it to her today. This is not a day for celebrating.

"Do you think we can forget about today and start over again tomorrow?" he asks her. His arms are bent at the elbow, his fingers interlaced, forming a cradle for the back of his head. While he waits for her response, he digs his thumbs painfully into the base of his skull.

Natalie turns to look at him. He seems to be speaking to the ceiling. She follows his gaze. "If that's what you would like."

"Don't you think it would be the best thing to do?"

"No," she says and sits up, hugging the sheet to her. "I don't think what happened was so bad we have to pretend it never took place but probably that's because it happened to you and not to me. From your point of view it makes sense. It's very painful to be caught failing or to be seen being clumsy. I can't forgive myself those things even if I'm alone at the time."

"If you're alone?"

"Yes. Stupid, isn't it?"

"Yes, particularly for a smart woman."

"But you see I don't mind it in other people. It makes them more human."

"No, that's not quite the way it works." He is still talking to the ceiling. "When you see someone failing it gives you a feeling of being superior, in control. I don't mean you personally, I mean in general. On that basis you can feel magnanimous. It's really kind of patronizing, though." He is lying very still with his hands folded on his chest like a dead king.

"You're right," Natalie says. She would like to kiss his hands. "I never thought of it that way but it's true."

"Yes," he sighs. "It's always a relief when it's the other person who is more human than you."

"Don't rub it in," she says, laughing.

"I won't if you won't." His voice is still solemn.

"Agreed."

"Can I see you tomorrow?"

"Yes, but early in the morning. Is that all right? I have to be at the hospital all afternoon."

"Nine?" he asks and looks at her for the first time, smiles at her for the first time.

"Nine," she says and smiles back.

Liberating herself from the sheets is her first problem. Getting dressed in front of him, her second. Tom solves them both by jumping out of bed and sprinting for the bathroom, shoulders high, stomach in, chest forward. In the interval, Natalie leaps into her clothes. In the hurried confusion of limbs, stockings and shoes, she catches her heel in the hem of her skirt.

"We're even," she tells Tom when he returns in a worn seersucker robe he must have owned since the days of summer camp. "I've just torn my hem. The back of my skirt is hanging down a foot." She pirouettes to show him.

"I've been hoping that at heart you were a slob like me."

"I hate not being perfect," she confides.

"We must have different definitions."

They exchange a long slow tender kiss at the door. Her

rhythm altered, Natalie decides to stroll home. The city has never looked so beautiful. The air feels indolent against her skin. Her sense of well-being is such that even a torn hem, grazing the backs of her calves for miles, even this feels like a caress.

CHAPTER

8

THE PHONE RINGS, DRAGGING GREGORY UP FROM THE BOT-
tom of his dreams. He can't quite make it to the surface.
Perhaps whoever is on the other end will give up before
he does. No such luck. He gropes for the phone, finds it
and says hello. His voice is thick and smudgy with sleep.

"Mr. Barnes?"

The voice is unfamiliar but urgent. "Speaking."

"This is the school nurse, Mrs. Link. I'm afraid Adam's
had an accident. Nothing too serious but it does require
immediate attention. It's his arm. I think it's broken."

Gregory gets to his feet. He thinks better on his feet.
He holds the receiver like a microphone, snaking the cord
out of his way as he walks. "Here's what you do, Mrs.
Link. Put Adam in a cab and have him pick me up in
front of our building. In the meantime I'll set things up
with the doctor. Is he in pain?"

"He's managing," she says.

Gregory touches the button on his watch. My God. 2:28.
He's been asleep all day. He presses the buttons on the
phone. The doctor will see them as soon as they can get
there. He runs his hand across his face, slinging his under-
jaw forward as he strokes his stubble. He needs a shave
but there's no time now. He throws on his clothes. Pockets
his keys and money. Shoots his cuffs. Flattens his cowlick.
On his way out he grabs the newspaper from the hall
table. He waits out on the sidewalk. 2:56. Where the hell
is Adam? He opens his paper and tries to read but a light
breeze blows up and interferes with its ballast. 3:01. He's

90

getting impatient. He doesn't like messed-up schedules. Adam should have been here long ago. He's worried. He goes to a phone booth on the corner and telephones the school. Adam left in a cab half an hour ago. He tries the doctor. Busy. Worrying about Adam is nothing new for him. Adam is his oldest son. Gregory's deepest fear is that Adam may be a loser. It's not that he wants his son to be a big winner. What he wants is for him to have the potential and the desire to be one so he has a choice. But Adam is a dreamer. Natalie was right. He shouldn't have been pushed into football. Gregory had insisted because football had changed his own life and, besides, his son is built for the game. At thirteen Adam is a replica of himself. The straight dirt-blond hair, the blue eyes, the solid compact build. There's nothing of Natalie in his looks. He can picture his son as a champion running back, but all Adam is interested in is drawing. He was probably daydreaming when his arm was broken. Gregory forgot to ask the nurse which arm. He hopes it's not the right one. He can't understand why the boy hates competition so much. His younger son, Steve, thrives on it. Competition is supposed to be healthy. Lately, though, Adam has taken to slumping down in front of the television set for hours on end. He sits there like a tired middle-aged man eating junk food and drinking Coke. Since Natalie won't allow that sort of food in the house Adam buys it himself and smuggles it in. Gregory has threatened to cut off his allowance if he continues spending his money to ruin his health but Natalie will never let him do that. He has tried talking to his son but Adam is like Natalie. He keeps everything to himself.

He dials the doctor again. The nurse tells him that the doctor is with Adam now. "Where are you?" she asks him. "The doctor is waiting to talk to you, Mr. Barnes." It seems that Adam took a taxi home but when Gregory failed to appear he went on to the doctor's office alone. "Resourceful," the nurse comments. "He was supposed to wait," Gregory tells her.

It's not that Adam disobeys deliberately. His behavior falls into that gray area between disobedience and not concentrating. Natalie always gives him the benefit of the doubt. So does Gregory. Natalie is lenient because she understands Adam, Gregory because he is so partial to his younger son that he indulges his older one to a fault.

There are times when he is overcome with the desire to sweep Steve into his arms and smother him with love. But he resists. Steve has Natalie's black curls, her slight build. He's in that androgynous stage, his features as delicate as a girl's. He could be taken for a girl were it not for his walk. His walk is pure boy. Gregory loves his son's walk. There is a little extra emphasis at the top of his toes, a slight hesitation, a hint of a swagger. It's not deliberate. The kid is a terrific athlete and a natural leader but he's not cocky.

Gregory hails a cab. Crosstown traffic is snarled. The cab comes to a standstill. He and the driver wait. The meter ticks on. At the corner the driver jumps the light, cutting off an old woman trying to cross the street. As they wheel past her she kicks viciously at the driver's door. Gregory wants to applaud. She is wearing army boots, a combat veteran. Her hair, live gray wire, crackles on her shoulders. Her eyes spark. The young man driving the cab screams at her to fuck off.

"Worm," she yells back. "Snake. Murderer." She grabs hold of his door handle, hangs on. "Defiler of old people," she screams into the open window. "Wait, wait until you're old. I wish on you someone like yourself."

The driver accelerates, trying to shake her off. She is a tough old bird, dragged along by her claws for one long heart-stopping moment. Gregory turns and looks out the back window as they speed off. He can see her chopping air in the middle of the street.

"Man, another crazy," the driver yells to Gregory through the partition. "This city is loaded with them."

Gregory wants to hit the young punk. He is a worm. He wants to grab this jerk by the collar and throttle him. He does nothing, says nothing, never gets involved. What is there to say, to do? Life here is often unbearable. Why get angry, take sides? Some days he longs for the kind, boring, hygienic streets of his hometown, yet when he's there he can hardly wait to leave. His limit is three days. He gets out at the doctor's entrance, stiffs the driver and walks away leaving his door open.

As it turns out, the break is clean and not serious. But it is the right hand. The fingers will have to be immobilized. When Adam comes into the waiting room with a white plaster wing in a black sling, Gregory feels a surge of flustering guilt. Adam is trying for bravery but his normally ruddy face is the color of ash. He stands in front of Gregory, mutely, a man waiting to be sentenced. Gregory doesn't know how to ease the situation.

"I fell down on my own arm before they could tackle me," Adam says in a trembling voice. "I was afraid. There were so many of them and they were all coming at me." He shrugs, forgetting his injury, then winces.

He is Natalie's son though he is Gregory's double. The truth matters more than his fear of disapproval. The child is worn out. His eyes are dead. How and when did this happen, Gregory wants to cry out. Why haven't I seen this before? They spend so much time together. He cares about his family. He's not one of those workaholics, one of those deadbeats who uses family as window dressing. He loves his son.

"It didn't make any difference," Adam is saying. "They all jumped me anyway, even though I was already down."

The thought of Adam flinging himself to the ground to avoid trampling pains him. He puts out his arms. Adam takes a step forward, leans his head wearily against Gregory's chest. Gregory kisses his head, then takes his good hand, the one with which he cannot draw, and kisses that.

"Are you mad at me, Dad? Please don't be mad at me," Adam says into Gregory's shirt.

"Of course I'm not mad at you. I'm glad you're okay."

"Really?"

"Really."

"Are you disappointed?" he asks, burying his head in Gregory's jacket.

"No," Gregory lies, "I'm not disappointed."

Natalie is home when they arrive. Adam explains, Gregory corroborates. She uses the opportunity to point out the futility of football, of contact sports, in general. Then she bundles Adam off to bed with cinnamon tea and homemade cake. Gregory trails them anxiously up the stairs. He wants to do something to make amends. Standing in the doorway, he watches Natalie feed Adam. He announces that he's going to spend the afternoon at home with Adam.

"No games," Natalie begs in the hallway. "No winning and losing. Okay?"

"I thought I would read to him."

"While you weren't looking he grew up," she says, smiling, holding the tray between them.

"My mother read to me until I finished high school." He picks a crumb off the plate and pops it into his mouth.

"Your mother was a schoolteacher with a passion for nineteenth century habits."

"So what?"

"So read to him. I think it's a wonderful idea." She gives him a quick kiss across the tray. "It's a lucky thing you were home today."

"Yes," he says and kisses her back. She moves to the stairs, her head thrown back in its peculiar angled way. She never looks at the ground as other people do. As a matter of pride she feels her way to the bottom.

He goes to the bedroom to find a book. The books, walls of them, are in the bedroom. No good arguing about inconvenience, Natalie doesn't want anyone gawking at their library. She won't have their books on display downstairs. He reflects that she didn't get away clean after all. Some of her family's craziness rubbed off on her. He locates the Heinlein under H in the fiction section—his section of the fiction section. He removes it from the shelf, takes off its jacket as Natalie requires, and then replaces the empty jacket in the empty space.

Adam is skeptical when Gregory announces his intention, his eyes lingering sadly on the television screen as the image fades. But it doesn't take him long to get interested. Ten minutes and he is rapt. When he moves closer, pillowing his head on Gregory's chest, Gregory's heart convulses. He would like to read to his son forever.

Natalie looks in an hour later and finds them both asleep, curled up on the bed like lovers. She is surprised to find herself weeping at the sight. Through her tears she can see that the afternoon sun is about to strike Adam's window. In a moment the room will be blazing. She tiptoes over and pulls down the shade, pulls it down on the violence outside. She wants Adam to grow quickly through these years. His terror of physical violence is extreme, his yearning to please Gregory equally exaggerated. She wishes Gregory could understand this. Did Tom have these trials as a child? How she would like to be with him now. How she would like to know him. If only he would stop protecting himself. She will protect him. You can trust me, she wants to say, but it sounds so maternal that he might be offended. He offends easily. They will get there eventually. Nothing can stop them. Even her poor dying grandmother can't stop them though Natalie has tried to fling Hermine's illness across the path of her imagination. She pulls the door to Adam's room closed. Gregory's weary face, Adam's innocent one belong to another sphere entirely.

Over dinner she tells Gregory Laszlo's news. This is what Laszlo expects. Then Gregory can appeal to Laszlo to accept his help. This is the way the system works. Laszlo maintains his image, Gregory gets to please Natalie. Gregory appears to be listening. He has pushed back from the dining room table, a slab of smoked glass which separates them, and sits with his legs stretched out, his muscled calves straining against the backs of his trousers, his elbows balanced on the thin chrome arms of the leather chair.

Natalie studies him. How can they ever be close again? Suddenly she is in tears. A day for tears, it seems, sobbing, gulping tears. Gregory leaps up. His arms enclose her in the old familiar world. Solid warmth. She longs to remain there but she can feel herself dispersing. His arms don't work anymore. Whose would? She gets hold of herself.

"Hermine is dying," she offers as an explanation for her collapse.

"I know," he says. "The doctor called me. That's why he didn't want to let her go home. I've made some preliminary arrangements."

She loves Gregory for his grip on the world. His explanations correspond to the situation. They are so probable. So what if he stands judiciously apart? If he's lacking in imagination? She must stop finding fault with him. She must stop comparing him to Tom.

"What is the real problem with Laszlo's fund?" she asks.

"I don't know. Political, I suppose," he answers, running his strong fingers over the tines of the fork. "Laszlo says that the fund could develop into something important. If it really has that potential I doubt whether our government or Brazil's will let him get started. You know his background. He's been in contact with revolutionary groups all over the world."

Gregory sounds listless. His speech doesn't have its usual forward drive. He looks exhausted. "Why don't you go up and take a hot bath?" she suggests. "I'll run the water for you, if you like."

"No, thanks anyway. I think I'll watch a little television."

"Is there anything at all I can do?"

"No. Nothing I can do either. I'll just watch some television."

"I'll be up later. I'm going to work on Laszlo's manuscript."

It's quite late when she finishes. She can hear the television blaring from the bottom of the stairs. Gregory is asleep again. Just as she gets into bed he sits up and yells. "What time is it? We've got to get out of here." He is rigidly upright beside her. "Yes," he barks. "That's right. We go."

Natalie wants to wake him but she is afraid that the interruption will be worse for him than his dream. He often talks in his sleep. But when he begins to yelp, small shrill puppy cries, she shakes him. "What?" he says. He sounds lucid but there is an edge of hysteria in his voice. "I'm all right," he says. "Now you get some sleep or you'll be exhausted tomorrow. You know what you're like when you don't get enough rest." He turns away from her and buries his head under the pillows.

Only after an eternity of digital minutes (fourteen, actually) does he hear Natalie's breathing deepen and regularize. Only then does he chance getting up. Natalie is a very light sleeper and if she hears him she will insist on getting up with him. He doesn't want this. He doesn't want to worry her. He's very uncomfortable in his heavy robe and bare legs. He creeps to the closet for his pajamas and then shuts himself in the bathroom. In this white tiled, white floored, white walled cell he lets his body have its way, lets it shake. In his dream it was the whole earth shaking. Now that he knows it was only he, himself, shaking, he shakes even harder. He is finished sleeping for the night. He takes out a tranquilizer. He keeps them hidden because they worry Natalie. They worry him too, but they reduce the fear. After he takes one, the gulf which materializes to separate him from his fears is wide enough and deep enough to make him feel safe. The gulf is about four hours wide and deep. In four hours it will be seven o'clock, four hours closer to facing the facts, four hours closer to the truth that he has blown his career. By rushing the design he has destroyed himself. He has a scientifically trained mind, a mind which views the world as a problem to be solved. He has spent his life designing solutions. His success has led him to believe that he was his own best design. Not so. Now he will have to be redesigned. He believed in his instinct for success, its hallmark a restless but graceful energy. He has been forgiven much because of this grace in a business not known for grace or forgiveness. This business is a gambler's game and he likes the odds. Why not? Until now they have been operating in his favor. Until now he had a good chance to make it to the top, the very top. He is—was—being groomed for it. The very top is no longer a possibility. The world outside of work isn't exactly fraught with possibility either. But then it never was. Hard as he trained himself to love this other life, he hasn't had much success with it. Deprived of the focus of work he gets tired of himself, tired of others. He doesn't have close friends. People keep a certain distance. He senses they don't trust him. He knows he's smooth, too smooth for some tastes but that doesn't mean he's not trustworthy.

The fault wasn't in the design but in the rush. It could have been brought in for less. It would have been simple. The engineers begged for a little more time but he had to be first. His sense of timing failed him. He closes the bottle. The trench is opening up. His hands are steadying down. He tiptoes out of the bathroom and goes downstairs.

Natalie has left an open book by the side of the seating unit. He sits down and tries to get comfortable. The damn unit is unyielding. Well, it is better than their old couch. At least these cushions are permanently fluffed and plumped. He doesn't have to watch Natalie pounding them. The book is in French. He smiles at it, proudly. He is the one who urged her to finish college, to become a translator. He hates the idea of waste. Natalie has an abiding reluctance to try anything new, and an equal fear

of letting go of anything familiar. He leans back against
the unit and lets out a deep sigh. God, when this is over
let him have enough energy left for life. He doesn't know
what he means by this wish. Enough energy to pick himself up and start over? Enough energy for Natalie and
the children? In a way he made it to where he is in spite
of Natalie. She is certainly not the model company wife.
She fulfills the essential obligations, nothing more. The
men at work view her as "different." This isn't a compliment but neither is it a slur. She makes them uncomfortable. She has no small talk. She is not involved in
civic affairs. She is not a competitor. But the things which
unfit her for the role of company wife are the very things
he loves most about her. Fads and fashions don't touch
her. Her thoughts, her conclusions are all her own. She
doesn't suspect how often he has tailored himself to fit
the times. She thinks of him as flexible and resilient. She
thinks of him as fair because he always examines both
sides. Seems to examine, is closer to the truth. The final
truth is that he knows in advance which side of the fence
he will come down on. The vested-interest side. Years ago
he discovered that his private convictions would have to
be sacrificed. Remorse faded as his career advanced. Something that Hermine said to him recently, just before the
stroke that paralyzed her vocal cords, comes back to him
now as he contemplates the end of his career. He hears
her high, censorious voice.

"Gregory. A philosopher for whom I have the greatest
respect once said something like this: Life is often spent
with no end in view but success. It is possible to live and
to die this way so long as you never encounter a situation
which compels you to ask the question why and not the
question how."

Not how but why. Why does he love this nerve-racking,
ball-breaking business he is in, this all-or-nothing business
which takes all of his brains, wit and famous flexibility
and leaves him nothing, nothing but ecstasy? Is it the
ecstasy? The romance? The glory? There has been plenty
in his drive to the top. He is known as a winner. Was.
Right now, he wishes he could go back, be what he was
at the outset, an engineer on the bench. His drive then
was for perfection. He is beginning to feel sentimental.
It must be the pill. A few tears film his eyes. He wipes at

them with his sleeve and then lowers his head to his hands. He heaves. He shudders for his failure. If only. But he knows he can never go back. He has broken through into another part of himself, the part he calls freewheeling. Innovative. The best thing to be. Drugged on change, the faster the better, as long as he was the one in charge of progress. Ah, well, he's brought about real progress this time. He's innovated himself right out of his own skin. What can he do to remain competitive? None of his methods is working now. He's obsolete. Obsolete, on his own and terrified. On his own but not altogether alone. Thank God for Natalie and the boys. What he has is bedrock. Bedrock. He is a lucky guy. They will see it through. Things will work out. They have to. Anyway, the pill is working. He turns on a late movie, leans back against the extra-firm foam and puts his feet up on the matching ottoman placed there by Natalie just for him.

CHAPTER

9

NATALIE LIVES BY LONGING UNTIL NINE O'CLOCK THE next morning. Tom is waiting for her in his seersucker robe. Wearing no glasses at all, he squints happily at her. They embrace, she and this stranger with the weak blue eyes and the hawk nose and the long bones. Part of Natalie is embraced. Part is standing aside watching. The part that is watching is miserable. The embraced part is giddy. She will never be whole again.

Tom takes her coat and goes to the closet. He returns with a box. A present at nine o'clock in the morning? She is so excited and pleased that she also feels like a stranger. She rips open the package and pulls out a soft blouse of red silk. Loose, gathered, brilliant. She tears off her tired gray sweater and puts on her new red blouse. It blazes, glows. The sun could set in such a blouse. It warms her whole body.

"You're beautiful," he tells her. "You're as beautiful as the color red, more beautiful."

This time she believes him. This time it matters to be beautiful, to be wearing a sunset blouse. It matters more than anything else. She puts her arms around him and kisses his moving mouth. "Thank you," she says. She can't get close enough. She presses against him. He must hold her in his arms until she has to leave. They sit down on the couch.

"Just one thing," Tom says. "Let me take the elastic out of your hair. I want to see it loose."

In her madness, she lets him. Her hair is wild. Her scalp

is freed. Thoughts and feelings are freed. His hands, moving under her blouse, free the rest of her. "I love you," she says quietly. "I love you."

"I love you," he murmurs. He kisses the edges of her face, buries his hands in her soft cloud of black hair. "I didn't think it was possible to love someone so much."

He is covering her with kisses. He brings her to her feet. With one mad motion of his hands he heaves the cushions across the room and opens the couch. They fall onto the bed together in a frenzy of seersucker and silk. Tom is everywhere. He is over her, chanting her name, calling to her, pleading. She wants to touch him but she can't. Her fingers are knotting. She wants to answer his call but she can't. Her throat is closing. She can only whimper and thrash, hurl herself against each succeeding spasm. Against Tom. They batter at each other like a pair of worn out punch-drunk fighters. She finishes it with a scream. Tom collapses over her an instant later. When she cracks open her eyes she sees him looking at her. There is adoration on his face. She feels so valuable. Whole again. Famous. She wants to worship him in return.

She pulls up the sheet and lies there in her new blouse feeling like a queen. Cleopatra. "I feel like the Queen of the Nile in this blouse," she tells Tom. "I won't ever take it off." She turns on her side and gets as close to him as she can. His faded seersucker arm is around her. "I love you," she says, loudly this time. He squeezes her to him. The seersucker is soft against her ear. She loves him. She loves his faded robe.

"I love you," he tells her. "God, how I love you." They are quiet awhile.

"My grandmother is dying," she says. Her voice is hollow. "Any day now. I'm here because I can't not see you." She sits up and pulls back her hair. Sober. Leans over and picks her elastic band off the floor. "I shouldn't be here now. I'm trying to figure out a way to punish myself but the only real punishment is not to see you and I can't do that." He remains silent, breathing softly. "Was it all right for you?" she asks, lying back down.

"Yes," he says. "I was just wondering if you ought to leave now? I know how anxious you are and I understand."

"I know you do. Do you want me to leave?"

"No, of course not."

"Then I'll stay. Listen, now that we've been lovers do you think we can try to be friends as well. Do you think it's realistic to suppose that a man and a woman can ever be friends?"

"We can try. It's never happened to me before but we can try it."

"Laszlo would say that jealousy is bound to interfere."

"How is Laszlo?"

"Very upset. My grandmother. And then his fund is in trouble."

"That's too bad. Do you think he's right about jealousy?"

"Probably. Judging by his memoirs, he seems to have a vast experience in this sort of thing."

"He must be right. I'm jealous already. I've been jealous since I met you. Will you talk to me about your husband and your children? That might help."

"Yes, I'll talk to you about anything. I'm in your power." She kisses his neck. It is so pale and soft. Gregory's tennis neck is leathery and creased.

"Okay, what should we talk about?"

"Tell me what you think of me, why you love me. After all, we hardly know each other." She flings her leg over his.

"Why I love you? Have you got a few hours?"

"No. Try to summarize it," she giggles.

"Impossible. You resist summary. That's why I love you."

"Bravo!" she laughs.

"I will tell you about my jealousy though." He tells her how the name Gregory affected him. She laughs out loud at all the Gregorys.

"What a wonderful story," she says. She wants to match him, to be equally unguarded. "Now I'll tell you something. I do keep my books separate from his."

He is berserk with happiness but he receives this admission without showing it. Life with Barbara has taught him the value of private victories.

"Do you love Gregory?" He dares to ask this question now that he can claim a small share of her loyalty.

"Yes."

"The way you love me?"

"No. The way I love you is crazed. I never loved Gregory that way. I feel more like his sister. That's not exactly what I mean. What I mean is he's family. We've been through so much together. Do you understand?"

"I'm not sure but I think so."

"Don't you have that feeling about your wife?"

"No. Well, maybe yes in the sense that we've been through a lot together, most of it not good. Anyway, family is a negative for me, except for my daughter."

"What is your daughter like?" she asks, slipping her hand under his robe and rubbing his chest.

"I don't want you to think I'm exaggerating. I have that reputation, you know." He sounds grave.

"I promise I won't."

"Laura is sensitive and intelligent and beautiful. I think she's perfect."

"Laszlo is right."

"What?"

"About jealousy."

"Oh." He laughs. "I wish you could get to know Laura."

They are silent for a long time. Her hands on his chest are all reverence.

"I'm so happy and so miserable at the same time," she confesses. "What if my grandmother dies while I'm here?"

"I don't want you to go but I think you should."

"I don't know if I can see you tomorrow. I think I'd better stay at the hospital all day. If she died while I was here—" She cannot finish.

"Look, I'll be here all day. Just call me if you can get away. I won't count on it."

"Yes." She covers his face with small urgent kisses.

"Let me come down with you and get you a taxi."

"No," she says. "I'm going to take the subway."

"The subway? What for?"

"It's a lunacy of mine."

"Can I treat you to a cab so you can get to the hospital faster?"

"No. It's not the money. It's the idea. I'll explain it to you sometime."

"I think I understand already," he lies. He holds her in his arms for a long time. Neither of them says a word. She feels he is holding back Hermine's death with his arms.

"I'll see you tomorrow," she promises. "Somehow."

"Only if it's safe. We can wait a day or two." She gets up. He pulls her back down. "God, I don't want you to go."

After she has gone, he stretches out on the bed. The afternoon sun is slanting across the rumpled sheets. He smooths them absently, thinking of Natalie. He loves her so much that he feels endangered. She is his and not his. Not yet. And he wants her entirely.

Natalie finds Laszlo standing outside Hermine's door when she arrives, rubbing his eyes. Her heart quits. She leans against the wall.

"It's all right," he says, rushing to her. "The nuns threw me out for a few minutes. I just called you. Why was Gregory at home? Is something wrong? He sounded awful."

"There's a big problem at work."

"Nothing serious, I hope."

"Serious enough. He's thinking of resigning."

Laszlo whistles softly.

"Well, it hasn't happened yet. Maybe he won't do it. I'm more worried about his state of mind than his job. All he does is sleep."

Laszlo shakes his head, runs his fingers through his hair but says nothing. He has very little interest in the personal affairs of others.

"I'm supposed to be in Washington tomorrow," he tells her, "but I don't think I can chance going."

"No," she says, "I don't think you can."

"No, I suppose not." He sighs heavily.

"It doesn't make any sense to me. Why should the government want to prevent people from doing good?"

"It isn't quite that simple, *chérie*."

The nuns float out of the room and past them. "How is she today?" Natalie asks.

"Weak. Very weak," they chorus.

All her energy dies away. She has to lean against Laszlo for support. He puts his arms around her and pats her awkwardly on the head. "I don't know what I'm going to do when she dies," she says into his shirt. He is wearing one of his usual plaid ones. It comforts her to be pressed against it. "I don't want her to die. I'm a grown woman but I don't think I can manage without her." She is shaking. How much more shaking can her bones take?

"She's ready," Laszlo tells her. "She's had enough."

"How do you know that?"

"I know. By the way, you are supposed to have her diaries. She told me that after the first stroke and it slipped my mind. You know how I am. She said to make sure you read them. Now stop crying and let's go in and sit with her. She's weak but she's conscious."

Natalie's first impression is that the bed has doubled in size since yesterday. Then she sees that it is her grandmother who is reduced by half. All her vital juices are gone. In the driest places her skeleton is pushing up through her skin. It is so naked around her mouth and jaw that her lips, which are still their normal size, look gigantic. Flabby.

Natalie reaches through the bars and takes her grandmother's hand. It is weightless. She holds it tightly. Hermine's fingers curl around her own like a baby's. Natalie looks away. For the first time, she notices that there is no Mrs. Miller, no Wilhelmina. The other bed is empty, stripped bare. She holds her grandmother's hand so tightly that no one will be able to separate them. She has given up swallowing her tears. They are pouring down her face. She sits like this for a long time. She sits like this until she feels a pair of cool immaculate hands on her shoulders. The nuns. She gets up to leave. Laszlo follows. At the door she turns and watches the nuns begin their bedside ritual. Pulse, temperature, blood pressure.

Laszlo goes to the phone to cancel his appointment in Washington. She goes to the visitors waiting room. A few aides are yelling to one another in the corridor. She covers her ears. She will take Hermine out of here right now. She wants to but she won't. Too frightened of death. In this factory they are equipped and trained to handle it. They know how to keep it moving along. It can't be the familiarity with death that makes them so impersonal—she is unfamiliar and it is still impersonal—so it must be the fear. It turns them all, skilled and unskilled alike, into mechanics. No one is ever ready to confront death without a technique. But she has none. Faced with Hermine's death she feels herself succumbing to hysteria. A sick feeling is creeping into her head, gripping her by the heart, reaching down into her bowels. She has had enough of death in her lifetime. She knows what it means. After the shock and the numbness pass, it means searching for replacements. Otherwise, how can you live? Where is your future? And it isn't a matter of love. Love is replaceable, the greenest of emotions. But devotion is a ripening that takes years. Lifetimes.

Natalie reaches into her pocketbook for a compact. Some powder, a little lipstick, an attempt to reintegrate before she returns to Hermine. She examines her face in the small hand mirror. What she sees there today is no different from what she has seen before. Ha! She laughs aloud at the folly of her observation. Time. If only it gusted like the wind so you could feel it, so you didn't have to wait until death forced you.

The doctor pokes his cheerful, tranquilized face into the room, startling her. She snaps her compact shut guiltily.

"Ah, Mrs. Barnes. I've been looking for you. She's slipping away from us. It's for the best. Another day, I think." He sits down and pats her hand.

"Can she still recognize me?"

"That's hard to judge. Better not to say anything in front of her that you wouldn't want her to know. There is always the possibility that she can understand." He gets up. "By the way," he says, "I've spoken to your uncle. If I were you, I'd keep an eye on him."

"What do you mean?"

"He strikes me as being quite unbalanced."

"Laszlo is fine. He's a bit eccentric, that's all." Her voice is cool.

"Good. I'm glad to hear it. Give my regards to that fine husband of yours."

Natalie walks slowly down the hall. Hermine is still sleeping. "I'm going to leave," she tells Laszlo. "Will you be all right alone? I'll be back soon."

He jerks his head up sharply. "Of course I'll be all right. What's the matter with you? Why do you ask?"

"The doctor suggested that I keep an eye on you."

"That idiot! He knows even less about human emotions than the psychiatrists."

"What happened between you?"

"Nothing. I merely told him what I thought of him."

"Laszlo!"

"Well, it's done and I don't want to talk about it."

"I'll be back very soon."

"Yes." He moves to the window and presses his forehead against the pane.

Natalie hurries down the corridor.

He doesn't hear Natalie leave. The pressure of the glass pane against his forehead has catapulted him into the past. Hermine is striding across the small, dark kitchen toward him with a knife in her hand. She grabs him wordlessly by the collar and, gripping him tightly, applies the flat side of the broad knife to the egg swelling up on his forehead. He is squirming to escape. He fears his head will burst. His older brother, George, stands in the doorway, laughing. This scene, recurring as it did so often, is as firmly fixed in his mind as a principle of logic. Cause and effect. He collides with some object therefore Hermine arrives with her knife therefore George laughs.

Many years later George would laugh himself out of Hermine's good graces, out of their poverty and into a bourgeois marriage and an academic life. Later still the Germans would shut his lovely, laughing mouth. The rest of them would escape by peddling the jewels belonging to Natalie's mother, Vera. Their flight would be so real, the guilt so complex and cutting that nothing else in his life would ever approach its intensity. Though on the surface he is alive and big with motion, underneath, in the deeper, quieter current which runs through him, he knows he is not capable of as much sustained affect as the characters in the driest of existential novels.

His mother moans. Laszlo turns from the window. Hermine is looking blankly through him, her eyelids fluttering restively. Where is she now? With her one never knew. Her lips part, stretch. A smile? Impossible, yet there is a curious tortured gaiety in her face. Perhaps it has always been there and he has overlooked it all these years. What he sees now recalls the triumphant, sinewy, heavenward stares of the early Christian martyrs.

Another and deeper moan. He moves quickly to the bed. Wilhelmina is there before he reaches it, breathing heavily, coat thrown open, retrieving her forgotten Bible from the nightstand.

"Your mother be all right, Master," she says, looking

down at Hermine. "God has granted her some little time
yet."

Wilhelmina's eyes are pools of pity, her voice at once
consoling and wise. If he could summon up an explicit
passion, a wailing primitive agony, he would offer it to
her as a tribute. The rending of clothes, the beating of
breasts, the tearing of beards, these are acts she would
respect. All he can muster is a melancholy smile. The look
of pity in her eyes deepens to include him. He is the first
to turn away.

Discomfort is the single sensation Natalie receives, has
always received at the threshold. The apartment is neither
pleasant, personal, nor comfortable. One small dark room
follows another. It is particularly dark in the late afternoon. She stands still a moment, looking around. No
amenities, no privacy. The bathroom is in a corner of the
living room. The living room serves as Laszlo's bedroom,
his bed covered with a faded Indian throw. The kitchen
is between the living room and the only bedroom which
once Natalie shared with Hermine. The furnishings are
old. The room smells decayed. Some warped shelves are
buckling under the weight of their musty books. The
heavy, old-fashioned desk at which Natalie used to do her
homework is piled high with yellowing newspapers. She
runs her fingers over the back of an ornately carved desk
chair and onto the frayed damask, tracing the pattern
from memory. Ladies on garlanded swings. A clumsy
mahogany chifforobe in which Hermine keeps her papers
and other things of value to her—faded pictures of her
own parents, of Natalie's parents on their wedding day,
of Natalie as a baby, an old clipping describing the Mad
Hatter's strike which she led as a young organizer in
Hungary—takes up the other end of the room. The place
is more of a mess than usual. Natalie rolls up her sleeves.

She starts in the kitchen. The water burns her hands.
She scrubs until her arms ache. She changes the beds. The
sheets are pitiful. They tear if you touch them. She will
buy new ones tomorrow, gay and flowered and soft. New
blankets and towels, perfumed soap. She dusts and
polishes and vacuums, launching an all-out attack, rubbing at the aged, cracked walls, the dark, gummy floor.
The place will shine. She works until it does. By that

time, it is dark outside. She feels better. She has exhausted herself, exhausted her sadness and, temporarily at least, exhausted even her fear. Though it is against her principles and against Hermine's, her exhaustion is so complete that she taxis back to the hospital.

CHAPTER

10

NATALIE AND LASZLO SIT TOGETHER BY THE SIDE OF THE bed, Natalie turned toward the window. The day is heavy with smog, the city capped with it. The wind is emptying garbage cans, raising grit to menace the eyes. She swivels to face Laszlo. His face is dark and melancholic. He is breathing heavily.

"Do you realize that in the course of my life I have buried a father, a brother and now a mother?" he asks. "Everyone I ever loved except for you is under the ground."

"Shh," Natalie says. "The doctor says she might still be able to understand."

"So? You think she doesn't know what's happening to her? She's always known what was happening. A brilliant woman. A woman who gave up every shred of self-interest, the most spiritual person. Imagine, a woman like this tormented by the fear that she wasn't pure enough!"

"Spiritual? But she rejected God all her life."

"Don't be stupid," Laszlo says, getting to his feet. "Her spirituality was the most striking thing about her. I said spiritual, not religious. Religions are systems. She rejected all systems." Abruptly he tilts his head back and presses a finger under his nose.

"Another nosebleed?" Natalie takes a tissue out of her bag.

"Damn."

"Hold this to your nose for a minute," she tells him.

Then she takes some ice from the bedside pitcher and wraps it in Laszlo's bandanna.

He presses it to his nose. These nosebleeds are chronic. Thin-walled capillaries too close to the surface. A chronic blessing really, an escape valve for his soaring blood pressure. She wipes a trickle from his beard.

"All right now?" she asks.

"Almost."

Natalie is still thinking of his last words. Spiritual? No, she wants to tell him. Wrong. Self-sacrificing? Yes. Puritanical? Yes. Undemonstrative? Yes.

Laszlo has recovered. This was a short one. "She was always spiritual," he continues. "Why do you think she gave up on all the things of this world? Trade unionism, Marxism, anything and everything that smelled of the collective? Even on us? I'll tell you what I think. It's impossible to live a life of faith and a real life simultaneously. One just pulls you away from the other. Everything you put your faith in in this world disappoints. The biggest blow of all: the failure of love as a solution to human problems. She gave up on the love and clung to her duty. I consider that spiritual." As he concludes, there is a scream from the bed. To Natalie it sounds like a smothered shriek. It finishes Laszlo. Through it all, he has never once broken down. There has been hysterical confusion, panic even, but no tears. Now he is weeping, holding his face in his hands and rocking up and down.

Natalie experiences a moment of singular clarity. She knows she must never laugh at Laszlo again. Who is she to have been laughing at him and why has he allowed it all these years? She takes her own children more seriously than she takes him. She has been insulting him all her life. What if her opinion doesn't matter to him? What if he thinks of her as an empty laughing girl? There is no other explanation for it but this one is painful. She looks down at her lap and waits for him to finish.

"I want to tell you something," he says, and his voice is hoarse. "I found out a few months ago that she was dying. I'm sure she knew it too, but she wouldn't talk about it. We were in a taxi on the way back from the doctor's office. I don't know what came over me but I found myself saying, 'Look, Mother, we've been together nearly sixty years and I know we care about each other deeply but we've never told each other so. Well, I'm going to say it now. I love you, Mother.' "

Natalie is holding her breath. She cannot exhale for fear the pain in her heart will spread, incapacitating her. Laszlo tries to go on but cannot. His mouth is caving into his beard. He squeezes his lips together, an attempt to stop the convulsive motions of his face.

"She looked straight ahead the whole time," he continues after a moment. "She nodded but she didn't speak. 'Please, Mother, say it,' I said. 'It's not so hard, you'll see. You'll feel better. I do.' She wouldn't," he tells Natalie. "She closed her eyes and shook her head," he says through his tears. "Not a word."

Natalie doesn't have a word for him either. What is there to say? She goes over and puts her arms around him, presses his head to her chest, strokes his wild hair. She knows she should phone Gregory. He would want to be with them. She doesn't move. She would rather finish it alone with Laszlo.

It takes another few hours. Hermine lies on her side, facing them. Her face has the pallor of death. Natalie is surprised to discover that there is such a thing. The pallor of death. Hermine's breathing is very shallow. She is deflating slowly from within. When she is empty, a sheet is pulled over her face. The sheet is more actual than any coffin. To think that though she and Laszlo kept the watch, they do not know exactly when Hermine died. It seems important to know, yet the moment came and went undetected.

Laszlo is mute, insensate. "Come home with me," she begs him. She is pleading for herself. He will keep her from Tom. She hates herself.

"No," he says. "It's better if I'm alone for a while. And there are the funeral arrangements to make."

"Gregory can take care of them."

"No," he says and he sounds angry. "It's my place to make them."

"I'm sorry," she says. "I thought you might not want to go back to the apartment alone."

"I'll be all right."

"Of course you will. Come later, then, for dinner."

"Yes. Dinner is good. I'll be there for dinner."

Laszlo leaves her in the lobby of the hospital. There

is nowhere for her to go. She knows where she is going. She will go hating herself but she will go.

Tom answers the phone on the first ring. "Yes," he says. "Hurry."

When he opens the door for her she falls against him, trembling. Her hands search frantically through the layers of his rumpled clothing. She knows what she is looking for but does she really believe he has it hidden somewhere on him? What she wants, the thing for which she has come, the thing for which she is searching, deeper than his clothing, deeper even than his skin, the thing she needs back and now, is her old lost familiar self.

"I shouldn't be here," she tells him. "I don't belong here now."

He is kissing her face. His hands are cupping her face, his fingers covering her ears. She cannot hear what she is telling him. Perhaps she has not told him yet. She says it again, yells it. "She's dead. She died."

"I love you," he is telling her. "I'm glad you came here. This is where you belong."

She cannot hear him. She is reading his lips. "What am I doing?" she asks as they lie down together. "I can't be doing this now."

"Shh," he whispers. "Everything will be all right. I promise."

Afterward, he fixes her a cup of tea. She sees that it is a red tea, tea the color of her new blouse, tea made of rose fruit and hibiscus blossoms. He adds amber honey and stirs. He hands it to her. It is a beautiful deep red drink. Without being asked he brings her a second cup. He waits on her. He serves. Clears. Anticipates. What is there to anticipate? She has no desires. The color has gone out of the tea. And she knows that her blouse, hanging in her closet at home, has also lost its color. The color red has died. How can she be as beautiful as a dead color? The comparison has no meaning. She is not beautiful. She will never feel beautiful again. The queen that she was is dead.

"I must go home," she tells Tom. She says this but she doesn't move. She is incapable of motion. She knows she is frightening him. He helps her. He dresses her, combs her hair. She submits. The ritual is appropriate to a dead queen. He takes her home in a taxi. She offers no resistance. Her principles are dead. He has coiffed and animated her. She needs him. She needs to be home. She needs Gregory. She needs her children. And Laszlo. No. She needs none of them. She needs Nana. She needs her grandmother.

Gregory and Laszlo are waiting for her. The boys are waiting. The boys look smaller than usual. Their eyes are darker and rounder than usual, their skin paler. Gregory takes her coat, leads her to the den, seats her as carefully as if she were a blind visitor.

"Where have you been?" he asks. He is fixing her a drink. She never drinks. "Drink this," he says.

She pushes it away.

"Drink it, darling. You need it. Where were you?"

"Walking."

"Walking?"

She sees him exchange a worried look with Laszlo. They have forgotten that she is sighted.

"I wanted to be alone. I sat in the park for a while." The lies are growing. She is growing more inventive. Soon she will be a master of the art of lying.

"It's raining out. Pouring. You're hardly wet," Laszlo says.

"What?"

"Your shoes are dry," Gregory says.

"They are?"

"Where were you? We've been so worried."

"Church. I went to church after my walk. I wanted to be inside a church. I took a taxi home from church. I didn't think Hermine would mind, about the church, I mean. She will never forgive me for the taxi. It was quiet there. I lit a candle for her."

Silence. "I'll fix dinner," she says into the silence. She puts down her untouched drink.

"No," Gregory says. He sits down next to her and takes her hand. He presses her fingers to his lips. He presses her drink back into her hand. "I've ordered some food in," he tells her. "The boys are going to take care of everything. They want to do it for you. Now be a good girl and drink your drink."

She is a good girl. She drinks it up. She is still empty

but now the emptiness is a few degrees warmer. "Laszlo," she says. He looks up expectantly. She cannot remember what she wanted to tell him. His hair is so gray. When did it turn so gray? He is wearing his old wool suit. It fits him now. When did he get so thin? They are all shrinking. They are all shrinking! Only her sons' eyes are growing. The two boys are standing at a distance. Clearly, they are waiting for something. She studies them. She sees Adam struggling to fit himself out with the right expression for the occasion. She sees Stephan looking down at his sneakers, rubbing the sole of one over the toe of the other. She puts out her arms. It is all she can think to do. Stephan springs across the bare polished floor and drives himself at her waist, her breast, her neck. Adam hangs back. He waits for an opening. When he is sure that Stephan is through, he arranges himself on her free side, holding his broken arm out of danger. She embraces them both, smooths their hair, kisses their cheeks. They are themselves again. A smile from her and they are restored. Who can do this for her? They run off to set the table. She can hear them in the kitchen arguing over who will clear, who will wash.

Ten minutes later they announce dinner. They wear towels over their arms. They pretend they are waiters. She pretends Hermine is still alive, that Tom does not exist. Laszlo pretends to eat. Gregory pretends he is wide awake.

Before Laszlo leaves, he tells her he has brought the diaries. They are in her study, on her desk.

The day is unusually mild for November. Still she is cold. They are only five. That is two too many for Gregory. Against his wishes and better judgment the children are present. Laszlo officiates at the graveside, if what he is doing can be called that. In the deliberate absence of a priest, Laszlo leads them. He leads them to share his belief that their tears are out of place. Natalie is the only one crying. Hermine was an old woman who led a full life, he says. Natalie wonders if he means full only in the sense of suffering. The correct emotion, he tells them, is one of gratitude for having her among them for so long.

"To whom?" she asks. "Gratitude to whom?"

He looks puzzled. "Ah, what do I know? Just gratitude. Not to anyone or anything. To her memory, if you like."

Natalie is not satisfied. The lack of formal closure bothers her. It is like a play without a final curtain. In an attempt to ring down one of her own, she refuses to leave until the grave is entirely filled. The two over-dressed diggers sweat under the bright sun and her scru-tiny. Their glasses steam up and have to be defogged every few minutes. It is taking forever. Gregory has had quite enough. He marches the boys back to the car mut-tering under his breath, "It's barbaric. It's too much." It is too much for her also but she stays where she is. Laszlo stays with her.

"It's the wrong sort of cemetery," she tells him as they wait it out.

"What?"

"It's too fancy and suburban. Look!" She stretches her arm toward the landscape. "Grass, big trees. Grand-mother belongs in Brooklyn or Queens, in one of those cemeteries you see from the highway, the ones that are old and decayed and so crowded that the headstones look like tenements. This could be someone's yard." She points to the pile of leaves and a rake standing against the near-est tree.

He smiles. "This was Gregory's choice, not mine. He bought it. It's your plot. There's room here for all of us. He said he didn't want Brooklyn or Queens because of the vandalism."

Gregory is right, of course. And what does it matter anyway?

Laszlo comes back to their apartment for coffee. He drinks it in his own fashion, throwing it scalding hot down the back of his throat. A few drops linger in his beard. Then he leaves. Gregory waits for the boys to change their clothes. He will drop them off at school on his way to the office. Natalie is left alone facing a desert of an afternoon. She vows not to make the phone call. She will force herself to do some work on a play that has been smuggled out of Hungary. She is translating it with-out charge for a group of new refugees, young actors who drive cabs to eat and to learn English. Their intention is to hire a hall and perform it in English as a memorial to its author.

She opens the door to her study. The room is dark and

airless, a cubicle off the kitchen. When she pulls up the
shade she will be facing a courtyard which is also dark
and airless. When she sits down at her desk she will be
facing a play which is equally dark and airless. She has
translated the literary efforts of many refugees. Most of
these efforts are poor. It would seem that oppression is no
guarantee of good literature. What is not poor, on the contrary, what is rich and unvarying is the passion. Even the
poorest manuscript has this passionate rage.

The shade escapes her hand and flies up out of reach.
It flips over and over on the roller until its spring is exhausted. Then it settles back down to cover most of the
window. She doesn't feel up to reviving it. She puts on
the overhead light instead. In the gloom, her desk looks
bulkier than usual. When she sits down she sees that it
is covered with a colony of small leather-bound books.
The diaries. She cannot believe their number. She counts
them again. Sixty. She opens the first one. The date inside, written in Hermine's elegant calligraphic hand, a
girl's hand, reads 1917. The last, which might have been
scratched by a child, says 1977. She begins with '77. She
will save the girl for last.

Vivianne is at home when he arrives. She sets aside her
work, pushes her reading glasses onto the top of her head
and rises to greet him. "Well?" she asks, taking his hand.

"What do I know? Perhaps it would have been better
to say nothing. I think Natalie was disappointed. I wasn't
very uplifting. Gregory was pleased by the brevity. Ah,"
he sighs, "there is no rhetoric left for these occasions. All
the old words are worn out."

"Not worn out," Vivi says. "It's that they have no
longer a common meaning."

"Whatever the reason, burial is an anachronism. Cremation is more sensible. And it demands less pretense." He
sinks into a chair and waves away the brandy she offers.

"Cremation? You are serious?" She shudders.

"Yes," he says. "I intend to be cremated. Can you think
of a reason why not?"

"It's too final," she says.

He laughs. Here is comedy of a high order! To discover, in such a moment, that Vivi is a woman with
whom he could linger a lifetime—to perceive, in the next,

that the true legacy of all his years of "mobility" is a consuming restlessness—and, to understand, in the end, that for him motion is sanity. The joke turns out to be serious, after all.

CHAPTER

11

HE HASN'T SEEN NATALIE FOR TWO DAYS. THE GRAND-mother who was never quite alive to him is dead. Tom knows she won't call him today, the day of the funeral. He doesn't dare call her. Her house will be full. Mourning fills a house. She will be full of remorse for the other day. He is full of joy for the other day but he doesn't dare disturb her remorse. He is full of joy because of what she gave him. She put herself in his hands. She said Here I am. It was as if she couldn't wait to get rid of what she had been hanging onto for dear life, all her life, until that moment. When it was over, when she had given what had to be given and given it with an urgency that could be heard in her breathing, she blanked out. She suffered a sort of cerebral anemia. Her red corpuscles deserted. She paled. Leaked color into the room. He could see it happening. She might have been unconscious but she wasn't. Her eyes were open the whole time. She said yes to the tea. She took it. He saw the level in the glass cup drop. But she was suffering an insufficiency, of that he was certain. It lasted so long he began to worry. When, finally, he understood that she was in a state of shock, he dressed her, combed her hair, put her in a taxi and took her home. He paid the driver and got out on her corner where he waited until he saw the cab reach her door, saw Natalie being received by her doorman and assisted into the building.

His own home is the wrong place for him to be this morning. Barbara is gone, out running, getting in shape for the marathon next year in Central Park, lapping ten miles a day these days and keeping up with the men. It's beyond him.

"What do you have to prove?" he has asked her.

"Nothing. I have nothing to prove to my friends. Just to my enemies and the people I don't know."

"Okay, you've made your point."

"Then feel my thighs. Just feel them. And my gluteus maximus."

"Your what?"

"My ass muscle."

She put his hand on the bulge in her rump, on the tree trunks her thighs had become. He felt. The touch of her skin had always given him an abstract pleasure. Barbara is hairless, poreless. Her skin is velvety. He felt another whole Barbara emerging from inside the old velvety one. A sinewy Barbara. A musculature of Barbara. A Greco-Roman Barbara. The running was doing something for her, it was. He congratulated her and meant it.

One thing the running is doing is cutting into their time together. For the moment this is a relief. The other thing it is doing is forcing him to make the bed. Make it if he doesn't want to come home at night to an unmade one.

"Leave it unmade," Barbara says when the subject comes up. "I don't give a damn. Or get up when I do and I'll help you. I'll be glad to."

This morning when he bends over to tuck in the sheet his toe hits something. He pulls. Something heavy resists. He gets down on his hands and knees and squints into the darkness under the bed. He doesn't believe what he sees there! He tugs them out. Twin weights! She's lifting weights? The goddamn things are really heavy. He tries to lift them. He can barely get them over his head. He wonders how long she has been at this. He shoves them back under the bed. He dawdles. There's nowhere he wants to be, nowhere that's possible. The day holds no promise. He dresses. He makes coffee. He collects the mail from the hall. He's on low idle. *The New York Times* informs him it's going to publish his letter-to-the-editor. This pleases him. Anything which has the double distinction of being in the public interest and making his father sweat pleases him. The day after tomorrow. Good. Great. He's warming up. Plans are jelling. He'll spend the day doing some of the uptown galleries. He'll catch one or two museum shows. Who knows, he might even see her on the street. Her apartment, after all, is in the neighborhood.

He is about to step into the elevator when he realizes that it is his phone that has been ringing so persistently. He steps back, fumbles like a madman for his keys, manages to get the door open, to race across the room and pick up the phone just in time to hear the caller click off. He tells himself that it could have been anyone but he knows for a fact that it was Natalie. He tells himself that it is highly unlikely that it was Natalie. Impossible. Why should she call him at home? Because she tried the studio and he wasn't there. Why should she call him at all today? Because she needs him. He rips off his coat, closes the front door and sits down to wait. Perhaps she'll try again. He'll give it half an hour.

He is sitting in the kitchen drinking coffee and reading the paper when he hears the front door open. He hears the laughter. Their laughter reaches him a few seconds before they do. They are Barbara and Eric. When they do reach him he sees that they are dressed in nearly identical blue warm-up suits which would be fully identical if Barbara's were zipped closed as Eric's is. But Barbara's jacket is open to the waist and Eric has his hand in the opening.

Several things happen at once. Tom sees them all with pellucid clarity. In the instant they spot him sitting at the kitchen table drinking his coffee and reading the paper and looking up at them with unconcealed shock, Barbara yanks her zipper partway up. Only partway because in that instant Tom sees the zipper catch Eric's fingers. He sees Eric pull his hand out and wring it. He hears their laughter stop. He sees their grins blur then dissolve like skywriting.

"OhmyGod," Barbara says. She wheels around and runs from the room with her hands over her face.

This leaves him with his friend.

Eric says: "I don't know what to say." He rakes his cropped hair forward. He fiddles with the zipper on his jacket.

Tom says: "Neither do I." He sits at the table, motionless. He sits like a judge on the bench waiting for the defense to sum up. He looks at Eric over the top of his glasses.

Eric says: "This has nothing to do with *our* friendship. Nothing whatsoever. I hope you understand that." He shifts his weight continuously like a novice on the high wire looking for his balance.

Tom says: "No. I don't think I do. Maybe you could explain." He takes a sip of cold coffee.

Eric says: "Well, it's kind of hard to explain." He looks down at his wedge-soled New Balance 320 running shoes.

Tom says: "You mean what you want is for me to take it on faith?"

Eric says: "Yeah, I guess so. I guess that is what I want." He cracks each of his ten knuckles.

Tom says: "Well, as a general rule, there's not much I take on faith." He makes a show of ruffling the newspaper.

Eric says: "I can't blame you if you don't." He sighs and clasps his hands behind his back.

Tom says: "Listen, morality and friendship aside, shouldn't you have been a little more discreet?" He stands up and faces Eric. Eric takes a step back. "Relax," Tom says. "I'm not going to hit you, for godsakes."

Eric says: "Barbara called but there was no answer. She let the phone ring a long time to make sure." There is a hint of accusation in his voice.

Tom says: "Do you lift weights together too?" He pumps his arms from shoulder height into the air and down a few times to illustrate his question.

Eric says: "What?" He looks at Tom for the first time.

Tom says: "Never mind. Why don't you go in and say goodbye to Barbara. I'll say goodbye now. I'd rather not see you again." He sits down and pretends to read his paper.

Eric says: "I'm really sorry about this, Tom. I'd give anything for it never to have happened." He backs his way out of the kitchen.

Tom says: "Yes, I know what you mean." He doesn't look up from the paper.

Tom hears Eric knock on the bedroom door and announce himself. He hears the door open briefly, then close. He hears the front door open and close. Then silence.

Outside, the usual white noise. Sirens, jackhammers, traffic.

He is glad Barbara fled the room when she did. He is glad she spared them both. He remembers the time they took Laura to see an R-rated movie. Though she hadn't seen it herself, Barbara's kid sister had assured them it was okay for a thirteen-year-old. Her own children had seen it. A few bad words, a minimal amount of nudity. Nothing to get worked up about. The group-sex scene caught them off guard. He froze in his seat, every hair on his body standing up. Barbara gasped, then, spontaneously, threw her coat over Laura's head.

"I don't want you to see this," she whispered urgently through the layers of wool and interlining. "I'm going to kill Aunt Carol."

Laura stayed quietly under wraps until Barbara rescued her. He didn't interfere. In fact, though he wasn't sure that Barbara had done the right thing he was so relieved not to have to watch his daughter digest the sweating, panting, snorting tangle of parts that he thanked Barbara later.

"Well, honey," he said to Laura as casually as he could manage when it was over, "what did you think of the film?" For an answer she burst into tears and ran down the block alone.

He knocks on the bedroom door, announcing himself. Barbara doesn't answer. "I just want to know if you're all right," he yells, pressing his ear against the door, listening for signs of life.

"Yes," she answers softly.

"I'm leaving now," he tells her. "I'll be back around six. Let's have dinner out tonight."

"Okay," she says. "Whatever you want."

He walks to Madison and turns south. He feels a bit peculiar. High instead of low. He could almost leap in the air and click his heels together. Not from happiness, from something else. He has been handed some extra energy. He has come through a bad scene and he has handled himself like a sage. He feels extremely civilized. Barbara bolted. Eric fumbled. But he rode it out with tact, firmness and even a little wit. Okay.

When he thinks about it, as he is doing now, he knows he has always known about Barbara. He has even known when and with whom. He is sorry it is out in the open. It just complicates everything. But that is Barbara's way, wooing disaster. Well, perhaps everything is simpler now. It will certainly be simpler to get out of his marriage if that is what he wants and, suddenly, he does want it. He wants to marry Natalie. He is certain, absolutely certain. He can live the rest of his life and never meet anyone like her again. She is his Beatrice. He cannot imagine a future without her. Oh, God! How she curled up against him and pleaded Here I am. I need you. I want you. How she made herself small enough to fit without rearranging him. He is enough for her. He, the simple fact of him, is enough. Her abandon the other day was total. It was unique. What Natalie had was a single private convulsion in his presence which moved her from one place to another place entirely. His desperate hope is that it moved her closer to him. This is what he has to find out and soon if he is to keep his sanity. In the meantime, one thing he has found out through Natalie is that sexual liberation does not depend on fucking everything that moves or even having the desire to. This discovery makes him feel more than adequate. It makes him feel superior and he is not about to resist the feeling. Eric and Barbara are just a pair of losers. He pushes his glasses back up on the bridge of his nose and moves confidently down Madison Avenue, a bull loose in his blood.

It was her idea to bring Eric home. Normally after their morning run they go to his apartment though it's geographically inconvenient. The running is also inconvenient. It bores her now. What she likes is the idea of having run ten miles. She also likes Eric and he likes the actual running. She also likes the small group which assembles every morning regardless of the weather. A small band of hardy men and one woman. She tells them they are more reliable than the postal service. This falls flat but usually they laugh at her jokes. They treat her like one of the boys. She is hooked on this treatment. She loves to be among men, the only woman among the men. She expands, can feel herself blossoming. She most enjoys being among men of the world, the sort of men who gather at Tom's father's house. She likes the casual talk of men who control things. It is not idle time she is passing. She is there to learn something. What she hopes to get from being among them is an understanding of the mechanism which determines success. She hopes to isolate what it is in people like these that enables them to actualize their fantasies. In other words, she is there to find out what it is that she is lacking.

She cannot believe how badly she behaved this morning. Bringing Eric home was stupid but abandoning him to Tom was cowardly. She doesn't like to think of herself as cowardly. Eric looked devastated when she opened the bedroom door to him. She wanted to ask what Tom had said but one look at his face silenced her. He said goodbye and I'll see you at the reservoir tomorrow. He couldn't wait to get away. Why does she bother with him at all? He is a terrible lover, constrained and passive. Oh, he has good manners and a beautiful austere apartment but a part of him is missing. They talk about his travels, his projects in foreign lands and her career possibilities. Following Grunewald's advice, she is pressing her nearest and dearest for help. Eric listens. He pinches his thin lips together with two fingers and thinks hard about her career possibilities. He hasn't come up with anything yet.

When Tom knocked at the door she panicked, couldn't speak at first for her terror. Eventually, she managed a faint acknowledgment. She was in a swoon on the bed. He was telling her that he would be home at six and would like to have dinner out. Her second response was fainter than her first. Was it possible that they weren't going to have a giant flap over Eric? That Tom wasn't going to walk out on her and move into his new apartment? That there would be no crisis?

She opens the door and peeks out. He is gone, really gone. She heats the leftover coffee. While it comes to the boil she undoes her braid and shakes her hair out. That is better. She braids her hair for running. For life she needs to feel it heavy around her face. Her hands are still shaking too hard for her to manage a full cup. Besides, it's bitter. It boiled. She didn't catch it in time. Her timing is way off. She pours her coffee down the drain. She sees it all again, sees it as it must have looked to Tom. Eric, little playmate, his hand bouncing her breast. Her zipper nicking his hand. Their clumsiness and their terror and their guilt. And Tom watching it all. Oh, how shoddy.

She leans over the sink and closes her eyes. She sways, droops on her long-stemmed legs. The picture doesn't fade. Something elemental remains. Humiliation. Humiliation is elemental. There, she has made a discovery. Why do all her discoveries bring her closer to the edge? Surely some of them should give her strength. Well, she won't be seeing Eric again. She can't face him. When he thinks over what has happened he won't want to see her either. Caught and shamed and chastened like two small children.

She rinses out her cup and leaves the kitchen. In forty-five minutes she has to be dressed, groomed and seated at an important luncheon. A fashion show for one of her favorite charities. She sighs sharply, pulls out a dress, a cheerful bright blue one. She steps into her boots, slaps on some makeup. The disguise is a failure. She can see right through it. She prays no one else will.

Her table is filled by the time she arrives. All her guests are assembled. There are the usual faces, the usual greetings, gossip, laughter, cruelty, champagne. Do they see the blond at the next table? Well, she's the one who sucked off Freddie at Orsini's last week. Gasps! How? Well, my dear, she just slid under the table to pick up her napkin. It took her a while to find it. They were in the darkest corner. How did the story get out? She told someone. He's embarrassed to death. A few more divorces in the offing. A few new affairs. She vows never to tell anyone what happened this morning. Still, she is frightened of trusting her own promises. She has broken them before.

"So, Mrs. Rilling," Grunewald says, rubbing his hands together. "How does it go?"

"It's doesn't go," Barbara answers, unable to meet his eyes. She relates the morning's disaster to the air conditioner over his head.

"So," he says, when she finishes, "finally, he caught you. This is very bad. Let us hope it is not irreparable."

"I don't need you to tell me it's bad," Barbara yells. She has had enough humiliation for one day. "I'm not stupid. I may be insecure and impulsive and self-destructive but I'm not stupid."

"Why did you take such an enormous risk?" he asks, his eyes fixed on hers.

She looks away. "Is that all you have to say? Why? Why? Why? That's all you ever say."

"What would you like me to say?" he asks. His voice is gentle.

"Oh, God, how should I know?" she asks, near tears, her panic, her feeling of loss, increasing by the minute. "I'd be the last one to know." She drops her head abruptly, pulling her hair across her face like a curtain.

"No," Grunewald says, softly. "Not the last to know but certainly the last to admit what you do know."

"And what could that possibly be when I don't know one single goddamn thing worth knowing?" she asks through her hair. "I couldn't even get myself accepted at graduate school, any of them. And, believe me, I tried."

"I believe you," he says.

"I should have told you that when I first came here, but I couldn't," she says, head still down.

"This is just as good a time to tell me. Perhaps even better. When someone is ready, there are always new alternatives."

"Do you really believe that?" she asks, drawing her hair off her face, lifting her head to look at him.

"Yes," he says.

"I wish I knew what they were." She sighs, aware of the flatness, the fatigue in her voice.

"Soon," Grunewald says.

She senses a new intimacy in the room. And a new danger. "Is that a promise?" she asks him with a weary smile.

"No," he says, returning her smile with one of his own, "just a prediction."

CHAPTER

12

THE FIRST FEW MORNINGS NATALIE WAKES UP PUZZLED by a feeling of blankness. It takes an instant for the memory of Hermine's death to return. When it does, it smothers her like a shroud. Under the shroud Hermine is immensely dead. Her death crowds all corners of Natalie's life. In this mood, her passion for Tom strikes her as a tyranny. He calls her every day. Her phone goes off insistently each morning at ten like an alarm clock. She gropes blindly to silence it so she can get back to her grieving. She is unwilling to be disturbed for anything as marginal as romance. Or sympathy. Laszlo and Gregory also hover in their own ways. They speak to her in the lingo of loss, offering her little messages of hope, like pills, every few hours. She cannot tell them to shut up. She cannot tell them to leave her alone. Her training keeps her from speaking out. She hides in her study. When they knock at her door she speaks to them through the crack as one might to a salesman. Only the children are welcome and not merely welcome but necessary. Her appetite for them is ravenous. But she has overestimated her capacity for solitude. After a week in her study wearing two sweaters and a pair of gloves she recovers some of her warmth for life.

"Let's take a drive," Tom suggests. "I've planned something for us to do today." This is their first day together in a week.
"Where?"

"I want to surprise you."

How she has grown to love surprises. This much she has learned about herself. "Someone might see us."

"Not where we're going."

They take the Holland Tunnel. "I'll be back by dinner, won't I?" she asks.

"In the early afternoon," he promises.

"Newark?" she gasps as they leave the Jersey Turnpike. "Yes."

Newark. She has never been here before but it reminds her of Detroit. She has gone there with Gregory. Another combat zone. The same rumble underground. The same shortage of weaponry with which to fight off hysteria and panic. Tom is concentrating on his printed directions. "We may be lost," he tells her. Large sections of the city are still alive, if one can tell such things from a car window. Those that are alive are alive to squalor and chaos. Other sections are quiet but it is the quiet of death. "We're here," he announces in one of these.

He pulls her up the museum steps. He is so eager. She loves his eagerness. His eyes are full of expectation. He moves with the urgency of a pilgrim. There is no admission fee but he makes an offering anyway. Art from the Alaskan Tundra, he tells her. The Eskimos of the Far North. A banner proclaims: SURVIVAL.

He has brought her to the right place. He has hit the right note. She knows this instantly. She could fall to her knees and kiss his hands for being so sensitive to her mood, for being so precise in his estimation of her needs. How can she thank him for bringing her here? They walk slowly through the galleries. He holds her hand but doesn't talk. She feels he is reading her mind as Hermine used to.

There is one piece that stops her cold. It is a carved wooden grave mask. A memorial to the dead. Everything in it has been reduced to essence. What remains in the wood is as harsh and elemental as the pit of the grave itself. She stands in front of the mask for a long time trying to wrest from it some formal truth. She needs such a truth, a shared truth. She needs it now. Tom stands behind her. His hands rest lightly on her shoulders. They are alone in the gallery. It is very quiet, quiet enough for her to discover that they are breathing in unison. Rising and falling together. She cannot walk away from the mask. She waits in front of it. She has an apprehension that she is on the edge of something, that the richness which awaits her just beyond it is worth any risk. She would risk even clumsiness to get there. It is a moment in her life without precedent. She feels herself expanding. Her skin is stretching to contain her. She holds her breath. Tom exhales without her.

Nothing happens.

They return from Newark to Tom's couch. They sit somewhat apart. He looks at her for a long time. She enjoys it. Finally, he reaches over and caresses her face. She kisses his fingertips as they explore her lips. Then, possessed, she takes his hands and places them over her breasts.

He kisses her, drenching kisses. His lips gallop across her eyelids, her mouth, her flesh. He brings her to her feet and stands her against a wall. He skins off her clothes. She hangs naked against his wall. Excitement leaves her. She squeezes her eyes shut. His scrutiny is lethal. She longs to be perfect. Short of that, he must close his eyes. She waits for release and when finally he holds her she cries out and presses herself against him as much to obliterate her own nakedness as to touch his. She loves his body, his long hound's bones. She loves its imperfections. They calm her. His body is long and lean and full of middle-aged hollows. It is these shadowy hollows that she kisses. She leans him up against the same wall. She is halfway up his legs, her mouth forming slow kisses, when he drops to his knees and grabs her. He rolls them onto the bare floor. He rocks her back and forth on the hard wood. Her spine will shatter. The pain is sobering. Let it be over soon. It is.

"I'm sorry," he says.

"It had nothing to do with you," she lies. "I can't stop thinking about Hermine."

Food is not on their minds. They have invented a different kind of feast. Day after day, week after week, three weeks to be exact, and they are still falling on one another like gluttons. She is bruised and aching. Her jaw hurts. Her lips are cracked. Some days it pains her to move. "Kill me," she begs, knowing he will understand her shorthand now. "Yes," he breathes. "Yes."

The moment of death. The killing off of every extraneous sensation but the sensation of each other. In reaching for this, she knows they have lost all reason. They flaunt clichés. She arrives nude under a prim raincoat and presents him with a large crystal obelisk. He buys her a black chiffon nightgown. He slathers her with perfumed oils. Orange. Almond. Sandalwood. They read about sex in groups, sex with drugs.

"We're novices," he announces. "Children."

"We'll stay that way," she tells him.

Nevertheless, they feel competitive. They are driven. They are barbarians. They amaze themselves. How much more deeply into the science and art of passion can they go? They are sitting on his prayer rug. It is their island. Their island is rimmed with a sea of books, books shipped in from all centuries, all cultures, books filled with annotated, illustrated erotica. They are preparing for a long siege, arming for a massacre. They are out for blood. They will sack and pillage. They will kill each other with invention. They will try it all. The sounds of their love are the sounds of murder. There is only one disquieting note. On the ground of a conflict of interest, she disqualifies herself from attending any more of his lectures. He is both relieved and hurt.

"I've borrowed a house for us in the Berkshires," Tom tells her.

She laughs. "Impossible. How can I be away overnight?"

"Why not?"

"Why not. I'll try."

Gregory works it out for them. He leaves for California. Silicon Valley. How inventive she has grown. "Here's what I'm planning to do while you're away," she tells him. "Laszlo has borrowed a house in Massachusetts. We're going up for two days with his secretary to put the finishing touches on his manuscript."

In his innocence Gregory worries only for the children. They will be taken care of, she assures him. The children don't worry her but Laszlo does. She must tell him. It won't be easy. Lying has become easy but she must face Laszlo with the truth. She discovers she cannot face him. She does it on the phone.

"Do you know what you're doing?" he asks.

"No," she answers. "But I have to do it anyway."

"Be careful," he warns. "It's not the answer you think it is."

"It's out of my hands for now," she tells him. "I wish it weren't."

"Then don't make any decisions until we talk. Promise me that."

"I promise."

"Now give me the name and phone number, just in case."

She gives it.

He is silent.

"Thank you, Laszlo," she says. "I'm sorry to involve you. There wasn't any other way."

"Yes," he sighs. "I'm sorry too."

Laszlo hangs up, shaken. Natalie? His secretive, upright Natalie? The news stuns him. He takes it badly. He wishes Vivi were here but she is in California on business and not due home for at least another month. Though she urged him to stay on in her apartment during her absence, he has retreated to his own. Hermine's. Unable to lighten his mood, he wanders from one sad, dull room to another. Foolishly, he had imagined Natalie safe from the terrors of narcissism, free of the painful ecstasy. He shakes his head, hitches up his trousers. Even Natalie?

He turns his attention to the letter in his hand. "The business is advancing slowly," Vivi writes, "but I am convinced it will be one day very successful. I have so much drive and a positive attitude. Here in the sun I radiate energy. I spend my free time at the beach where I find much pleasure. California is a children's kingdom. *Les petits,* they are very spoiled only they do not seem to know it. I wish you could come for a while. That would be a great streak of luck. How do things march with the fund? And the book? Promise to write, *chéri,* and tell me everything."

There is nothing to tell. The book "marches" well. He smiles at the word. She is determined to master the English language and will allow no French between them. However, his life, mummified in print, seems curiously static; that is, if one is willing to allow for a presumption of havoc within stasis. Well, if he hasn't moved forward, at least he is not guilty of backtracking. At least running in place has kept him free of bourgeois flab.

The fund, however, *ne marche point*. It is stalled, its future in doubt. It has fallen victim to the usual bureaucratic complications, suffering from the acid effects of confusion and delay. A wasting disease. The Washington lawyer has assured him that with the proper treatment they can prolong its life, but Laszlo knows the long-range prognosis is poor. They both know it. Nevertheless, they medicate—Laszlo out of inertia, the lawyer for his fee. Strangely, he feels little concern for the fund; less for his own future.

He puts Vivi's letter aside, promising himself he will write to her later. Kicking off his shoes, he goes to his cot and stretches out. After so many months in Vivi's airy flat, he is unaccustomed to the darkness here. His return to the old apartment was a bit like breaking into a tomb which had been sealed for centuries. He found the relics intact but the air bad. Or perhaps it is just that he is not used to the starkness of living alone. It takes a strength and imagination beyond his power. Hermine could have done it. She lent solitude the kind of majesty which occurs naturally in forests and mountains and seascapes but rarely in places as impoverished as this one. Whatever meager heroism once existed here has disappeared with her.

He turns on his side, stares at the wall. He should call Washington, should write to Vivianne, should give up this apartment, should make an effort; but between the recognition and the action lies a dense, humiliating torpor and though the habit of work is strong, it is no longer strong enough. He spends the rest of the day motionless on his narrow cot.

Tom picks her up early in the morning. The air is crisp enough to break. They take the longer scenic route even though they know they have missed the full radiance of autumn by a few weeks. The leaves that remain on the trees are frail. The slightest wind detaches them. Tom drives with one arm around her. When they can take this separation no longer, they pull off the road. "What if someone comes?" she asks. For an answer, he pulls her out of the car and into the woods. He backs her into a stand of trees.

Some of the towns they pass through have the self-conscious quality of a picture postcard. These bill themselves as the Real New England. But nearer to reality and to their destination is an abandoned mill town. An ancient, weathered brick hat factory dominates the imagination as once it dominated the town. Hundreds of gaping holes through which the wind now blows once reflected life. The old glass panes have been vandalized. The oak doors are shattered. The interior gutted by fire. Tom finds it an appealing sight. History in ruins. For her it is more like life in ruins but she doesn't tell him this.

The road they are following curves along the river. Boys float there in rubber boats. They hurl stones at the passing cars. "Bucolic charm," Natalie says. They both laugh. Today everything is funny.

A few more miles and they pass a famous paper mill. It turns pulp to rag and rag to fine stationery. The mill sullies the river but looks paternal and benevolent. A Victorian papa. Crowns and turrets. Ivy has a secure hold. The windows are greenly, serenely bearded. They pass the entrance. An enormous sign announces: SAFETY FIRST. ONLY 16 MAJOR ACCIDENTS THIS YEAR. The number 16 swings freely on its hinges. It is removable. Changeable.

"What's major?" she asks Tom.

He shrugs.

She imagines the missing limbs and digits sheared off like branches.

"Just a few more miles."

They turn onto a dirt road. Trees overhang it. Dry leaves shower the car like rice. Natalie can see a large white house at the end of a steep drive. It has a sloping roof and many small shuttered windows. The exterior is freshly painted. Inside, the house is warm and dark and cluttered. The clutter is artful and selective. The walls are whitewashed and the fireplace is tall enough for a man to stand in.

"Whose house is it?" she asks.

"My parents'," he says. "Mine, someday. They believe in dynasties."

The house has its smells. Rough timber and mold. Tom lays a fire to subdue the mold. They go upstairs to unpack.

Their bedroom is an illustration from an old-fashioned children's book, canopied and ruffled. Tom flings his clothes into the drawers. Natalie arranges hers neatly. Tom is growing impatient. He turns the contents of her suitcase upside down on the bed and drags her from the room.

"I need some coffee," he tells her after the tour. He goes to the stove.

"What are you doing?" she asks.

"Roasting the beans the old-fashioned way." He uses a simple tin pan with a built-in paddle. "It was my grandmother's," he tells her. He turns the beans constantly. It is tedious work but he looks exhilarated. The smell of roasting coffee brings her to her feet. She embraces him dumbly from behind. She is embracing the woods, the farmlands, the villages, the whole incorruptible world. She feels a global euphoria.

He turns and kisses her. "Coffee first," he says.

He puts the beans into a small electric grinder. He throws a switch and in a moment they are rendered to granules dense as sand. She is rendered to granules, feeling each separate cell in her body come to life. She has never been so alive, so glad to be anywhere. It is this mass of penetrating gladness which distinguishes her time with him from time spent any other way. She unbuttons his shirt, kisses his chest. He leaves the coffee and brings her to the fire. He undresses her in front of the flames. He stokes her. Under his hands her body heats up obediently. The house is silent as they join. Only the fire cracks. Separate flinty sparks burst from the fire and crack. It is no use, all their straining, however energetic or inventive. They will never have enough of each other. They can keep this up until they burn away all the excesses, until they are down to bone, bleached, scraped bone, no flesh left to cushion them and it will still not be enough. This incendiary craziness separates them from everyone. Who can get near them? Their fire throws too much heat. They fan it with lies. The lies singe Gregory and the children and Laszlo, Barbara and even Laura. They don't care. She has become such an expert liar that she has nearly forgotten how to be truthful. Ah, but what is the difference? Lies or truth, she will never be free again no matter what she chooses to say.

Later, Tom takes her for a walk. He moves her along

briskly in a rush to cover all the territory of his life. Their feet crunch on leaf drifts. He stops suddenly. He strips a large piece of bark from a birch tree and hands it to her. "I used to write letters to Laura on this when she was little. Here, take some for the boys." They peel together. He furrows his brows in concentration. "It's bad for the trees," he says as he gives her another large sheet, "but it's for a good cause."

They walk on. "This is our compost heap," he says, pointing to a small clearing. Her nose has already told her. It smells rank. She turns her head away.

"Do you mind the smell?" He is incredulous.

"Yes. I gather you don't."

"No. On the contrary, I like it. It's just a kind of organic stew on simmer."

"I like your description but I still don't like the smell."

The woods rustle. Tom puts his arm out in front of her. A small quail struts regally out of the thicket. It stops a few feet from them. It stands still as death. A dog yammers in the distance and the quail bolts. Natalie is reminded of herself.

Tom says, "I want you to marry me."

Natalie struggles for an answer. She cannot tell him her other life has its weight. She cannot tell him that her selfishness and deceit appall her, that her guilt is equal to her passion. He would never understand. She says nothing. She squeezes his hand instead.

After lunch they spend an hour bagging leaves which reminds her in turn of Marie Antoinette playing dairymaid and of Hermine's scorn for the idle rich. Then Tom tumbles her in the leaves and she forgets Marie and her grandmother and lets herself feel like a movie star. How she loves romance. Romance and surprises! As they frolic, nature cooperates. The sun shines steadily. A delicious smell of the earth's crust baking. Sparrows hog the feeder. Jays dive for spilled seeds. A male cardinal streaks a small portion of the sky red. They are playing in a celluloid world. The real world never looked like this. Then they see it. A butterfly. It shouldn't be here. It's the wrong time of year. But it is here. She shouldn't be in pain, cradled in the leaves with Tom's hand under her bulky sweater. But suddenly she is. An out-of-season butterfly has destroyed the day.

"What's the matter?" Tom asks.

"A slight headache," she says. "Too much sun."

Tom fixes dinner. While he cooks, she reads poetry to him. Reading poetry to one's lover is contrived and self-conscious and she has contrived to do it. So what? They can get away with it. They can get away with anything. She wants to show off a little, to educate him. Two Hungarian poets have actually made it onto the pages of the *New Yorker* and one of them has her maiden name. She feels strangely close to this poet whom she doesn't know. She wonders if Laszlo knows of him. Perhaps they are related. She feels related to him through his poem. Tom doesn't like Várády's poem, "Chairs Above the Danube."

"It's too depressing," he says, in Russian-accented syllables. "Promiscuity, suicide, freedom, tyranny." He confesses he is not a lover of poetry.

"I thought we shared everything," she says.

"Not this poem, we don't." He has missed her irony, too busy basting his quail. "The grapes," he mutters. "Where did I put them? I hope there's no buckshot in these birds," he says, turning them over. "My father is responsible for these murders. If you come across any lead pellets, spit them out. Don't be polite. He shoots at close range."

The wild rice is steaming. Natalie reads him the second poem. "Mr. T. S. Eliot Cooking Pasta." He loves it. He loves particularly the last stanza.

> Still, the most gripping moment
> comes when the macaroni
> are broken in two with a dry crackle:
> in that, somehow,
> one recognizes oneself.

He beams, hugs her for this poem. "Now," he says, "if all poetry could be like that! You know, though, that macaroni should never be broken before cooking."

"Would you sacrifice and break it for a poem you loved?"

"Of course," he says. "Wouldn't you?"

"Yes." She laughs. "If it were a good enough poem."

"What about for a bad poem that you love?"

"Are you making fun of me?"

"Just a little."

"More than a little."

She is bewildered and hurt. She gets up to set the table. She wants to be doing something concrete. He follows her, hangs over her, directs the action. They work in silence a few minutes, only a few. Nothing can restrain the force of their passion for long. Wisdom dies on her lips in the face of it. She apologizes for whatever she has said, whatever she has done, whatever she is that has offended him. He puts down the wooden spoon on which his quail is balanced and takes her in his arms. He apologizes for giving offense, for taking it, for future sins, for sins not yet dreamed of, for peeling grapes.

They stuff themselves at dinner. They spit lead pellets. They can hardly eat for laughter. He makes her take off her blouse. He paints her breasts with the quail marinade. Her breasts are not a beautiful enough canvas. She dissolves into adolescent gawkiness. She cannot tell him why. The heavy pleasure in her own body is gone. The world returns. Nothing has changed. This succession of fucking and sucking—there, she has thought the words while cold sober—has changed nothing. She is plunged into sadness.

There is no avoiding bedtime, bathroom time. The tub is oversized. Natalie pours in a gallon of bubbles. They try the required things but they are too clumsy for such aquatic feats. They will drown. They dry each other. That, at least, is more graceful. She puts on a new nightgown. It is French, bias cut and red satin. She feels she is following the stage directions for a script. Why did she buy it? It emphasizes more of her imperfections than her naked body. She tightens every muscle and poses. Tom loves the gown as she knew he would. She bought it for him. It is real satin, not a synthetic. It cost more than a dress. Her frugality is gone along with her common sense. She regrets this.

Tom makes love to the gown. She feels like a voyeur. When he removes it, she sighs with relief. He takes this for excitement and turns her over. He vibrates his fingers slowly down the center of her back. She feels a pulse begin to beat in her spine. At the base of her spine his fingers flutter to a deliberate stop. His fingers brush her skin like butterfly wings. He knows her body. She merely inhabits it. Very gently, he eases across their last threshold. "Oh," she cries, dying. "I can't live without you."

She hears a loose shutter banging. He is still over her. He screams. He has never screamed before. She feels as though she owns him. He sinks his teeth into her shoulder. She would like him to bite her through. She twists out from under. She turns to face him. "I love you so much," she says, clinging, and clinging, can't love him enough. How?

"Marry me." He twines their fingers.

She ruffles his hair, kisses the tip of his nose. "Why?" she asks. "Can't this be enough?"

"Because you understand me better and disappoint me less than anyone I've ever known."

He is leaning over her on one bony elbow. His intensity is luminous. She cannot match it. She cannot even try.

Hours later she is still awake. When Tom fell asleep, she moved out of his embrace. She cannot sleep with a hand across her. She needs distance and privacy and her own pillow to sleep. She has none of these. She lies on her stomach, legs slightly apart, face turned away from his, gripping the edge of the sheet with her fingers. The house whispers and moans. It is after two o'clock when she feels the first pains. Oh, God, no. Too much dinner? A surfeit of guilt? A few lead pellets? Or a self-willed punishment? She wouldn't put it past herself. She tries to find a comfortable position in this strange narrow bed. There is moonlight seeping in around the shade, light which outlines the sleeping man next to her. His hunched, unfamiliar back offers no refuge. The next spasm is a killer. A giant fist. An intestinal tornado. She stifles a groan and sits up. Worse. She bolts the bed. The next moment she is in the bathroom spilling up her whole body, gasping for air.

I may not live through this, she thinks. She cannot go back to bed. She lies down on the tile floor, sweaty, ice cold, limp. She covers herself with a towel. When the squall moves to her bowels, she knows she is in for real destruction. A narrow but violent path is being run clean through her.

At dawn there is a knock on the door.

"Good morning," Tom says. His voice is buoyant. "Come out of there at once. I want you unwashed and unbrushed."

"Good morning," she groans.

"Are you all right?"

"No."

"What is it?"

"My stomach, my head and everything else."

"May I come in?"

"No."

"Do you want a doctor?"

"No."

"Then come out or I'll call one."

She takes a quick look in the mirror and gasps. A drawn, pinched, gray face. She sticks her stringy sour hair under the faucet. She barely makes it back to bed. Her hair is dripping. She is ruining his mother's polished floors. She cannot look at him. She lies there racked while he stares sorrowfully at her. She feels homeless. She wants Gregory.

"Maybe sleep will help." He tucks her in and leaves the room.

When she comes to, Tom is reading in a chair. "Better?"

"A little. What time is it?"

"Two."

"My God. We have to leave. Gregory will be home this afternoon." Her arms and legs won't coordinate. He brings her clothes. This man is always dressing her. She is a strong woman, yet she is always collapsing in his presence. Another regret. "I'm so sorry." She longs for the leaves and the bubbles and the red satin gown. "I don't want you to see me like this."

"Just pretend I'm a doctor."

"I wish you were or that I knew you better."

"Knew me better? May I call you tomorrow? I'd like to get to know you better."

"Are you sure? The next time might be worse. I might die in your arms."

"I'll take my chances."

"All right. But only because I don't want you to re-member me like this." Like what?

The car ride back to the city takes years. Natalie is ter-rified of losing control. She has a dizzying headache. She keeps toppling over in the front seat.

"I don't understand why you won't lie down in the back," Tom says.

"If you've never been carsick, you won't understand about back seats. Everyone in my family gets carsick."

"You could try it."

"No, I couldn't." Further speech is impossible. She cannot tell him what is keeping her in the front. She can barely admit it to herself. She is in the front seat so that if this volcano in her intestines erupts again she will be able to leap from her side of his speeding car onto the highway. It won't matter whether or not she survives the fall.

She arrives home before Gregory. The boys tackle her at the door. She is so glad to see them she wants to weep. They take her suitcase, help her upstairs to bed, tuck her in, bring her tea. She marvels at their efficiency. They stand by the side of the bed, adoring but anxious. She is never sick.

When he arrives home Gregory is also anxious and ador-ing. He is also distracted. He shoos the boys out, kisses her goodnight, tiptoes from the room. Why is he tiptoeing? Oh, how glad she is to be home. Home. "How did things go in California?" she asks.

"It's a long story," he says. "I'll save it for when you feel better."

CHAPTER

13

THE LONG STORY IS JUST TOO LONG. HE HASN'T FOUND time to tell it to Natalie in full though he has summarized it for her. It is reducible to this: The microprocessor, that microscopic computer laid out on a fingernail-sized square of silicon, has short-circuited his career. He knows he is being neurotic about his situation. Not to be made president of the company is not necessarily the end of his professional life. But for him it is. If he loses his momentum it will all be over, the romance, the freedom, the creativity gone, what's left not worth having. A middle management job. Pressure from above. Jealousy from below.

He puts his stubby feet up on the kitchen chair, flexing and extending each one. His arches give him trouble. The tops of his feet are chronically tender from being pressed against the roof of his shoes. He slips off his shoes and bends forward to massage his feet. The effort—all effort—exhausts him. His fatigue is bone deep. He is thoroughly depleted, living well beyond his strength and resources. Sleep doesn't help. Black hours in which bridges collapse, fires rage, boats sink, the earth opens.

He would like to tell Natalie about his dreams but she has been very remote since Hermine's death. There is suffering in her face. When he tries to comfort her she backs out of reach. This hurts. He is used to being able to console her. If it weren't for Hermine's death he wouldn't know what to make of her behavior. The diaries obsess her. Sometimes, walking in on her unannounced, he

142

catches her pressing her palms into her eyes to stop the tears. At other times, she sits perfectly still and stares into space. Then there are the sighs, deep and painful, so deep they can be heard all over the house. He resents the diaries. They are intruding in his life. It is as if Hermine herself has come to live with them. 1963 is face down on the kitchen table. He would like to look at it but he knows it is private. He sighs and stands up. What he needs is a vacation. He can't remember his last one. A few days in the sun would be a good thing for all of them. He will talk to Natalie about it tonight.

Natalie says she can't leave, even for a few days. He must understand. "The publisher is screaming. We're past the second deadline already. Laszlo promised them a finished book when he signed and we haven't got it pulled into shape yet."

"I thought you finished it in Massachusetts," he says.

"They want other changes. They're never satisfied."

His disappointment must show because she says, "Look, why don't you go anyway. Take the boys. Their Thanksgiving vacation starts in a few days. Laszlo can stay here with me and perhaps we can finally finish."

He is on the verge of protesting, deterred at the last moment by the look of unremitting finality on Natalie's face. It's no good pleading his case in a situation like this. He shrugs and says, "Okay. Do what you want."

She gives him a hug and a kiss, the first in a long time but when he tries to prolong it she pulls away and runs off to the kitchen where she has something cooking. He follows. Next to the stove is 1962.

She is too busy to talk, rushing with dinner because they have tickets for a play tonight. It is a version of Euripides' *Trojan Women*. It is written in a made-up language, ancient Greek mixed with bits of African and Amerindian tongues.

"Amerindian?"

"Yes. It's short for American Indian. By the way, there won't be any place to sit down. There aren't any seats."

"No seats?"

"No. The audience is expected to move around with the actors."

"I don't go to the theater to have something expected of me."

"This is experimental. It's different. The play opens with a procession. If we're not on time they won't let us in."

"Does the audience have to be in the procession?"

"I don't know. We'll find out when we get there."

"I can't face it tonight. I have too much on my mind. Why don't you go without me." He tries not to sound angry although he is. Her compulsive intellectual explorations make him furious. She is so damned elitist, so unrelaxed in her tastes. She has no tolerance for the ordinary. The ordinary makes her ill.

"Experimental," he says and shakes his head. "What you need are some antibodies." He looks at the boys. "We should tie her up and drop her in front of a television set for one whole viewing day."

"Great idea," Steve says. He jumps up and slaps jubilantly at Gregory's open palm. He and Adam hop wildly from one square of kitchen flooring to another.

"Settle down," Natalie orders them. "I thought you didn't mind my going alone," she says to Gregory.

"Of course I don't mind. I was only clowning. Just promise me you'll take taxis."

"Yes," she says. "I promise."

As soon as she leaves, Gregory settles into bed with Stanislaw Lem. He enjoys science fiction and Lem is masterful. When he hears the scream he jumps to his feet. A book falls from his chest onto the floor. He glances at the clock. 10:46. Asleep again. More wasted hours. Another high-amplitude scream. He heads for the door. Steve is standing in the hall shaking.

"Where's Mommy?" he wails. He looks too fragile to support the weight of his grief.

"What's the matter?"

"I want Mommy."

"She'll be home soon."

"No. I want her now."

"What's the matter? You can tell me." He takes Steve into his arms. The soft black curls, the tearful eyes break his heart. He squeezes his son hard.

"I had a bad dream." He squirms to get loose.

"What was it about?"

"Mon—sters." He is gulping and hiccuping and shuddering.

"What kind of monsters?"

"Terrible ones. Worse than anything on television. Worse than the movies. They threw me off a building."

"Did you watch a scary program on television after I fell asleep?"

"Yes."

"Why? You know you always have bad dreams afterward."

"Adam was watching and besides, it wasn't scary then. It was sort of funny. You know." His sobs increase. He can hardly breathe.

"Listen," Gregory says, desperate to comfort him, "let me tell you something that frightened me when I was your age. Well, actually I was only seven."

"What?" He rubs his eyes.

Gregory can feel the expectancy. Daddy as a boy. Fairy tales. "Well," he begins, "it was a radio program. We didn't have TV in those days. This young scientist discovered a serum and he decided to test it out on himself first. You see, he wasn't sure what he had discovered. At first nothing happened. There were no changes. But after a while he noticed that he was hairier and that his arms were longer and that his head was a different shape. Then he knew for certain what he had only suspected before. He was changing into an ape. He told his beautiful fiancée what he had done—she was a scientist too—and she cried but there was no antidote."

"What's an antidote? I know but I can't remember."

"Something that makes it all better. Anyway, they began to work on one. His fiancée helped as much as she could but time was running out. He bought a cage and he made her lock him in it at night just in case. Then one day when he looked in the mirror he saw that he was all covered with hair and he knew that he would never be a man again. He broke out of the cage that night. He just pulled the bars off."

"Like King Kong."

"Yes. And then he went out and killed someone, some

stranger. Afterward, he returned to their secret basement laboratory and crawled back into the cage. His fiancée was waiting. She had finished the antidote and she injected him. Two big tears rolled down his cheeks and she understood that he had done something terrible. Then the police burst in. They had trailed him from the scene of the crime. They shot him. While he was dying he turned back into a man."

"That's not scary," Steve scoffs. "It's stupid. An injection can't do that. Anyone knows that. Mine was much worse. There were these terrible monsters all around me. They dragged me to the top of a building, a big building. I couldn't even fight back because they paralyzed my arms and legs with a ray gun. And they didn't have any ears so they couldn't hear me screaming not to do it."

He is crying again. Gregory carries him back to his own bed and sits with him. When he is sure that Steve is asleep he goes to Adam's room where he adjusts the blankets and opens the window.

Natalie doesn't arrive until twelve. "I had a terrible time getting a cab," she explains. "I had to take the subway."

"The subway at this hour? Are you completely crazy?"

"Yes," she sighs and sinks onto the bed.

"Natalie?" he whispers hours later when he hears her stir.

"Yes," she says, instantly awake. "What's the matter? Can't you sleep?"

"I'm too worried." It's not so hard, talking into the darkness.

"Don't be worried. We'll manage. I know we will."

"Put your arms around me."

She does as he asks.

"I love you," he says into her nightgown. "I love the boys."

"I know." She kisses the top of his head. His cowlick springs back against her lips and escapes. It's not reasonable that one corkscrew of hair should cause her heart to break but it does.

She offers to pack for Gregory out of guilt. He accepts her offer with good-natured reluctance. He would much rather do it himself. Packing for him is a simple matter, simple because the choices are as limited as his wardrobe. Winter or summer, he dresses the same way; only the weight of the clothing separates one season from another. His dress shirts are pale. They have french cuffs, narrow collars and are all cotton. His sport shirts have epaulets, bone buttons, flap pockets. His suits are either navy or gray. All wool in the winter, a blend in the summer. Some are pinstriped and some are not. He has no more of anything than is absolutely necessary. She could pack for him blindfolded. At the ties, she hesitates. Alongside the stripes, solids and foulards of her choosing are some of the most hideous ties ever designed. Dozens of them. These Gregory has bought himself. He doesn't respond well to criticism of them, however sensitive or veiled, and though he wears them infrequently he will not give them up. This makes her wonder about all the safe, neutral things which fill his drawers and closets. It makes her wonder. She leaves the suitcase open on the bed, leaves him to deal with the ties.

Stephan can wear Adam's summer clothes from last year. She takes them out of the cedar closet. She loves the smell of cedar. She has a passion for closets. When she was a child—she cannot identify the year or the place but perhaps the diaries will help her there—she used to hide on the top shelf of the linen closet, close to the ceiling, and stay there for hours. She has no memory of the closet or its contents, just the feeling, a feeling of snugness that she has never been able to duplicate.

Glancing at the inside of the closet door, she smiles. On this door the boys' heights and weights are marked off and dated. Twice a year she measures them against it and records the data with colored inks. This door, along with Gregory's collection of ties, has followed them from one home to another. This door is very important to the boys. Sometimes they fight over who will get to take it when they grow up and move out. When Stephan's suitcase is filled with Adam's old clothes she puts it in the hall. Gregory will have to improvise a wardrobe for Adam. Either that or buy him the necessaries when they reach the Keys. It can't be helped. Rather, she can't help it—it being a recently contracted amnesia for domestic details.

She drives the three of them to the airport and waits to see them off. Before their plane leaves the ground, she is a million miles away.

CHAPTER

14

TOM SAYS, "THANKSGIVING ALONE? WHAT ABOUT Laszlo?"

"Laszlo's deserted me. He's going to the country with his new secretary."

"What's she like?"

"I don't know. He won't talk about her."

"I have to show up at an old friend's. A yearly ritual. I don't see how I can get away."

"Don't be silly. It's not important."

"Of course, it's important. Look, I have an idea. Why don't you come with me?"

"You're out of your mind."

"Listen, the invitation's no problem. They're my oldest friends. We just have to figure out the—the what? Help me. What do we have to figure out?"

"The reason for my being there."

"Yes. Let's work on that. A logical reason. A plausible one. Plausible is the key word."

"Tom, it's out of the question. Barbara will be there."

"No, she won't. She's spending Thanksgiving with her parents. They live up near Laura's school."

"It's an awful thing to do."

"No worse than what we've just finished doing—or what she's done to me."

"Yes, it is. This is premeditated. Stop tickling me. I don't want to laugh."

"Quiet. I'm thinking."

"No, I won't be quiet. It's wrong."

"Agreed. But let's do it anyway."

"It's more than mischief, you know."

"How about this? You're interviewing me for some Canadian magazine. You're a writer from Quebec. A Quebecoise, a believer in secession. That should be lively. Your name is Simone de Barnesoir. You don't speak much English, you don't know anyone in the city and I took pity on you because it's Thanksgiving. How's that?"

"Terrible. Stop making me laugh. It's not funny."

"But I want you to meet my friends. That's not unusual when you're planning to marry someone."

"Tom!"

"Will you marry me, Natalia? May I call you Natalia? When I first met you I wanted your name to be Natalia."

"Yes, if it makes you happy."

"And the other question?"

"You promised not to ask."

"I'm going to ask until you say yes. Rilke says a woman loved who yields is still far from being a woman who loves. If you love me, you'll marry me."

"I do love you."

"Enough to be with me on Thanksgiving?"

"Yes."

"Good. I'm glad something's settled."

"You look like Rose Red," Tom tells her as the taxi stops to pick up her escort. Jean Pierre, a close friend of Tom's and a visiting European, is small and narrow and flawlessly dressed.

Who is Rose Red? she wonders as they shake hands. She feels Jean Pierre's scrutiny. When he is through examining her he allows himself a discreet smile. Natalie can tell he is a practiced conspirator, a professional. His manner assures her there will be no slipups. He will carry his end. She hopes she can hold up hers. Why did she agree to come? Why does she allow Tom to experiment with her?

Tom briefs them. Their hostess is Antonia, the host George. Editor and publisher, a formidable team. Among a certain type they are original. Their charm is unarguable. They have money, breeding, brains and taste. They abhor notoriety.

Antonia opens the door. She is short and wide, wide

enough to remain stubbornly frontal even when she turns.
Full faced she is handsome and alert looking. Her profile
has less character. She is kind but brusque, rushing them
into the living room where, beaming like an exhausted
relay runner who has done her part well, she hands them
off to George. With fists on hips and head thrown back
she returns to her post at the door.

There are many parties or, perhaps, only so many, but
they all have this feature in common. Pleasure Compelled.
Impossible for Natalie and what is impossible for her is
uncomfortable, even hateful. George, with all the charm
and intelligence of a prewar Viennese, cannot relax her.
Tom takes her education in hand. He pulls her into the
ocean of laughing vacationers. She hangs onto him, dragging her feet, protesting, but he has a merciless look in
his eye. She tries not to flail. At the edge of a large group
he abruptly deserts her. Startled, she wheels about to follow him. An obstacle presents itself. She gasps and presses
her forehead. What she had taken for depth and a far
corner proves a solid mirrored wall. Has anyone noticed?
She doesn't dare look around. This problem of perspective
is not any more amenable to solution now than it was
when she first met Tom, involving as it does the idea of
a loss of position. She is bewildered. A bump is rising.
Before she can panic, Jean Pierre is murmuring at her elbow, guiding her. He is indispensable. She will recommend
him for promotion. They join a group, Jean Pierre with his
arm around her. Where is Tom? She cannot see him but
his laughter reaches her.

Her disorientation is complete. She is not here as anyone she knows. She is here as the translator of Jean
Pierre's latest book. Zealous to play her part in this charade convincingly she speaks to Jean Pierre in French.
His English is excellent. A glimpse in the mirror reminds
her she is costumed for the role. She is dressed entirely and
unfamiliarly in clothes of Tom's choosing, dressed in his
gifts. Over the red silk blouse and narrow black trousers
she wears a brilliant Chinese robe, antique. Her hair is
pulled back and held by a pair of carved ivory elephant-
head combs. Around her neck a string of jade. Eyes
rimmed in kohl, lips berry stained. Her reflection excites
her. Her costume excites her. She allows it to impose its
character on her, permits herself to feel languid, smoky. It

is a masquerade. Their circle is conversing in splendid French. She can hide the banality, the vulgarity of her position behind the brilliance of this language. She is persuaded to speak. She hears herself describing her Hungarian playwrights, their struggles. Gradually she becomes aware of interest, even admiration centering on her. Faces press closer. Oohs and aahs. Jean Pierre lets his arm drop, smiles at her, pushes her forward like a stage mother. He can recognize an opportunity for triumph when he sees it.

She is borne into the dining room on a wave of radiance. She feels immodestly proud. Her breasts swell and her nipples are airbrushed with silk. She doesn't disown them.

Jean Pierre holds her chair. Tom is across the table talking to a woman in a red dress. Around her neck, suspended on a filigreed leash, hangs an enormous silver elephant festooned with ceremonial bells. This musical accompaniment makes her hard to ignore. She is a pretty woman with pale hair and friendly blue eyes but Natalie can't forgive her the tintinnabulation.

"Who is that next to Tom?" she asks Jean Pierre.

"*Sa femme,*" he answers, eyebrows arching. His first unguarded, tactless moment. "Barbara."

She gasps. *Mais il me l'a dit, il me l'a promis,* she wants to scream at Jean Pierre though she hasn't enough wind left for swallowing. She clenches her hands under the table. Jean Pierre escapes to the woman on his left. Tom, her traitor, her free and easy traitor, won't raise his eyes. He attends to Barbara. She feels lonely and degraded. The situation won't yield to excuses or interpretations though now she understands his sudden earlier departure. Around the table twenty civilized multinationals are working their teeth through turkey and pigeon and goose, breaking the smallest bones with relish. Tom is no exception.

Later in the living room Tom brings her a cup of coffee and an apology. He rotates a brandy snifter between his hands.

"She showed up at home in tears as I was leaving. At the last minute Laura decided to spend the day at a friend's. I've never seen Barbara so upset."

"Why didn't you call me? I wouldn't have come."

"I know. That's why I didn't call."

"I see."

Jean Pierre approaches. Barbara is on his arm. "I've just been boring Jean Pierre with a description of my new hobby," she says.

"Jogging or singing?" Tom asks.

Barbara doesn't answer. "I'm part of a choral orgy on Christmas Eve at Avery Fisher Hall. Everyone who buys a ticket gets to hum along with Handel," she says to Natalie. "Have you and Jean Pierre known each other long?"

"Natalie is going to translate my new book," Jean Pierre answers for her, back on the job.

"I didn't know there was one. Tom never tells me anything. Congratulations."

"Thank you."

"Into what language?" she asks. It is unclear to whom she is addressing the question.

"English, of course," Jean Pierre answers.

"What are your languages?" she asks Natalie.

"French, Russian and Hungarian."

"Tell me what Jean Pierre's new book is about." She takes Natalie's arm. Her tone is confidential.

"I think he'd better tell you himself. I haven't seen it yet."

"Do you do fiction as well as criticism?"

"Yes."

"Have you translated any famous authors?"

"Not famous here but some of my work is from Hungarian into French and Russian."

"How interesting! Now, Jean Pierre, you come with me. Tom can entertain Natalie. I want to introduce you to a giant in paperbacks. It can't hurt to meet him."

"What did I tell you?" Tom asks as they move off.

"She's not as bad as you make her out to be. She's friendly and warm."

"You're being very perverse tonight."

"Because I don't agree with you?"

"Yes, I suppose so."

"That's childish."

"Yes. I know it is. But you're supposed to agree with me about the important things."

"Show me where it says that."

"Right here." He taps his head.

"What about here? What does it say here?" She points at her heart.

"That you can feel any damn way you please and I'll still love you."

"I'd like to believe that."

"And I'd like to take you in my arms right now and prove it."

"Just to get even with your wife?"

"That's a nasty thing to say. Why would you say a thing like that?"

"Can't you guess?"

"No, I can't."

"You're right. It was nasty."

"Are you sorry?"

"No, I don't think so. Let's not talk about it anymore. Tell me who Rose Red is?"

"Rose Red was the love of my childhood. She had jet hair, milky white skin, full red lips and mysterious dark eyes. She was as good as gold and she had a sister who was equally pure. The sister was called Snow White. Snow White looked like a Swede. She never interested me. I always preferred Rose Red. I think it's the Brothers Grimm. I've forgotten the plot but not Rose Red. We'll read it together sometime. Now say you forgive me. I'm sorry that you're so upset." He has walked her to a quiet corner of the room. He is leaning against the wall. Her back is to the other guests. He looks over her shoulder, scanning the crowd. When he lowers his eyes he reaches over and slides his hand inside her kimono.

"Stop that," she says, taking a step back. "You're crazy. Remember the opening scene in *The Portrait of a Lady*? Just a look, as I recall, but it was more than enough to give away their relationship. Tom, I can't stay any longer. I want to go home."

"You can't walk out on Jean Pierre. He has those perfect European manners. You'll force him to leave and see you home."

"I'll just slip out without saying goodnight to him."

"Don't go yet."

"Don't go? I should never have come."

"All right. I'll call you first thing in the morning. Tonight, if I can manage it. I love you." He reaches for her again.

She backs away, stepping as carefully as if the living room were mined. It takes her a long time to get to the front door.

Tom's demands are escalating. Reflecting on this in bed, face scrubbed, gowned in prim white, her hand absently stroking the quilt, she knows she must call a halt. She has lost her sense of the limits. Tom rewards her for her part in these experiments. He buys her presents. It is possible that she has become addicted to his bribes, to his taste, seduced by the elegance of the offerings. Among the gifts he has pressed on her with his long articulate fingers is his prayer rug. It hangs on the wall of her study. He has penetrated her sanctuary. He shares everything, even his mental associations. He is unstinting and generous, gifting her with himself. All the conversations she has ever longed to have they are having. They have even the longing in common. And yet. And yet what? Nothing concrete. Vague feelings. Moments of profound unease that come and go; flashes of sorrow, sorrow beyond dreaming, which occur when they are together, often when she feels closest to him, moments which require all her vitality to get through. Perhaps she is more like Hermine than she knows and what causes her to sicken is an overdose of unearned pleasure.

She is having these thoughts at two in the morning with the diaries strewn across her quilt like a child's toys, near at hand and reassuring. So many small brown Lincoln Logs, building blocks. Think of the possibility in such a set of blocks! But no possibility here and not reassuring either. Quite the contrary. Hermine's character and spirit make the reading a joyless enterprise. Constriction is the key, a choking off of life, deliberate strangulation. Hermine was high principled but she was also censorious and cranky. No compassion. How she hurt them. What about the hurt? Natalie thinks of Laszlo, poor Laszlo pacing through life, trying to effect Hermine's goals, to earn approval from her stern judge's mouth, Laszlo made odd and urgent by her remoteness. The thing is, she was so secure in her own counsel. How? Oh, what's the use. Natalie is too tired and oppressed to puzzle it out. It can wait. She calculates that if she continues to run the diaries at her present breakneck speed, knees pumping her back through time, by tomorrow her mother will be alive again. In a few days, she will discover her father. She will see him as a resistance fighter, as a young husband, an adolescent, a child, an infant. In a short time, she will witness his birth, that is, if she can stand Hermine's reflections that much longer.

"We live in an age characterized by the failure of all Grand Ideas. Small works of personal conscience are the only alternative."

"The interpreters (authorities-in-charge) of these Grand Ideas actively promote the growth of ritual and symbol which they then use to manipulate the faithful."

"The only true source of authority is the good deed itself, voluntarily done. The rest, by definition, is self-aggrandizing."

"And though it is difficult, it is lonely, indeed, it is often barren, to live without ritual or symbol, nevertheless it is necessary, for only by such trials can one develop a sense of justice, of responsibility, can one attain qualities of daring, of imagination, of kindness. Only under such conditions is true strength forged."

This last entry seems written especially for her, a message from Hermine. Natalie kicks her feet up and down under the quilt and sends the diaries flying. Sleep is out of the question. She is too tense. Gregory's remedy is television. A handsome, straight-nosed, curly-headed blond god comes into focus. He wears jodhpurs and boots, a khaki shirt unbuttoned to the waist. He carries a whip, sits alone on the stage in a director's chair. Has she stumbled onto a late-night blue movie? No. He gives his occupation as Animal Tamer. He is being interviewed by an earnest, off-camera voice:

"Is it possible to feel really safe working with fifteen tigers at one time? I mean, you are literally surrounded by them. You must have quite a relationship with your animals. They must love you. You must love them."

"Love?" the Tamer says. "Love?" He gets to his feet, plants his gleaming boots wide apart, crosses his muscular arms over his broad chest. The whip in his hand twitches reflexively. His blue eyes are very strict. He looks directly at Natalie. "Love is too dangerous. I have to respect my animals. They must respect me. That is all that can be asked for or given in safety. And even then, one never knows." He shrugs. "There are always the imponderables."

"You," Natalie says, winking at him, "may be the only philosopher I have ever understood." She clicks off the remote as he prepares to enter the arena. She has enough imponderables of her own to worry about.

CHAPTER

15

TOM CALLS NATALIE AS SOON AS HE WAKES UP. IN ANticipation of making contact with her, his heart varies its normal rhythm. The resulting weakness in his limbs is compensated for by a spurt of sudden high-quality psychic energy. Contact with her makes him feel unique. Important, significant, significant enough so that he begins to wonder how the world will manage when he's gone. Thinking of Natalie, he mourns the inevitability of his own death. It is a pure, romantic affectation. Actually, he is terrified of death. He and Barbara went to England one summer where they "did" the graveyards, the requisite rubbings. They gamboled through picturesque cemeteries in the Cotswolds, picnicked at quaint ones in the Lake District declaiming Gray's "Elegy" and Tennyson's "Crossing the Bar" and Matthew Arnold's "Memorial Verses," not from memory but from a slim volume of graveyard poetry they found at a second-hand bookseller's in London. They toasted their youth and good health in dozens of these garden spots. Only when they reached Scotland were they hit head on by the real thing. Scottish cemeteries are raw. Cold. Grim. In Scotland death is a dour matter. The sheep concur, cooperate. Across the length and breadth of the land, heads down, jaws working, they mow the acreage. They denude even the cemeteries, exposing a Grim Reaper behind every headstone. In Scotland, Tom discovered that reaping was more than a poetic gerund.

There is no answer at Natalie's. He hangs up and dials

again. Still no answer. Where is she? She has ruined his whole day. He gets up, goes to the bathroom, dials again after his shower. He shaves and redials. He breakfasts. He is on an alternating current. An hour later and still no answer. He will not last the day. He fidgets, paces, tries to read. He doesn't know what to do next. He checks with the phone company. There is no problem on the line. He is dialing for the last time when Barbara returns home.

"Hi," she calls out from the foyer.

"Hi," he answers, putting down the phone. He is glad to see her, grateful for the diversion. She sounds cheerful enough. She's been on good behavior since their "episode."

"Is there any coffee left?" She's getting closer.

"Yes," he says as she enters the kitchen. "I'll heat it for you."

"Thanks."

"How was your run?"

"Not great. I ate too much last night and I didn't sleep well. I woke up with a headache."

"You certainly have an iron will. I don't see how you can do it every day."

"It's just desperation. If I had a job I'd probably give it up, the running, I mean. Speaking of interesting work, what did you think of Jean Pierre's mistress?"

"Jean Pierre's mistress?"

"Well, it was obvious to me. I think she's very attractive. But unfortunately she has that aloof European manner. You know what I mean? 'Our civilization is older and therefore better than yours' syndrome. Do you suppose she's any good at what she does?"

"How would I know?"

"I thought Jean Pierre might have spoken to you about her."

"No. Not a word."

"Does she live with him in Paris, do you suppose?"

"How would I know that? I haven't the faintest idea."

"You're a gold mine of information this morning. Don't men ever talk to each other? Don't answer that. I know they don't."

"Why are you so interested?"

"Well, I admit I am curious. There's something mysterious about her. She's fascinating to look at. Her clothes were incredible, weren't they? Costumey but incredible.

Without those exotic clothes she might be plain looking. Did you notice her kimono? I'll bet it cost a fortune. And those combs in her hair? I wonder if that's her real hair or if she's had a permanent. I felt we had something in common when I saw her combs. Not too many people wear antique elephant jewelry. Didn't you find her interesting?"

"I suppose so. She's quite intelligent."

"I'm not talking about her intelligence. I mean overall."

"I don't know. I haven't given it any thought."

"It doesn't require thought. They make a gorgeous couple, don't they?"

"They're probably miserable just like everybody else."

"You mean just like us."

"I didn't say that. You did."

"That doesn't mean you weren't thinking it."

"I wasn't. I don't think of us as being miserable."

"Ha!"

"Look, let's drop the whole thing. This is getting us nowhere."

"Neither is our marriage."

"I was on my way out. I'll call you later if I don't hear from you. Maybe we'll go to a movie tonight."

"Yes, sir."

"What are you doing today?"

"I don't know. Nothing much. It's Thanksgiving weekend and everyone's away. Maybe I'll go shopping. I'm in the mood for a new dress."

He calls Natalie from the studio. He holds his breath. Seven rings. His lungs will burst. He holds out a little longer. Eight. Nothing. He hangs up and inhales greedily.

Her sense of the limits is gone. Shot. She is as reckless, as precisely lunatic as Tom. She has lost the will to edit her behavior. She is ungovernable. The phone has been ringing all morning. She has vowed not to answer it. She must make a stand somewhere, even a melodramatic one. She is not herself this morning. Melodrama is clearly not her style.

She gets back into bed with 1959 and '58 of the diaries. She has had her babies. That was last week's news. Any page now she will be getting married to Gregory. But

Gregory and her babies don't exist. They are in Florida. How can she believe she is married, was ever married? How can she believe in her motherhood? It must be true. Hermine has faithfully recorded all the events and Hermine never lies. She reads that Hermine was disappointed in Gregory, certain that he will make her life too safe, too comfortable. She is fearful that Natalie will never grow to womanhood as his wife. She concedes his sincere love, his good manners. But what of his morality? His ideology? Of what use is private virtue to the revolution which will feed the world? By four in the afternoon she has not even met Gregory. She picks up the phone on the first ring.

"Where the hell have you been?" Tom yells. "I've been out of my mind all day."

"In bed," she answers. "Having an attack of conscience."

"I'm uptown, on your corner. Don't move. I'll be there in five minutes."

When she opens the door he falls on her like a drowning man. He succeeds in pulling her under.

When they surface he says, "Don't ever do that to me again."

"No," she says. "I won't. I can't. What am I going to do with you?"

"You're going to marry me."

"I told you I don't want to talk about marriage. I am married."

"You can get a divorce."

"I can't. I don't believe in divorce."

"Neither do most people until they have to get one and sometimes not even then."

They are talking about divorce in her marriage bed. Her marriage. An institution with a life of its own, a will of its own. She will have to divorce Gregory and her marriage both. She doesn't have the fortitude for it. Through the open bedroom door she can see the linen closet. She would like to be in there, hidden away. Another dozen volumes and perhaps she will be. Perhaps Hermine knew all about her secret place. The thought pains her.

"For I'm going to marry Rose Red," Tom is singing in

her ear. He sits up. "Does one of your kids have a copy of *Grimms' Fairy Tales?*"

"I'm sure there's one somewhere."

"Go look for it, please." He pushes her playfully off the bed.

"Page two hundred ninety-eight," she tells him when she returns with the book. He takes it from her.

"Christ," he says, reading. "Imagine not remembering that they were named for the rosebushes outside their front door. Here," he continues, "this is the important part. 'These two children were as good, happy, industrious, and amiable as any in the world, only Snow-White was more quiet and gentle than Rose-Red. Rose-Red would run and jump about the meadows, seeking flowers and catching butterflies, while Snow-White sat at home helping her mother to keep house, or reading to her if there were nothing else to do.' "

"I'm a lot closer to Snow White, no matter what you say."

"That's just your opinion. What do you know? You'd be the last to know. Lie back. I'm going to read this to you. It's not very long."

He is a compelling reader. All the things she loves about him come through in his reading. Enthusiasm, wonder, curiosity, energy, magic. She closes her eyes and sees the two sisters, the cranky dwarf, the bear who is a prince in disguise.

Near the end, Tom interrupts himself with a groan. "Oh, no, the prince can't marry Snow White! I don't believe it! That jerk would rather marry the housekeeper than the one who chases butterflies?" He scans the next page. "It's true," he says. "Rose Red gets a brother who's manufactured for the occasion. I didn't remember it that way at all." He looks deflated. It's as if the star witness for his case has recanted at the last moment. The Brothers Grimm have defeated him. "So much for fairy tales," he says, closing the book. "By the way, speaking of misleading memories, when was the last time you read *The Portrait of a Lady?*" He turns on his side to face her, takes the hand nearest his and kisses it.

"Why?" she asks, raising their joined hands to her lips.

"Last night you mentioned the opening scene. Remember?"

"Yes."

"Well, the scene you described wasn't the opening one. I looked it up when I got home. The one you mentioned took place five or six hundred pages into the book. And it wasn't a look that gave away their relationship."

"It wasn't?"

"No," he goes on. "Isabel did catch her husband and Madame Merle looking at each other but what moved her from suspicion to certainty was something else. A breach of etiquette. Gilbert Osmond was seated while Madame Merle stood. Pure James!"

"Don't blame James. He was just reporting. And by such trifles the gods do bring us down." She delivers the last line in mock stentorian tones.

"Who said that?" he asks, laughing.

"I did. I just made it up."

"You didn't."

"Yes, I did."

"Sounds authentic to me."

"It is."

"Well, authentic or not, it certainly is a depressing thought."

"I'm sorry."

"Me too. But it's okay. The most lovable thing about you is your obsession with the meaning of everything. If only you were as obsessed with me."

"I am."

"You can prove that anytime you're ready." He looks at the clock. "Shit, I have to go." He leans over and kisses her kneecaps.

Smiling, she watches him jam his feet into his loafers, the backs of which are permanently flattened, watches him struggle, hooking his index finger like a shoehorn, to pry them loose. She feels a sudden violent upwelling of love, a surge too strong to suppress. If only she were a believer, she could defy the gods, throw over her own quiet, cramped life, and take her chances with him in the howling wilderness.

CHAPTER

16

CHAOS. NATALIE, TRYING TO PICK UP GREGORY AND THE boys at the airport, has blundered into the midst of a demonstration, a holy war on wheels against the supersonic transport. One placard reads: "God is on the side of people not planes." The demonstrators have their headlights on in the bright sunshine and they move as slowly as a funeral cortege, three lanes wide. They take precedence the way death parades do. It is their right as mourners. No one may pass and they are required to stop for nothing. It is hard, sad work, holding back progress, as hard as holding back grief, and the strain shows on their faces. They stare grimly ahead over their steering wheels into a future doomed by scientific advances. They have lost all peripheral vision, see no paradox in blasting their own horns to protest the noise level of the SST, in poisoning the low-lying air with their engine fumes to protest the threat of ozone starvation to the outer atmosphere. What is one to do? It is not useful to get angry. Nevertheless, the hostages of today's demonstration are. They improvise a protest of their own, leaving their stalled cars to kick at the demonstrator's tires, to bang on their rolled-up windows, to yell profanities. One man, more original than the rest, hurls himself onto the hood of one of the lead cars and has a temper tantrum.

It takes forty-five minutes to reach the parking lot, another fifteen to find a space. And then she doesn't actually find one. What she does in the spirit of the moment, in the spirit of anarchy, is abandon her car in a restricted area.

She is very late. She was late before she left home. Gregory will think she has met with a fatal accident. She locks her car and runs across the road to the terminal, dodging cars and buses and the angry signals of an airport policeman. She cannot find her family in the returning holiday mob. She may never find them. She should be able to pick them out, they should stand out for her, but she can't and they don't. She fights her way to the luggage carousel. A redcap tells her that all arriving flights are late. He points to the flight board. The plane is just now landing.

She runs up to the arrival area, feeling light-headed. She hasn't eaten, hasn't used her hand, hasn't seen Tom in two days. He and Barbara are with his parents in the country, in the land of quail and canopied beds, his presence required in lieu of an apology for his letter to the *Times*. Old as he is, he is still standing in corners.

She awoke early yesterday thinking how grateful she was for the chance to be alone. But it was no good. Within an hour there were signs of the onset of a headache, an ominous throb in her left eye, a sensitivity in the bones of her face. She took a pill, put some water on for coffee. While the water came to a boil she drifted through the empty rooms with a cleaning rag. A thin tissue of dust covered everything in the deserted apartment, bringing to mind the ghost towns she and Gregory had visited with the children last summer, provoking thoughts of mortality.

When the smell reached her she dropped the cloth and ran to the kitchen. The scorched handle broke off when she grabbed it but the kettle itself remained in place, its bottom melted onto the electric burner. None of Hermine's remedies worked. Her palm and fingers sizzled and swelled. She felt a wire of pain draw up from her hand and thread itself deftly through her throbbing left eye.

Eventually, the sun set. She slept badly. She squeezed vitamin E capsules onto her hand each time she woke, Gregory's sworn remedy although it hadn't saved his mother. Sunday passed in silence, the emptiness increasing as the pain did. In the early afternoon she relented, telephoned her doctor. He was out of town. His service directed her to the emergency room of a nearby hospital. There, a young doctor told her she was doing nicely but to expect some problems once the healing began, something about the skin being too tight. The drive to the airport was difficult. She had to guide the car with a single hand.

She joins a pedestrian traffic jam in the arrival area, holding her hand up to keep it from being jostled. Gregory will be distraught when he sees it. It's bound to call up the episode of his parents' death. She and Gregory had been married only a brief time, a matter of months, when the accident occurred.

The call came from Gregory's youngest brother in the middle of the night. She had to shake him awake. He could sleep through anything in those days.

"I think it's serious," she said as she handed him the phone. His brother's voice had been urgent, grim.

"When?" he asked his brother. "How bad? Yes, as soon as we can get there."

Then he hurled the receiver to the floor and curled into an agony on the bed. She crawled across the twisted sheets to his side. "What is it?" she asked, stroking his buried head.

"They were on their way to the lake when a heavy fog blew in. The plane crashed on landing. The airport there has always been substandard. My mother is critically burned and my father—," he gave one black, appalling cry, "my father is dead. They found him strapped to his seat with a broken neck, a hundred yards from the plane. A hundred yards," he repeated, his tone suddenly and confusingly impersonal.

The special emergency burn unit was marked as such by the pervasive smell of singed chicken skin. The smell made the nightmare real for her, cut through all her defenses, clung to her clothing, seeped into her pores. The smell of her own burned hand, these many years later, is enough to revive it all.

They waited their turn among the weeping to speak to the resident in charge. When he finished with the couple ahead of them, the woman screamed. She smashed her fists against his white coat, yelled murderer, murderer. The doctor looked dazed. He shuffled his papers for a long time until he found theirs. He read them the prognosis. His heart wasn't in it. He was very young and the woman had frightened him.

"Mrs. Barnes has a very slim chance of recovery," he

read to them. "Two-thirds of her body surface is covered with burns of varying severity."

They spared him the rest, made their way down the corridor to Gregory's mother's room. Gregory pushed open her door, hesitating only the barest tick of a second. Natalie followed. She closed her eyes at the threshold, waiting for Gregory to tell her when she could safely look, as he did for her at the movies. There was silence. A long silence. She opened her eyes to see him standing at the foot of one of the beds reading a chart.

"This is my mother," he said calmly.

Natalie glanced at the bed, at all three beds. She looked hard at all three occupants. She said no, said it emphatically, and ran to him.

"Yes," he insisted, as though she were not protesting the horror, only disagreeing with him. "The one on the left is eighteen years old. On the right, thirty-three. See for yourself. It's on the charts."

"No," she whimpered, sinking down onto her knees.

The three women were as alike as the batches of yeast dough her own mother used to prepare. The three faces had risen uniformly from their pans of burnt hair and doubled—no—tripled in size, overflowing their containers, increased beyond human scale. Any one of these creatures could have been Gregory's mother.

"Oh, no," Natalie said over and over. She tried to stand and found she couldn't manage it alone. Gregory raised her up. They stood together in helpless bondage, waiting, released from all other obligations. It took six weeks.

It is ridiculous to think she can ever leave Gregory. He is part of her. And they are all orphans now. She has joined Gregory and Gorky.

Natalie waves her good hand. They see her immediately. They run to her. They are bronzed and happy. They chatter and laugh. She keeps her bad hand draped casually in a scarf. It's not until she pulls one of their bags off the carousel and the scarf slips that Gregory discovers her burn.

"My God," he says and goes white under his tan.

"I promise you it's all right. I saw a doctor. He said it will be fine. It doesn't hurt. I have a prescription here, somewhere in my bag."

His color doesn't return. He remains unpersuaded. They bear her to the car. She is not to touch a thing, not to lift a finger. They are more careful with her than with her precious porcelains. Gregory detours to an all-night drugstore once they reach the city. No, it can't wait until morning. He runs in to fill the prescription. When he returns to the car and looks at her hand he shudders.

"How did you manage to drive to the airport?" he asks but before she can answer he says, "Never mind. I don't want to know. It will just upset me more." Natalie is tempted by martyrdom, the tendency tooled into her character. Not to downgrade it. He values stoicism but there is a limit. He shakes his head, remembering an episode some years ago in which a carving board, studded with iron spikes designed to cradle a roast, edged from the top of the refrigerator onto her head. She served dinner without mentioning it. Only when they were halfway through the meal did he catch her blotting furtively at a narrow trickle of blood. He thought his heart would stop. It looked to him as though her forehead had been split in two. Thank God, it was only the scalp. Eight stitches. She was planning to tell him, she explained on the way back from the hospital, after he had finished his dinner.

He glances over at her now. She looks dreadful, her face drawn into a wince. "Did the doctor give you a painkiller?" he asks.

"No," she says. "But I'm managing fine."

"Well," he says, "we had a great trip, didn't we boys?"

There is agreement from the back seat. "The weather wasn't too good but we got to be expert miniature golfers," Gregory says. "Also, we did a lot of walking in the rain. We are expert rain walkers."

"I thought up that category," Adam interrupts.

Natalie reaches behind her and strokes Adam's cheek with her good hand.

"We might even get a mention in the *Guinness Book of World Records* in the category of Rain Walking," Adam says. "Seriously, I'm going to write to them."

He and Steve exchanged comradely punches. Gregory and Natalie exchange a look of celebration. These marvelous children are theirs.

"Adam did a portrait of me, a sketch," Gregory says. "I'm going to have it framed and hang it in the office."

Adam reaches forward and puts his hands on Gregory's shoulders. "Not while Daddy's driving," Natalie cautions.

"It doesn't bother me," Gregory says. Doesn't bother him? He is so pleased at this show of affection he could drive right off the road.

"Hey, Mom, any calls for me while I was away?" Steve asks Natalie. He has an eager look, his favorite at the moment that dubious music, the insistent harmonics of a ringing phone. He lives on the instrument, answering every call, even the ones that have already been answered by someone else. He breaks into ongoing conversations from an extension with an expectant hello, hello. This irritates Gregory who can only growl at Steve to hang up, which offends Steve who obeys but sulks. His sulks are more irritating than his interruptions.

Gregory pulls up to their building. He helps Natalie out of the car. She cocks her burned hand in the air like a dog offering a paw. Her thumb is raw, swollen, reminding him of his mother's charred limbs. It is still painful for him to think about his parents' accident. He never saw his father's body. It was presented to him at the funeral home in a closed casket. He never inspected the contents. For years afterward, he dreamed that his father was still alive but had chosen to remain incommunicado, that the man he had buried was not his father but a stranger. He searched for his father through many dreams. He came very close to finding him but never close enough.

Natalie walks through the lobby ahead of them. Gregory is acutely aware of her separateness. She is uncoupled, detached, as disconnected as when he left. Enough, he wants to tell her. Hermine was an old woman. But he doesn't dare. Natalie has had a hard life. Hermine was both mother and father which entitles her to double the grief. He will give her a little more time.

As he unlocks the front door it hits him. Except for Adam's portrait there is no evidence that those few days in the Keys ever took place. The weariness comes on so suddenly that he has to stop midway on the stairs and put down the two suitcases he is carrying. Natalie is right behind him, warning him not to scratch the walls, reminding him that it would have been more sensible to take up one bag at a time.

"Shut up," he yells at her. "Just get off my back, will you. I don't give a shit about your goddamn walls."

He apologizes later when they are in bed. Natalie accepts and offers one of her own. She is contrite but cool, moving to the farthest edge of the bed. Her hand is propped up on an extra pillow. He wants to say something but he can't think what. She looks so hurt. "Did you remember to take your pill?" he asks after a while.

"No."

He gets it for her, brings her a glass of water, waits for her to finish the water. "Let me take the glass back to the bathroom so it doesn't leave a ring on the night table."

She puts her arms around his neck and cries, blaming it on her hand. "It doesn't hurt," he hears her say through the tears. "A good night's sleep is all I need."

"Me too," he tells her and with this lie he says goodnight.

Casting about for comfort in the days that follow is not easy. Her poor burned hand has gotten its share but there isn't much for the rest of her to live on. Tom and Gregory are baffled by her behavior. Put out. She knows they are withholding their seals of approval until she shapes up. By shaping up they mean different things. Tom knows that her malaise (his word—she prefers malheur) will disappear if she leaves Gregory and marries him. His patience is wearing thin. Gregory knows that her depression (his word) is temporary, having been induced by Hermine's death. In the interim, he is feigning patience but not understanding or approval. She is a trial to both of them though she tries not to be. When she tries not to be, Gregory shouts at her to stop playing martyr. Tom, on the other hand, tells her to be more stoical and take some decisive action. Both of them are trying to bring her along, each in his own way. She will have none of it. Why don't they leave her alone? She will get there in her own good time. Get where? Where can she go from here? She has reached the point of *taedium vitae*, the saturation point.

She has drawn away from everyone. Granted, it's not an army she's talking about. A handful only. But this handful is all she has. And, in a sense, it is an army. It's all male. There are no women in her life anymore. In her dreams there is still Hermine and occasionally her mother. She can't dwell on her mother. No amount of dwelling will ever put it right. She has never spoken about her mother to anyone and she never will. Anyway, her small private army has retreated or, perhaps, she has retreated or, perhaps, they are all exactly where they have always been. Whatever the high ground she has been defending all her life, she has lost it now.

"I'm sorry," she says to each of them each day. "I'm sorry." Tom is sorry, Laszlo also. Gregory too. It's one of those periods in life filled with missteps and apologies and anger. Obviously, she is doing something wrong. In his sorrow, Laszlo is edgy and difficult. He battles for his fund against all the odds. Detecting little signs of life, he keeps up the artificial respiration. Natalie tries for cheerfulness with him, with all of them. She does it gladly, grateful for the chance. Such chances are scarce these days. Gregory is still a lieutenant in the memory-technology war. He still dreams of being a general. Tom still dreams of marrying her. She has no dreams at all.

She is not a refugee for nothing, however. The price was perhaps too high. It is arguable. Tom argues it with passion. But she did learn something. Tom may not know it but she has this something in common with those Eskimos who tread the blue tints of the polar ice cap. Things have a way of shifting under their feet too. If isolation and cold and hunger are their elements, they have been hers too. She knows about survival. It would be easier if she had a shaman. But as much as she wants it, sincere faith today strikes her as a neurotic desire, a private fantasy. The Eskimos have it all over her there. Over all of them. Think of it this way, she consoles herself. In a century in which the nation's symbol, the bald eagle, must be pumped with antibiotics to keep it aloft, how can the spirit soar?

CHAPTER

17

IF IT'S A LIFETIME SINCE HERMINE'S DEATH, THEN IT'S another kind of lifetime since she and Tom tore holes in the sheets of white paper handed to them by that strange man, the Turk. It seems so long ago that she can hardly remember the man, the woman they were then. If today, six months later, the Turk were to give her that paper, she would know what to do with it. She would snatch it from him and without hesitating she would tear it into a thousand pieces. Tom, with the same undiminished verve, would probably punch out another sun.

It is with an equal amount of verve that he has dragged her up to Boston today to see an exhibit at the Museum of Fine Arts. Gregory thinks it is part of the course work. He doesn't know that she is no longer taking the course. Romans and Barbarians. This is the title of the show. It's a terrific title, one whose "polarization makes for high drama." At least this is the impression it made on one critic. The title doesn't impress her. She and Tom have enough high drama of their own and are not in need of any other. That is, Tom is not in need. She is but she doesn't know what sort.

She has tried to stop thinking and analyzing. "Beyond a given point, man is not helped by more knowing but only by living and doing in a partly self-forgetful way." She can't remember who said that. The stack of books by her bed yields all sorts of sage advice, all sorts of plausible systems of thought and logic such as: "The more man can take reality as truth, appearance as essence, the sounder, the better adjusted, the happier he will be. This constantly effective process of self-deceiving, pretending and blundering is not a psychopathological mechanism."

Natalie knows that Otto Rank is right. What she doesn't know is how to do it, to take reality as truth. Tom does it. He worships his aesthetics. Gregory does it. He has his technology. Laszlo does it. He had his projects, he has his book. Each feels that his reality is best. She feels that none of them has any correspondence with her life. She sometimes wonders if her object in reading all these erudite books isn't only to reduce the pile to zero. She has little hope that they will give her any more to hold on to than did Hermine's diaries. And, anyway, all the unsystematic insights she has collected, however rich, are confusing to an untrained mind. Nevertheless, she reads on. Her hope is that absorption may become a physiological reaction and out of this reaction she, like the sponge, can create a life.

To reassure Gregory and Laszlo she has learned to playact. Her cheerfulness is convincing. They are reassured. Their eyes say to one another, "She is over the worst." Even Laszlo seems over the worst. "Seems" because now and then Natalie senses that he also is playacting though he has reason enough to be cheerful now. His book is about to be released. The advance notices are excellent. He is in love. It is serious. Her name is Vivi. No, she was not exactly his secretary.

"I don't want to hear any criticism from you," he told Natalie. "I'm the virgin in this relationship."

"How long have you been together?"

"A long time."

"Then why haven't we met her? Why have you been hiding her?"

"You'll meet her as soon as she comes back from California. By the way, I sublet the old apartment. I'm moving in with Vivi. We've decided to get married."

"You? Married? I don't believe it."

"Nevertheless, it's true."

"I'm sure she's much too young for you. They all are."

"When I'm famous that won't matter," he joked. "Look at Steichen, Casals, Picasso!"

"You've made your point," she told him, laughing. "But that doesn't mean I'm convinced. Take that as a warning."

Over the long run, the effort of treating each other

seriously has proven too strenuous. They have returned by degrees to the old comfortable posture, that of ironic bantering. Unfortunately, warnings given in this modern style have little effect. Like blows delivered underwater, most of the impact is absorbed by the medium.

Natalie has told Tom she will never marry him. This is the direct action for which he was lobbying but not the outcome. He takes comfort in his daughter who is living at home again after a disastrous semester at boarding school. Natalie and Tom spend most of the daylight hours together at the studio. She has two husbands now. She is Snow White in duplicate, the flowers and butterflies out of reach. When she is sad, rather when she cannot help showing the sadness she feels all the time, Tom tries to joke her out of it. Her tearful laughter is rewarded with an embrace, a chuck under the chin.

"That's the girl I love," he says, chucking.

Phony words, phony gestures—ingenuity instead of honesty. What next? Will he co-opt the technique of the Ch'ien-lung potters, those preeminent imitators who could duplicate any substance in porcelain? Dust, rust, bronze, shells, ivory, jade, the eggs of birds, the grain of rare woods—imitations which fooled the eye but cheated the heart. This thought burdens Natalie, for she knows as well as any scholar that once refinement and simplicity give way to pyrotechnics, then the art itself is in decline.

She is subdued most of the time. Tom doesn't notice. Gregory doesn't notice. Adam does look at her now and then as though she were a stranger but he doesn't say anything. Perhaps she is only imagining it. Perhaps it is only natural that he should look at her this way now that he is turning into a man. He has thinned out and his voice has dropped and he has a row of dark fuzz along his upper lip. He will shave soon. Yesterday he asked their permission to pierce his ear. He wants to wear a gold earring. A gold earring? She looked helplessly at Gregory. If she had expected him to thunder and rage she was wrong.

"Well," he said, "it's not my idea of beauty but if it's what you want, go ahead."

Gregory has changed that much since he left his job and started law school. He left even though the company offered him a perfectly respectable place in the hierarchy. She is glad for him, though in her opinion he has only traded one game for another. Nevertheless, this new game has rejuvenated him to the point of passion. He takes sides. He has developed what Hermine would call an ideology, a luxury he never permitted himself while he was with the company. It was bad for business. He is going to school and working as a consultant for several other firms in his field. He is very busy.

They are both very busy. Natalie is working on an adaptation of Giraudoux's *La Guerre de Troie n'aura pas lieu.* When she is finished it will be set to music, very modern music, music which drives her to screaming madness when she hears it. She is trying to learn to accept these abrasions and others, trying to become more tolerant, trying to force herself to bloom out of season. Otherwise she may turn into another Hermine. This fear haunts her along with others. Perhaps they are all part of the same fear. When she tries to grasp herself whole, all she can come up with are bits and pieces of her grandmother. For this reason she is trying to give up thinking about herself. She fears she is growing morbid with introspection.

Tom does not approve of morbidity. He has told her so. Morbidity requires drastic measures. He has suggested therapy. Natalie tells him he has missed the point. She may not know specifically what she needs but what she most emphatically does not need or want is an intensive investigation of her own personal unhappiness. All the analysis in the world hasn't helped people to discover who they are, no less why they were put on this earth in the first place, and never mind the problem of death. She tells him this.

Hermine, who spent a lifetime searching for the answers to these questions, never got close. It was her grandmother's conviction that her own early, pioneering analysis was the single most destructive thing in her life. She referred to her analysis as a wedge driven between herself and a larger world view, between herself and God which took all her strength and most of her life to chip away. "How can I continue to believe in sexuality as the root cause of all human unhappiness?" she wrote when she was thirty-five. "I would rather die now than live by such an absurdity." And later: "Having given up God, am I to be condemned to search for meaning inside myself when I have never been able to endure my own littleness?" And: "Have I exchanged my soul for my self? If so, then I have made the same bad bargain as Faust."

Natalie has not raised these questions with Tom. His interest is limited to matters of a purely aesthetic nature. She has learned that the "meaning of life" and attendant subjects bore him. Possibly this is because the meaning of life is not visual. Or possibly because he has never allowed himself to feel fear. Only outrage.

When she broaches the subject with Gregory, he assures her that he has no objections to her going to church. She can even take the boys. It would probably do them some good, particularly Steve. Met with such sweet reasonableness, Adam declined to pierce his ear. She is no different. Well, yes she is. She is not testing the limits, at least not Gregory's. It is not Church she wants.

At the moment, Tom is leaping about in front of her with delight. He cannot get over the variety of the objects on view. "Prodigious," he says. Natalie is not as astounded by this sweep of empire. She knows about Man the Maker even if that Man doesn't interest her right now. She wonders if Tom's enthusiasm is genuine or if it is habit. His enthusiasm is what she fell in love with and here she is questioning it. She will never learn. She will never change.

"I like the title," Tom tells her. "As an attempt to organize the chaos, I think it works."

Natalie can sympathize with the motive if not the title. "I see your point," she says.

They are being guided past an endless variety of tight-lipped Roman portrait busts, past amulets and coins, past pottery and plaques and jewels from all over the empire, past mundane household goods and sublime architectural fragments, past all this by yet another member of Tom's legion of male friends. This one is a curator. They all lunch together. While the men talk shop, she flips idly through the catalogue. On the last page she finds a translation of a Cavafy poem, "Waiting for the Barbarians," a poem she hasn't read for years. She rereads it and then is sorry she did.

When they finish lunch, Tom and his friend get up. Tom is eager to have another look at the show. Natalie refuses. Tom insists. Natalie refuses again. She is not sure why but she feels physically unable to re-view the relics of that exhausted civilization. Tom is annoyed with her, scowling, the same scowl that appears on his face when he complains to her of his father. He leaves her sitting in the cafeteria and goes off with his friend. The show has inspired him. Dead civilizations are his meat. He would like to get it down on film, weave a documentary around it. He is itching to get back to the city, to make some phone calls. There is no doubt about his inspiration. He can hardly sit still in his airplane seat. He's up and down the aisle every other minute. He'll make his calls when they get home. Home means the studio. House means his home with Barbara. He gives the driver the address of the studio. But suddenly Natalie wants to go to her own home. She has two homes and no house. Tom is too high on his new idea to object seriously. He kisses her goodbye with gusto. He has forgotten he is angry with her. He drops her off on her corner and yells, "See you tomorrow," from the moving cab.

In the middle of the lobby, Natalie is overcome with dread. She knows it's dread because it is identical to the feeling she used to experience every day as she got off the elevator and began her walk to Hermine's hospital room. Cavafy is right. There is much worse in store for the human race than the Barbarians. They would be a kind of solution. The dread persists though upstairs everything is as usual. She puts dinner on the table, as usual. She serves the three of them, as usual. Adam waves his hand under her nose and says, as usual, "Hey, Mom, wake up. Remember me? I'm the one who eats carrots but hates squash." He switches plates ostentatiously with Stephan and they all laugh, as usual. They all eat, as usual. She can only try, which is not usual. Swallowing is so difficult she feels she has not been genetically endowed with the gift. But she continues to try. And because she knows that one thing follows from another, that beliefs about reality affect real actions, she continues trying to work, trying to sleep, walk, talk, love, live. Though she is exhausted and gaunt and hollow-eyed from trying, she still has the habit of self-discipline.

She is most successful at the working. Those involved in the play, *Tiger at the Gates*, its English title, are pleased with the results. But she suspects that a time is coming when even her work will no longer be possible. Then, if she can't work, how will she earn her safety?

Natalie is disintegrating. Perhaps that is too strong a word for it but that is what comes to mind and Tom trusts his first impressions. He doesn't know what to do with her, for her. Life is too short, he wants to tell her but is stopped by the look on her face. She wears a tragic face.

The look of doom on her face is beginning to make him feel guilty for being happy. It disturbs him for other reasons as well. He knows her despair has nothing to do with those things in life that worry most people, things like money, fame, success, failure, family problems, etc. He thinks she thinks she is in mourning for the human condition. Her questions lead him to this belief. He just can't get worked up over the human condition and the fact that she can disturbs him, leading him to wonder if he might not be somehow deficient. He tries not to think of it this way but lately, now and then, he feels a twinge of jealousy. Since he is trying to be candid with himself, he also has to admit that every now and then he also feels a flare of resentment not unlike that which he has permanently with regard to his father. They are both so damned certain. He can't comfortably dismiss either one, much as he would like to. They are both so damned disengaged. They might as well not be there with him. And yet, he can't conceive of giving her up. He is trying to adjust. Natalie does make it easy, he will admit that. She is not the kind of person to wreak havoc when miserable. On the contrary, she is more docile and desirous of pleasing than ever. Sometimes she is so docile, he is bored.

If he were asked to date this new development in their relationship, he would have to go back to that day in Boston when she refused to go through the Roman exhibition a second time. She wouldn't give a reason. Her decision struck him as being selfish and arbitrary.

"Are you playing Freud before the spectre of Rome?" he had joked as he tried to pull her to her feet. She had given him a blank look, forcing him to explain how Freud fainted dead away each time he tried to approach the Eternal City, how Jung did the same while buying tickets for the trip, how even Luther had had to beat a fast retreat.

"But Goethe called Rome a place in which to be reborn," she had countered, smiling. "Perhaps I'm not yet ready for that."

In his opinion, she needs some professional help. He has come around to believing in the usefulness of psychiatry. His own wife is living proof. He would like to tell Natalie this but he knows he won't because it would be traitorous to use his wife as an example.

"Even if it doesn't help," he tells her, "it can't hurt."

"Believe me," Natalie answers, "it can."

She refuses to elaborate. She has gotten very secretive. For a while he felt she had opened to him entirely. Not anymore. And though she doesn't argue with him neither does she accept his opinion as the last word. Not anymore. Neither does she attend his lectures. They haven't discussed these issues. The proper moment never comes. Overall, however, he is content. Laura is at home and Barbara is working. She has gone into the commercial end of the real estate brokerage business and she is doing very well. All those contacts she made over the years are paying off. Her lunches these days are business lunches. She is in the big leagues, renting thousands of square feet of office space over her eggs Benedict. She is easier to live with now that she is gainfully employed. The money is good, one source of irritation done away with. When she finds the time, she plans to look for a new apartment. When she finds the time! So many things have happened to Barbara. She has graduated to twelve-pound weights. She is still running. Contrary to her own prognosis, she hasn't given it up. What she has given up is singing, and complaining and, possibly, just possibly, now that she has a solid career, she has given up the old extramarital one. This suspicion is based on several observations: She is wearing a bra again although she claims it reflects only a requirement of the job and not an ideological shift. She isn't as sloppy or as crazed or as temperamental. She drops fewer names and they hit the ear with less of a thud. She is anxious to visit his studio.

Actually, Natalie's state of mind is the only cloud on his horizon these days. Cloud is too strong a word but he can't think of another. Today, for the first time, he is feeling mutinous. He has made an excuse not to see her. Instead, he is lunching with a group of friends whom he hasn't seen in months. A nice, easy, casual, witty, amusing lunch. Not until he sits down at the table where they are all assembled does he appreciate just how cloistered he has been this past year, the scale of his confinement. He smiles at them all, all his friends with their upturned, expectant faces. He wants to applaud them. He pulls out a chair, takes a deep breath and prepares to be brilliant.

CHAPTER

18

NATALIE HAS NO DOUBT THAT THE LONELY LOVELY LEAP into faith suggested by her bedside Kierkegaard is too broad a jump for her unathletic self. However, it does suggest an attitude which appeals to her nature precisely because it is difficult, if not impossible, to achieve. It sticks in her mind. Unfortunately, what also sticks is the knowledge that even its creator, a man who possessed a mental agility which, by any standard of measure, renders hers insignificant, never himself managed this broadest of all jumps.

Natalie is as far along as this: She can acknowledge life for what it really is. Demonic. Terrifying. Her education began with Hermine's death and, in some way she hasn't fully worked out, was completed during the course of her relationship with Tom. False as her earlier strength may have been, she was attached to it and even now would welcome it back. Since it is obviously not going to return, what she needs to discover is how she can put her terror back in the universe, in outer space, the dimension to which it properly belongs and which may or may not be large enough to contain it. On some days she is sure it is not large enough. Yesterday, for instance, was such a day.

Yesterday, the rush-hour subway for which she waited was late and undersized and overcrowded. After the train pulled out, the man next to her raised his arms from his sides. When his hands were shoulder height she saw that he held a penknife in one of them. He opened the blade and calmly pointed it at her throat. Faced with impending violence, with personal cataclysm, she had no choice but to scream, to try to get away. The faintest nudge of a doubt, the doubt that she might be wrong, a doubt she has had all her life in relation to her appraisal of others, kept her silent, motionless. A minute later, the train gave a body-smashing lurch. The man with the knife helped her regain her balance, apologized for having fallen on her. She saw then that his knife was only a small blunt blade similar to the one Laszlo used for cleaning and trimming his nails, the very job which the courteous stranger proceeded to get on with, his nail crumbs flaking onto her coat. She has not told either Gregory or Tom of the episode. She tries not to think of it herself.

So here it is: her naked terror. There is a place she suspects would be perfect for its cold storage. Stephan is reading to her about this place now although in truth all she understands of what he is reading is his uncontained excitement. This may be partly due to a full mouth. He is eating breakfast and simultaneously reading to her from *The New York Times*. She wonders if an understanding of the mysteries of space such as he seems to have, with or without his mouth full, would make it any easier to leap from the edge of the known world into *it*, as Kierkegaard suggests one do.

The place to which she would like to consign her dread has a good name. Also it is a star. This makes her feel very comfortably disposed toward it. She can appreciate the poetry of stars. Through the ages they have been an appropriate place for terror, certainly more appropriate than subways. Radio astronomers call this particular star the Vela pulsar. It is so named for the constellation where it was found. It is the second pulsar to be identified optically, that is, as Stephan explains with milk dribbling down his chin, identified in terms of visible light. These are the kinds of newspaper articles she skips but there is no stopping Stephan who has lately decided to become an astronomer-astronaut. He continues. The first pulsar to be identified optically, he reads to her, was in the Crab Nebula. She will stick with Vela. She hates crabs, the image a part of the debris of childhood nightmares. Since Vela is the dimmest star ever photographed, Natalie reasons that it would welcome the energy generated by her terror to increase its light. There is easily enough energy in her terror to bring Vela's paltry eleven pulses per second up to and perhaps even past the thirty of the Crab. She would like to see the Crab outclassed.

"I can understand the symbolism," she confesses, "but not the content."

"Try to think of Vela as a fluorescent tube."

"That doesn't help me at all."

"Fluorescent light isn't constant even though it looks that way."

"It isn't?"

"No. It blinks on and off so quickly that the eye can't perceive the difference." He says this between bites of his fingernails, bites so rapid and sweeping that he might be playing the harmonica for the effect it gives.

"Perceive?" she asks him. "How do you know the word perceive? You're only twelve."

"Cut it, Mom. It's perceived as constant because the human eye has something called the persistence of vision."

Persistence of vision? She has been deceived all these years? Nevertheless, the idea of the persistence of vision is soothing. What gives her a curious kind of comfort is not that the Vela pulsar originated in a supernova, and here she interrupts herself to confess to her son that she has no idea what a supernova is, but that this same supernova was recorded by the Sumerians some six thousand years ago.

"Mom," Stephan says with unconcealed amazement and jam on his nose, "I don't believe a person can live in the twentieth century and not have heard of any of this."

"You may be right," Natalie tells him and wipes his nose in return for which he swipes at her, "but I know something about the Sumerians and I'll bet you don't."

She tells him what she knows. He is bored out of his mind. Sumerian literature is rich and varied. There are myths and epics. This is the bait. Stephan is a lover of heroes. She tells him that while there was never exactly a Sumerian people but only Babylonians and others, there is a Sumerian language and it is the oldest written language in existence. These facts make him fidget but then she can appreciate that a child who feels comfortable in the infinity of space is apt to be a little cramped inside history. "How did we make this optical identification?" she asks. "And why did it take so long? We must have improved on the Sumerians."

"I'm not sure. Our science teacher hasn't gotten to that part yet. Why don't you ask Dad? He knows all about this stuff."

"Well, with both these pulsars," Gregory explains over dinner, pleased and surprised by her interest, "the flashes could only be detected by using a computer that controlled the sensing system so that it was able to scan the area in tempo with the assumed flashes."

Assumed and in tempo. This is what interests her, what she focuses on. This and the persistence of vision.

"Does it make any sense to you?" Gregory asks. "That's about as simple as I can make it. I'm sorry."

"Enough sense," she answers. She has what she wants out of the lesson. The flashes were assumed before they were actually seen. And the light was so dim it couldn't be detected with the naked eye. Symbolism has always mattered more to her than hard facts. In this respect, at least, she hasn't changed.

For a reason which she suspects must be connected to Vela, she doesn't feel as bleak as usual. At least Vela is alive in a continuous present, a present which unlike her own has been proved to contain both the ancient past and the distant future. She is determined to ignore Gregory now that he is telling her what she does not want to hear, telling her that there is proof that the pulse rate of the Crab Nebula, which was discovered around 1050 A.D., is *slowing* down. She prays that this is not the case, that pulsars don't die, that the fault lies not in our stars but in ourselves—and in our tools of measurement. Even Gregory laughs. As for her, it is her first smile in a long time. What also makes her smile is the crazy, totally unfounded, truly weird notion she has just come up with that Vela, an ancient pulsing, constant star of light, is female.

In the weeks ahead there are other things which make her smile. Spring is one of them. It is unseasonably warm for spring. Buds of dogwood and cherry and apple open synchronously, revealing petals as unblemished as newborn skin. The streets smell of excrement. She ignores it, breathing deeply (even the notion that spring is a loaded pleasure gives her pleasure) as she strides down the block to the market, a small neighborhood grocery that she has dealt with for years. The two brothers who own it see her rarely. Usually she telephones but today she wants to be there, to make small talk, to pinch the food. Today the brothers are pushing artichokes. She buys them even though they take too much time to prepare. She buys them just because they are being pushed on her in such a friendly way. One of the brothers gives her a few tips on how to minimize the effort. The tips come straight from his mother who at eighty-two still puts up her own tomatoes and speaks only Italian. She has never needed to learn English. Why? She plans to return to Italy to die.

Natalie takes the tips, the artichokes and the rest of her purchases and goes home to cook. She hasn't done any serious cooking for a long time, not since Tom began cooking for her. She did make him some strudel once, hot, peppery cabbage strudel. It's a pity they never cook together. It's not her choice. Tom can't tolerate sharing the kitchen. It breaks his concentration. His concentration makes him a good cook but not an inspired one. She has never told him this.

The act of unpacking the produce puts a smile on her face. The immediacy of this still life which has created itself on her counter makes her want to laugh aloud, to draw a deep breath and laugh. She has seen this same display a thousand times but today the beauty of its concreteness is undiluted, an absolute in its own right and compelling enough to make her forget her longing for those other absolutes which never materialize.

She picks up an artichoke, drops it. A speck of blood appears on her thumb. She sucks at it impatiently. There is work to do. Laszlo and Vivianne are coming for dinner. Tonight, for the first time, they will meet her.

With his hands resting lightly on her shoulders, Laszlo moves his companion forward a step. "Natalie," he says, "this is Vivianne Péffert."

Natalie is stunned. Vivianne is not the person she expected. She is not beautiful. Neither is she young. There is as much relief as shock in her discovery as she scans Vivianne's face. The delicate woman with olive skin and straight, thick, dark hair standing opposite her smiles warmly. Natalie smiles back.

"Hello," Vivianne says and offers her hand. She is sweet voiced.

Natalie takes it and says, "I'm so glad to meet you at last."

"I too," Vivianne says and smiles again.

Her face is compelling, the eye color so unexpected. By rights such eyes belong in another complexion. The pale blue eyes of a blond have no business here. Nevertheless, they are here and they glitter like the cold blue of early winter mornings, the imperial sky blue of her porcelains.

"I'm dying to discover everything about you," Vivianne says. "I have heard only the most wonderful things from Laszlo. I want us to be great friends."

She has not yet released Natalie's hand. Now, as she tightens her grip, Natalie feels that Vivianne is extracting a promise from her. Strangely, she doesn't mind.

"Laszlo hasn't told us anything about you. You'll have to start from the beginning."

"I'd like nothing better. I'm a born exhibitionist. Wait until you know me."

Vivianne's eyes are transparent. They appear backless. Natalie crosses the deep blue outer rim and risks the iris. There is no further barrier. On the contrary, she has the sense of being invited to look through Vivianne's clear eyes into her soul—a pleasant if fanciful notion.

"LuLu, come here," Vivianne calls to Laszlo. He is wrestling with the boys. "And bring my shopping bag."

She reaches into the bag and pulls out a pair of Adidas, the sneakers of Stephan's heart. She ties the laces together and slings them around her neck, wearing them as casually as if they were pearls. She doesn't mention them. She acts as if the whole world wears size six sneakers in just such a fashion. Stephan's eyes are popping. He looks to Natalie who is equally puzzled. Vivianne continues to rummage in her bag. When Stephan can stand it no longer he asks, "Are those yours?" fearful she will say yes, they are.

"I thought you would never ask," Vivianne answers. She bends her neck, inviting him to unyoke her. "I'm Vivianne," she says, "and I've been wanting to meet you for a long time."

"Thank you," Stephan breathes. "How did you know?"

Vivianne points to Laszlo. Stephan turns and gives Laszlo an excited hug.

Adam gets his own membership card to the Museum of Modern Art. "Thank you," he says and shows it to Natalie with the intense nonchalance of a teenager flashing his first driver's license.

"Thank Laszlo," Vivianne protests. "I chose but Laszlo told me all about the two of you."

"It's no one's birthday," Stephan volunteers.

"We're celebrating our engagement," Vivianne says.

"And the launching of your business," Laszlo adds.

"What business?" Gregory asks.

"Tell him, *chérie*," Laszlo says to Vivianne. He walks over to her.

"No, you do it, LuLu." She puts her arms around his waist, kisses his cheek. "Boast for me."

"Very well, *idiote*. If you insist. Even among Americans Vivianne is conspicuous for her energy," Laszlo says. "She is a born entrepreneur. Imagine, exporting sea urchins!"

"Sea urchins?" from both boys.

"Yes," Vivianne breaks in. "You know them?"

A chorus of nos.

"They resemble small rocks covered with the quills of a porcupine. Ugly little creatures to look at but delicious to eat."

"You eat them?" Stephan asks.

"You Americans, no. But we French adore them. They are very dear in France just now. A great demand and a disappearing supply. My plan is to take them from California—there are millions of them in the water there—and fly them fresh every day to France." She claps her hands.

"The problem has been with the government," Laszlo explains, holding one of her small hands between his own. "In fact, that is how and why we met. We had the same lawyer. Vivianne lacked only the export license. Today, finally, after months, she received it."

"Bravo, LuLu," Vivianne says. "It's because of you that I got it. I'm certain. He knows so many people," she tells them.

"How did you think of the idea in the first place?" Gregory asks.

"I went to Stanford University some years ago as an exchange student. There I stepped on one." She laughs. Her laugh is musical.

Natalie is dazzled. Vivianne's spontaneity is so infectious that if Natalie has not yet gotten the disease itself she has certainly caught a severe case of longing for it. She studies Vivianne during the evening. Vivianne has a capacity for pure motion, motion which is not frenzy, the motion of a plant growing toward the sun, the motion of a life lived with trembling intensity in the present. Compared to Vivianne she feels joyless and cramped.

Vivianne eats almost no dinner. She is too excited. "She lives on enthusiasm," Laszlo tells them.

"Did you grow up in France?" Adam asks.

"Yes, but I had a strange childhood. Shall I tell you about it? I'm shameless." She laughs again. Natalie laughs back in antiphony, then says, "Yes, tell us," too eagerly, before Adam can answer. She blushes. Vivianne turns a full radiant smile on her. "You have a wonderful smile," Natalie says in confusion. "And beautiful teeth."

"Thank you. I'm very particular about my teeth."

Natalie laughs. "As though being particular could produce that mouth," she says to Laszlo.

"Go on," Adam urges.

"Very well," Vivianne says. "I am one of four. There are two brothers and a sister, all older. My father held a very important position with the Bank of France and we lived quite well in a small suburb of Paris. In those days, my father was handsome as a god but he had what we called black moods. I don't remember much of it. I've been told my mother was a saint. She did her best to protect us from him when he got that way. He must have been deteriorating for years but she refused to see it. She is loyal to him even today and he is dead two years. Well, to come to the point, one day at work he tried to kill a man, to strangle him, and he almost succeeded. Can you imagine, in the main office of the Bank of France? It's such a snob place, so stuffy."

No one is eating except Laszlo. Gregory's fork is suspended over his plate. Natalie is leaning forward. The boys are transfixed.

"After he was committed they discovered that his junior staff had been covering for him for years. He hadn't been able to do the simplest work. I can tell you, they found there quite a mess. Can you imagine, sick as he was, his juniors adored him enough to protect him from his superiors? He must have been very unusual."

"What happened to him?" Stephan asks. "Did he go to jail?"

"No. He was sent instead to a private sanatorium. Fortunately, the Bank agreed to continue paying him his full salary. The problem was that it took most of the money to keep him in that place and the five of us had to live on what was left. We were very poor while he was living in luxury with good brandy and Havana cigars and a personal psychiatrist at his elbow. I remember visiting him once and he was wearing silk pajamas with his initials on the pocket. My mother wouldn't hear a word against him even though we were so poor that she had to sew all our clothes herself. She wouldn't hear of moving him to a state institution."

"Is he still there?" Adam asks.

"No, dear," she reminds him gently. "He died two years ago."

"Did he die there?"

"No. He went into that place when I was seven and came out when I was seventeen. He was still handsome but still crazy. A week after he came home to live, my mother borrowed some money and sent me to a boarding school. My brothers and sister were out of the house by then. My mother lived alone with him until he died, nineteen years, and for all those years she lived in fear of her life. You see, he tried to kill her and she wouldn't report it because she knew he would be locked away again for the rest of his life."

"Did he try to strangle her too?" from Stephan.

"No. He put small amounts of poison in her morning tea. She found out about it because she began to feel ill and the poison showed up in a blood test. She never ate or drank anything again without great fear. At night she slept with her door locked and a chair propped under the knob. While he was alive she never told anyone. She wanted us to believe he was cured."

"Did you get teased while he was in the asylum?" Stephan asks. For some time now he has been out of step at school.

"Yes," Vivianne answers.

"Me too," Stephan says under his breath. Only Natalie hears him.

"It got so bad that we had to move to another village. But eventually everyone there found out. You see, my father had been a prominent man. I hated him all my life for that. Anyway," she says, managing a smile, "my mother is a changed woman since his death. She has a real life now. Finally, after all those years, she has friends, she goes places and does things. She was his jailer, you see, which meant that they were both in prison."

There is silence when she finishes. It is only after she is gone that the bomb she placed in their dining room goes off. Fragments from the explosion will be imbedded in Natalie's mind forever. When the boys have been put to bed and she and Gregory are doing the dishes, he says to her, "I like Vivianne but I find it hard to believe that story she told us. Do you suppose she's not as—well, you know what I mean, not as—"

Natalie lets him struggle. She is in a rage. "Are you trying to suggest that she's a liar?"

"No, not a liar exactly. I think maybe she exaggerated the story out of proportion to the events."

"What for? You think she needs to make her life more interesting? Can't you face up to the fact that people live with one kind of violence or another all their lives? Just look at us!" she orders him in a voice that doesn't sound anything like her own. "Two perfectly normal people, aren't we?" Her voice breaks with anger. She clears her throat and goes on. "Your parents died in an air crash. They were burned and broken. Remember, you were actually afraid to look in your father's coffin for fear of what you might see? Look at my father. Shot to death. And my mother, part of her jaw eaten away by cancer. My God, you read the papers. Four of them a day. Look what's happening. Death and torture. It's happening. Real people are being maimed and killed. Babies are thrown off rooftops every day. And you have the nerve to question Vivianne's story? By comparison to some her childhood was tame. What does it take to make things real to you? Are you going to keep your feelings buried forever?" She ends with a shout, her fists clenched around the dish towel.

"All I said was that I thought she had exaggerated a little. You hardly know her so why are you overreacting like this? You're not yourself tonight," Gregory says in a calm, even voice.

For an answer, Natalie hits him. She hits him but stuns

them both. "Well," is all Gregory can say as he stands there, rubbing his cheek. Natalie can think of nothing to say, nothing that he would understand. And she's not certain she would understand it either.

CHAPTER

19

"WELL?" LASZLO ASKS.

"She's marvelous," Natalie answers, cradling the phone between her neck and shoulder so that she can finish rinsing the breakfast dishes.

"Good. I knew you would like her."

"When are you getting married?"

"Soon. We haven't picked a date yet."

"Gregory and I would like to give the wedding."

"I don't know. I'll talk to Vivi."

"Nothing formal. Don't worry. Just a few friends here at the house."

"I'll see. I'll let you know. By the way, what's going on with you? I don't like the way you look. You have dark circles under your eyes and you're far too thin."

"Everything is fine."

"That's not what I'm asking. Your friend?"

"Oh." She puts down the sponge and takes the receiver in her hand.

"Well?"

"I'm still seeing him."

"Still?" His sigh is one of deep, hoarse disapproval.

She waits, leaning weakly against the edge of the sink.

"Do you want to talk about it?" He sounds reluctant himself.

"I can't."

"I've told Vivi. You can talk to her."

"Laszlo!"

"She's very sympathetic. She's the perfect one to speak to. She doesn't make judgments."

"That's not the point. Besides, everyone makes judgments."

"Well, then, hers are softer than most. *Elle a vécu, tu sais.*"

"Yes, I'm sure she has but I don't even know her."

"That's why it would be easy to talk to her."

"No."

"All right," he sighs. "Just tell me one thing. Are you thinking of leaving Gregory?"

"No."

"You're certain?"

"Yes."

"Good." This time his sigh is one of distinct relief. There is a brief pause and then he says, "I'll let you know about the wedding soon."

Natalie replaces the receiver and returns to the sink. The phone rings again immediately.

"It's only me," Laszlo says. "I forgot the main reason I called. I have to be in Washington for a few days next week and Vivi is going with me. I want you to come along and keep her company. I'll be very busy and she doesn't know the city at all."

"Laszlo!" she protests.

"Think about it," he answers rapidly and hangs up.

"I have to go out of town for a few days next week," Natalie tells Tom the following morning. They are stretched out in the garden on canvas lounges, one of her gifts to him.

"Why?" he asks, sitting up, screening his eyes from the sun with his hand.

"A scheme of Laszlo's."

"What does that mean?" He pulls on his sweater.

"Vivi and Laszlo and I are going to Washington together. Laszlo is determined that Vivi and I get to know one another as quickly as possible."

"That stinks."

"I don't want to go."

"Then don't."

"It's important to Laszlo. Besides, I know you have work you want to do."

"I'd rather be with you."

"You are."

He gets up and stands over her chair. His shadow covers her. "Come inside," he says.

"Not now."

"Why not?"

"I don't know. Later."

There is silence. Then he shrugs. "All right."

But it isn't. Natalie studies his face. The all right is only a front. Under its cover he is communing bitterly with himself.

After lunch he announces stiffly that he has work to do. She gets up, gathers her things.

"Stop," he says, crossing to the front door, taking her pocketbook from her hands. "Don't go, please. I was being stupid and childish." While he speaks he looks at the floor.

She sighs, careful to keep the sound concealed in her chest. What he can't know is that this simple confession has obligated her to him more profoundly than any show of love.

Natalie knows she has an instinct for engaging life alone, on her own terms, which means visible yet safely hidden. Her connection to anything communal is, by choice, tenuous. Outside of her family, she can point, though no longer with pride, to neither close alliances nor loose friendships. Tom is the first exception. Vivi seems determined to make herself the second. She will use any means at her disposal. She resembles Tom in this respect. The means they have in common are charm, energy, wit, openness and a talent for friendship. Vivi has kept Natalie in a state of happy disorientation since they left New York forty-eight hours ago. For the most part they have been alone. Laszlo joins them only for late dinners. Even then, he forms a backdrop for their conversational fancies. Their laughter bounces off him, amplified. Though he smiles at them, the motion of his lips is purely decorative. Try as they may, they cannot move him to share their delight.

It is Friday morning. Spring. Washington is enameled in shades of *rose d'or* and grass-green, the colors applied delicately to its unglazed stone surface in the style of Ku Yüeh-hsüan, as Natalie is just now explaining to Vivi.

They are waiting on line at the visitors entrance to the White House. Vivi listens patiently but without marked enthusiasm for the subject matter. There is a look of approval on her face for the speaker, however. Natalie, turning her gaze from the flowering trees to Vivi, catches it and blushes.

"A small enterprise but rewarding, *non?*" Vivi asks.

"Collecting?"

"Friendship."

"Yes." Natalie laughs. There is no doubt that Vivi sees the world aslant, yet how congenial the angle.

Vivi chatters on, building their friendship with words, darting back and forth with bits and twigs of her life, her feelings, herself. Her voice is high and pleasing. Birdsong.

"No," Vivi is saying as the line snakes slowly along the fence. "I don't agree. I think the problem is deeper. He's in a terrible depression. After we had dinner at your house, for five days he didn't leave the apartment. He played music on the hi-fi, only Bach, and sometimes he cried."

"Have you called a doctor?"

"Yes. He gives some pills but I don't think Laszlo takes them. He hasn't touched me since I return from California." She sighs. "He tells me it will pass, that it's happened like this before."

Vivianne's eyes are disturbing. Something has seeped in to dilute the blue. Into the sky also. A large cloud has moved across the sun. A gust of damp, raw air buffets the line. Vivi shivers, thrusts her hands more deeply into the pockets of her coat.

"Do you really care about seeing this?" Natalie asks, gesturing toward the building.

"Not really. I'm bored of being a good tourist. My eyes are tired and my feet hurt, both."

"Let's go."

"Where do we go?" Vivi asks as they sneak from the line like conspirators.

"How about a good, hot breakfast," Natalie suggests. The wind is blowing seriously now.

"Bon. Where?"

Natalie thinks a moment. "There's a lovely old hotel around here. Just let me get my bearings." She digs in her pocketbook for the map Gregory forced her to take. Gregory at the elbow of her consciousness. She smiles. Well, he would be pleased to know that she is voluntarily consulting a map. Gregory is a believer in accurate orientation in geophysical space. He refuses to ask for directions, preferring to put his trust in the professional cartographer. This is not merely stubbornness, he argues. His larger aim is self-sufficiency. Natalie studies the map. When she refolds it, there is on her face the confident, near-zealous smile of a convert.

The dining room is pleasantly full. While they wait to be seated Natalie scans the restaurant. For the most part, the patrons seem to be hard at work over their coffee and toast. Negotiations are in progress at all the nearby tables. The studied faces of people who want something from each other. Vivi wants something from her. She is quite open in her pursuit of it. Why can't she be more like Vivi? Why is she still so suspicious?

"This hotel is like Europe," Vivi comments as they sit down. "I feel very comfortable in the ambience. It's a well-known place?"

"I think so. Tom and I spent a day here once. It's his favorite hotel."

"Ah, yes," Vivi says. "Tom. You know, of course, that Laszlo told me."

"Yes."

"It's not finished?"

"Yes and no," Natalie answers. She doesn't lift her eyes from the menu.

"A difficult stage, *non?*"

"Yes. Very."

"I am in a difficult stage also," Vivi says.

"But I thought everything was decided," Natalie says, looking up, distressed.

"I haven't told Laszlo. I don't dare to tell him. I'm pregnant. Three months."

"But that's wonderful," Natalie says, closing the menu firmly and smiling.

"For me, yes. There is nothing more beautiful. All my life I wait for a child."

"Then why—?"

"It's Laszlo."

"Laszlo will be very happy."

"You think so? Truly?"

"I'm sure of it. Tell him," Natalie urges. "You'll see that I'm right."

"Perhaps. But I wait for the right moment. When he is feeling better."

"This news will make him feel better. I'm so happy for you, Vivi."

"Thank you." She smiles sadly. "I am equal parts happiness and superstition," she says, toying with her water glass. "I have a great fear. I don't deceive myself. I'm not young anymore." She lifts her head and looks piercingly at Natalie. "And this is work for young women."

"You'll be fine. You're strong."

"Oh, I don't worry for myself. It's for the baby." She shrugs. "What makes you think I'm strong?"

"I don't know. Your energy, I suppose."

"My energy." She shakes her head. "Before I came to the States I was so depressed I committed myself for a sleep cure."

"A sleep cure?"

"You don't know this treatment?"

"No."

"I went to a clinic in Paris and the doctors in that place put me to sleep for three weeks. That's five hundred and four hours. Imagine, I was awake for only fifty of them. So you see, here is the true source for all the energy."

"Did it help?"

"For the moment."

"I could never do it." Natalie shudders at the prospect. "All that time lost. It's like being dead."

"A bit, perhaps."

"Then you're very brave."

"No, not at all. Desperation often resembles bravery."

Natalie feels a rush of sympathy. It is a difficult moment for both of them. Vivi liberates them by laughing. She turns her attention to the menu.

"Let's order something delicious," she says. "Have you decided?"

"Yes."

Vivi signals the waiter with a wave of her hand. He acknowledges her request for service with a nod, and approaches.

If only, thinks Natalie as she prepares to give her order,

if only there were such simple, direct, unambiguous signals for friendship, if only a wave and a nod could do it. Words don't work for her as they do for Vivi. All she can do to convey her desire is to smile shyly and hope that the open and passionate woman sitting opposite her, this woman who seems to have experienced everything, can also read her mind.

CHAPTER

20

THERE ARE STILL MOMENTS WHEN LASZLO IS QUINTES-sentially himself. Natalie, crossing the foyer of her apartment to greet him, her arms opening, a smile forming on her lips as it does each time she thinks of Vivianne's news, catches him during one of these. His back is to her, his body in motion. He is wrestling with coat and hanger. As usual his lack of physical competence gives the scene a comical twist. Natalie's smile widens. Poor Laszlo! All his life beset by active resistance from the inanimate. When he has succeeded in subduing his coat he stuffs it in the closet. Once again the inanimate will have the last word. The coat slips from the hanger and slides to the floor. Laszlo turns and faces her. What Natalie sees shocks her, sends deep vibrations through her. What he has done is simple enough. Merely shaved off his beard, his moustache. Merely cut off his hair. Simple? Reckless. Carnivorous. Inexplicable. More than facial hair has been excised here. The landmarks by which to identify him are gone, the spacing between nose, lips, chin, ears eliminated along with the wild black bramble. What is this oversized Adam's apple? This long, scrawny neck, the neck of a goose? She tries to control her face.

"Don't make a tragedy of it," Laszlo warns.

"Vivi didn't tell me," Natalie answers.

"She doesn't know. I did it this afternoon."

"I suppose I'll get used to it. What made you do it?"

"A whim."

"It's quite a shock. You look so different."

199

"Badly, you mean."

"Yes, to be truthful. Awful. I think you should grow it back."

"No, I don't think I will."

To think, it is this smooth sallow mask she will have to embrace now. In the absence of a beard, Natalie notices for the first time just how hairy Laszlo is elsewhere. Hair at the base of his throat, on his knuckles, along the rim of his ears, poking out of his narrow nostrils, pushing up around his collar, curling over the edges of his watch face. When he sinks down into a chair and his slacks ride up, she can see that even his legs are mossy.

Vivianne arrives. She takes it in stride. "Well, at least now I know that I didn't fall in love with you for your magnificent beard." She kisses him experimentally a few times. "Yes," she pronounces, "it's an improvement. My nose doesn't tickle."

Laszlo's smile is false, perfunctory. He receives the remaining opinions, Gregory's and the boys', in the same fraudulent spirit.

"Natalie tells me the final word came in on the fund," Gregory says as he pours the wine. "Rough, but try not to let it get you down. Something else is bound to turn up."

"It's of no consequence," Laszlo says in a flat, strained voice, his despair as naked as his mouth. "I'm used to failure."

A short, precise, terrible pronouncement. Vivianne inhales sharply then presses white knuckles to her lips. She and Natalie exchange frightened looks. Natalie turns to Gregory, a mute plea on her face. He understands what is expected of him and intercedes.

"Vivi, Laszlo," he says, raising his glass. "I'd like to propose a toast to both of you. To a very happy marriage, as happy as ours."

Glasses are extended and meet. There is the clear ring of fine crystal. Then Vivi speaks. Her chin is trembling. "I want to add something to the toast. To the future of our child." She looks at Laszlo. "I am *enceinte*. Three months gone."

For a long moment Laszlo's glass hangs in space. Then he brings it down hard. "No," he says, and again and louder, "No." There is enormous momentum behind the second no. Tremendous. He strides from the room. Another moment passes. Natalie rushes after him. Vivianne follows, her face frozen, streaked with tears. Natalie flings out an arm to stop her. She points through the doorway. Laszlo is collapsed in a chair with his eyes closed, groping wildly for his beard like a blind man who has misplaced some crucial thing.

Vivianne runs to him. She kneels at his feet, lays her head on his sharp knees, wraps her arms around his calves.

Choking back a sob, Natalie retreats to the dining room.

She is still sitting there when Vivianne returns. They are alone. Laszlo has gone home and Gregory, pleading work, has retired to his study.

"Well," Vivi sighs, "there's no point pretending. He's not prepared for a child. He is so mistrustful of things domestic."

"What did he say?" Natalie asks.

"He apologized, of course. He says once he gets used to the idea he'll be as happy about it as I am."

"I'm sure he will."

Vivi shakes her head.

"Let's not say any false things. We both know the truth. I've known it all along and that's why I waited to tell him. I was afraid. He doesn't see the family as a true value, only a thing of economics. Nothing more. He's still a member of the loyal opposition." She smiles tenderly at the notion. "All I could do was to tell him how much I love him."

"And?"

"And then he asked me what I thought love was for."

"What love is for?"

"Yes."

"What did you answer?"

"To make life bearable."

"And?"

"And he said, what if it doesn't?"

When Natalie can speak she asks, "What are you going to do?"

"I don't know."

"The wedding?"

"I don't know. I think we should continue as we are. I don't need to be married. He said he would rather talk about it tomorrow. He was too tired tonight."

"And the baby?"

"The baby," Vivianne breathes. "I want to keep it so badly. I don't know what to do." She lays her head on the table. "I feel in such danger," she says softly.

Natalie bends over her. Touching her fingers to her own lips, she presses them to Vivianne's forehead. Vivi smiles sadly, a sidelong smile, her face still resting on the glass.

At the door they embrace. Though Vivi is over three months gone and increasing every day, to the touch she feels smaller than ever.

"Call me tomorrow," Natalie says. She puts her arm around Vivi as they walk down the hall. Vivi doesn't answer. She appears not to have heard. Natalie keeps her arm where it is, sensing she must hold on because Vivi is losing dimensionality, disappearing from her side.

"Vivi," she says, gently.

Vivi looks up, startled. "Yes?"

"Please call me first thing tomorrow."

"Of course."

As Vivi steps into the elevator, Natalie can see that she has begun to shiver. Under her bulky, oversized sweater, the narrow shoulders are drawn in. At last glimpse, Vivi is huddling inside her own crossed arms, trying to get warm. The intensity of what Natalie sees, Vivi's loneliness made so graphic, moves her to a deep sadness. Beyond any doubt, Laszlo and Vivi belong together. And yet, she muses, chilled herself by the thought, and yet, how precarious everything, even certainty, is.

Natalie can't concentrate on her book. She has read the same sentence a dozen times and it will not yield. She gets out of bed and goes downstairs, looking for company. Gregory is just finishing, gathering up his papers, shutting off the lights. There is something of the old-fashioned schoolboy, weary but staunch, in his appearance.

"Hi," she says, softly. "How did it go? Did you finish?"

"No. It finished me. This work isn't really designed to be completed, just to exhaust you and make you feel inadequate. It's meant for a younger man."

This is a conceit, Natalie knows. These days he thinks of himself as a "younger man." "Can I get you something from the kitchen?" she asks.

"No, thanks." He stretches his arms overhead and rotates his neck from side to side.

They walk upstairs arm in arm. Natalie waits until they are in bed, until the room is dark. "Gregory?"

"Hmmn?"

"Are you listening?"

"I'm trying but I'm absolutely dead."

"Oh."

"What is it?"

"It's Laszlo. I'm worried about what happened tonight. He's not himself." As she says this she knows it's not true. If anything, Laszlo is more himself than ever. Too much himself. Himself to the limit, past any question of degree. Dangerously himself. "Life is an offense against logic, dear girl," he used to tell her. "One must rejoice in that." And he did, then.

"I don't know how many times you've told me lately that Laszlo's not himself. Well, you better get used to it because whether you approve or not, this is obviously the new Laszlo. Christ, it was stupid of Vivianne to spring the news on him like that. What did she expect? Cheers?"

"Let's leave Vivi out of this. She's upset enough as it is."

"Leave her out? I don't understand you anymore. Face it, Natalie, you have one set of standards for Vivianne and another for everyone else."

"I don't understand what you have against her. She likes you."

"Come on. You know that's not true. I bore her to death. But you won't admit it because then you might have to question her."

"You sound jealous. I don't believe it."

"Jealous?" he snorts. "Is that what you think? Well, you can keep your precious, self-centered Vivi. And Laszlo too. Even his own mother couldn't take him."

He grabs a fistful of blanket and wrenches himself away from her onto his side, leaving her uncovered. The bed shakes with the violence of his maneuver. "I suppose you've been reading Hermine's diaries?" she asks.

"Yes."

"I see." What does she see? What has she ever seen? Everything? Nothing. "Scrutiny [her speciality] is of a lesser order than seeing." A notion of Tom's, out of context to be sure, but a custom fit nevertheless.

"Goodnight," Gregory says after a while from his side of the bed. There is a hint of conciliation in his voice.

"Goodnight," she responds, in kind, from hers, a canyon between them. What a large social lie sharing is.

A good night's sleep, Gregory's remedy for everything. Right or wrong, following his own prescription he has dozed off and she is alone. She's in for it now. The instant she closes her eyes the images come. She cannot find a way to turn them off. She tries to remember what Tom once told her about mental pictures. They are not kinds of paintings. They are not visual images. They do not have the form of objects. They are made up of movements, of attitudes, of gestures. Memories of these. At the moment the movements and gestures and attitudes are crowding her, moving in at breakneck speed. She is ambushed every night by these dreadful thought portraits. She puts a pillow over her head. Too late. The film is running, her eyelids a screen. She forces her eyes open. Her brain becomes the screen. Can you turn off a brain? Shrapnel is flying. A bursting charge of movement, gesture and attitude hits her. Her mother's face, half a jaw. Natalie sees the missing part, the hole where once there was a face. Funereal. Banked in gardenias. Heat and curled brown edges. She pushes the face away. A sheet takes its place. She peels it back as indeed she must, a long list of musts, every night the same long list. Hermine lies there, a fetal skeleton, all head. She presses her fists into her eyes. Why should she have to witness these deaths over and over? Her imaginings are bottomless, her panic Malthusian. Her children are getting closer. They hurtle by her outstretched hands and fall to their deaths. Who can live with such imaginings, such fears? She tries to imagine herself out of existence and fails. Poetry: One cannot look directly at either the sun or death. Very well, she will move toward the sun with her eyes closed. She will burn up in outer space if this is what it takes to die in one's imagination, if this is what it takes to sleep. She will speed up her pulse rate to eleven per second. She will pulse in tempo with Vela. She will merge with that rare celestial body if this is what it takes. And then if Gregory and his kind are right, if pulsars do die, if a good night's sleep puts everything right, she will have gotten her wish. In the meantime the movement, gesture and attitude which add up to a remembrance of Vela are bringing her a kind of strange comfort. Enough comfort for the moment. Enough so she can let go of her fears. Enough so that she can fall asleep.

CHAPTER

21

IF A MIND CAN BE SAID TO TWITCH, TOM'S IS DOING SO.
Waiting for Natalie puts him into this nervous condition.
They see each other twice a week. Twice weekly at
9:00 A.M. he is subjected to these unnerving mental tics
which make concentration on any serious work impossible.
The odd thing is that he doesn't miss her during the other
five days of the week. In fact, he's relieved to have his freedom back. But—a disquieting but—the sound of her key
in the lock still has the power to jolt him. With her arrival
all emptiness disappears.

He is worn out this morning. Barbara woke him at six.
Sex with Barbara has improved enough to exhaust him.
Early morning sex, which she prefers, numbs him for the
rest of the day. Twice a week at home. Twice a week with
Natalie. It's compulsory and it's an effort since his drive
has settled back to its normal low level. He has accepted
his nature. If only the women in his life would. He wonders why women assume all men to be highly sexed. His
theory is that each century produces a few rogues with a
talent for public boasting and this vocal minority gives the
rest of its gender a reputation for lust. The last thing in
the world he feels like doing is getting back into bed. The
thought of yet another morning shower makes him groan.
Today, he has a legitimate excuse. He can desist without
guilt. There won't be time enough. Within the hour he has
to be on his way uptown to attend a political send-off. A
friend of Barbara's is announcing her bid for a City Coun-
cil seat. His presence is not required but since Barbara is

chairing the finance committee it seems only decent that he put in an appearance. Barbara continues to amaze him. Yesterday, in a fit of strenuous good spirits, she whistled the entire cello part of Beethoven's Trio in B-flat Major, opus 11. She is a whirlwind of purposeful activity these days. She has given up running with her Men. Laura partners her now. His soft, golden, dimpled pet of a daughter is thinning out and toughening up. He is living with a pair of Amazons. No, they correct him. Not Amazons. Jocks! What next? he asks them as they bend over his side of the bed in their sleeveless T-shirts and satin track shorts and beribboned braids to kiss him goodbye. 6:30 A.M.! What next? Bullet-deflecting bracelets? Bionic knees? They are an impressive pair. He tells them so. Amazons have their virtues. They tell him they are entering the International Women's Marathon over the Fourth of July weekend. They will not be joining him at his parents'.

The sound of Natalie's key in the lock unlocks him from his reverie. He jumps to his feet. Once she is in his arms reverie is superfluous, Barbara is superfluous, even Laura fades from his mind.

She and Tom are having coffee. Tom is reading a "think piece" to her, a reexamination of the Whitney Biennial. The biennial comes off just as badly as it did the first time around, a review which Tom also read to her. Who needs another review, particularly if it draws blood? If it were Gregory behind the paper he would be reading to her about the latest development in chip computers. She is so sick of information. She wonders where the essay has gone. She hasn't come across one in a long time, at least not in a public place, not out in the open where anyone can have access to it. Even when an essay is bad it has moral posture going for it. The writer takes a stand. There is some tension. Some texture. Some thickness. This Tom would understand if she wanted to tell him. Life, she could tell him, life like certain sauces is improved by thickening. He would flash her an adoring smile, his star pupil. She can sound like him if she wants to.

She waits until he puts down the paper. Then she says, "I want to talk to you."

"Sure. What about?"

"About us."

"What about us?" He pours himself a second cup of coffee and raises it to his lips, raises his eyes to hers.

"I think it would be better if we stopped seeing each other."

His sip turns into a gulp and Natalie can see that he has scalded his tongue. "Shit," he says, slamming down the mug.

Natalie waits.

"Don't be an idiot," he says, rubbing his tongue with the corner of his napkin. "Why should we stop seeing each other?"

He seems to feel that he can't manage without seeing her. Natalie knows this isn't true but he is saying it over and over so he must believe it. What can she say? She wants to be truthful. She owes him the truth. The truth is that her feelings have changed. His have changed too, she assures him very gently.

"It was bound to happen," she says. "Things never stay the same."

"I know what my feelings are," he says. "I don't need you to tell me." He gets up and goes to the window. He stands there looking a little dazed, staring into the garden. "I don't believe this is happening." He takes off his glasses and rubs his eyes.

"I don't either," she says in a low voice.

He wheels around to face her, his glasses, forgotten, dangling from his hand. "Well, damn it then, do something about it."

"What is there to do?" she pleads.

"Forget you ever brought up the subject."

"I didn't invent the subject. It exists."

"I don't understand why we can't keep things the way they are."

"Things don't stand still. You know that as well as I do."

"Don't try to make me your accomplice in this. I don't want any part of it. You can take all the credit."

"I don't want you to be angry."

"What should I be? Happy? Would you rather I thank you instead?"

"What are you talking about?" She is in tears.

"I love you and you're telling me it's over," he yells.

"What kind of reaction do you expect? Some phony decency crap? 'Of course, I understand and it's okay.' Shit," he says and his voice breaks.

She bows her head. He stands there, shaking his head helplessly, his lips clamped together. There is a long, unnatural silence which she is afraid to break. He shatters it at last with a deep sigh. He replaces his glasses and walks over to her. He drops a weary hand on the top of her head and leaves it there. Her neck begins to ache from the pressure. All his pain is in his hand. It weighs on her.

"I'm so sorry," she says, reaching up to stroke his wrist.

A mutual sigh. "I'll never love anyone again the way I loved you," he says, taking her hand in his, sitting down next to her.

"I won't either," she says in a small voice.

Now that he has joined her in reading responsively from a text assigned centuries ago, things are smoothing out. In this text, love is eternal. Though they part, they will love each other until they die or until the fear of death forces them to look elsewhere for love. Perhaps he is already thinking about elsewhere. She is not mistaken. He said "loved," past tense.

They sit looking mournfully at each other, then at their laps. Finally, she rises to go.

"I'll see you here next week," he says. "I need some time to get used to the idea."

"So do I," she admits, grateful for the reprieve.

The intervening week is ruinous. In the terrible absence of love, Tom is forced to take a true reading of himself. It is a desperate piece of autobiography. For the first time in his life he broods. He has difficulty going to his studio. Once their cradle, it is now his graveyard. Natalie has buried her love here and urged him to do the same. He has tried but his own won't stay underground in spite of her predictions to the contrary. He discovers that his love for her is labyrinthine. He traces and retraces his steps but his memories are false guides, leading him only deeper and deeper into loss. In the end, he can find no way out.

Another loss: The irony he expects of himself, the irony he needs for insulation has deserted—a chilling piece of irony in itself. What follows is a moment of painful clarity in which he glimpses himself as he was before he met

Natalie, as he will be again without her—a man driven to persuade the world of his worth and doing it on technical brilliance alone. Not an easy thing any longer, for what he has lost along with Natalie is his continuity. He has suffered a major displacement. A fault has opened in his soul. He can feel the pain. He knows it is a serious fracture, one which is beyond his skill to treat.

He also knows that Natalie will never change her mind. He will just have to find his meaning in the future where he found it in the past, in the distraction of friends and work. If history can still be trusted, he should get some added consolation soon. He knows that what often follows on the heels of a great but impossible love affair is a burst of intense, creative energy. He isn't counting on it.

It goes on and on. Natalie has thought it ended but now, standing in front of Tom's door, fumbling for her key, she feels weak and sentimental. In a moment, she is facing him. He is dressed—no bathrobe—wearing a shirt she doesn't recognize. He looks confused, shy. Neither of them says a word. Finally, he takes her hand. He holds it silently. She can feel parts of her love reviving in the heat generated by their joined hands. She can feel her resolve weakening. She wants to say something which will dissolve the sudden monstrous formality which has arisen between them. He is Tom, after all. Tom. Nothing comes. What could there be?

"I'm going to fix us a farewell breakfast," he says, relinquishing her hand. "It would be inconsistent with our history to part on an empty stomach."

She receives a bright smile. Artificial light. His staginess brings her near tears. She wants to comfort him. She wants to tilt her body forward into his arms. She wants to return them to that brief, enchanted period when their love and preoccupation with it were of equal weight. Agreeing to see him again was a mistake. The week has just made things worse for him. He looks haggard, sunken around the eyes.

"You don't look well," she says.

"Neither do you," he responds, pouring her a cup of coffee.

"I know. I haven't been sleeping."

"Isn't there some way we could—"

"No," she interrupts, gently, staring down at her cup.

"I'm trying not to hate you," he says.

She looks up. Their eyes meet. His smile is genuine this time.

"But it's a struggle," he adds.

"One I hope you win."

"We'll see," he says. "I'm not sure I want to win it."

She shrugs helplessly.

"Well," he sighs, "Laszlo certainly was right."

She raises her eyebrows.

"You once told me he said lovers could never be friends."

"Oh, that." She tries to smile. "He seems to have managed it with Vivianne."

"I'd rather not hear about Laszlo's good luck," he says, moving toward the kitchen. "Is an omelet all right with you?"

"Anything," she says, although she doesn't see how she can manage solid food.

"If you prefer something else, just say so and I'll see what I can do."

"Oh, no. I meant an omelet would be fine. How is Laura?" she asks, raising her voice a little so he can hear her.

"Fine. She did something very touching the other day," he says, coming back into the living room with a bowl of eggs in his hands. "I must have been looking pretty miserable this week because at one point I overheard her talking to a friend on the phone. She was saying, 'I can't come this weekend. My father is really down. He hasn't even looked at his work so we know it's serious. My mother thinks we should both hang around and keep him company. She thinks he's having a crisis.' The kid never left my side. She even bought me this shirt as a present."

Natalie hears the catch in his voice. "Did it help to have her around?"

"Some," he acknowledges. "Not a hell of a lot." He returns abruptly to the kitchen, whisking vigorously as he goes.

Natalie wants to follow his dancing arm, embrace him from behind, end this charade. Instead she sips at her coffee with a pinched mouth. But when she hears the eggs sizzle as they hit the pan, she smiles. The sound is so right. She hopes he is smiling too.

He is just sliding a buttery, herbed omelet onto her warm plate with one deft Gallic maneuver of his wrist when the phone rings. He rushes to answer it. "Take the croissants out of the oven, will you," he yells with his hand over the mouthpiece.

"Yes," Natalie hears him say as she juggles the hot rolls. "Just a moment, please. It's for you," he tells her, eyebrows raised. "It's a woman."

Natalie drops the rolls on the table and goes to the phone. Vivianne is the only one who knows she is here. It must be an emergency. She holds the phone with two hands to keep from dropping it. "Yes," she manages to say. "What is it?"

Vivi is hysterical, sobbing something over and over. Laszlo's name. Natalie sinks down into a chair, tries to relax her grip on the receiver as she waits for the rest. After a while other words come through Vivianne's sobs. Natalie listens for a long time. "Where are you?" she asks, a lifetime later. "Stay there," she orders. "I'll be up in fifteen minutes."

Tom is waiting to learn what happened. Natalie tells him the story as cogently as she can. He is riveted. His eyes are bright with attention.

"Laszlo went back to his old apartment this morning," she begins. Though she is blind with tears she sees it happening as she tells it. She has Homer's gift. "He told her he needed something he had stored there. She had no reason to doubt him. He kissed her goodbye and left. He went straight to the closet once he reached the old place. From the closet he went to the bathroom. He had asked permission from his tenant to use the bathroom. A call of nature, he had joked. He went straight to the bathroom window and opened it. He wedged himself into the window frame—it was such a small window—and then he jumped twelve floors to the courtyard. After a while, the tenant became suspicious and forced the door open. The police came, an ambulance came. The body was moved to the morgue pending notification of the nearest of kin. In case of emergency, they were to notify Vivianne. They did. She's waiting for me at home now. We have to identify the body." Her timing is perfect. She reaches the front door as she concludes her epic.

Tom puts his arms around her. Thank God he doesn't speak. Natalie waits for what she thinks is a decent interval before she moves out of his embrace and excuses herself. She is very conscious of the front door closing behind her. The sound she hears over and over as she sits in the cab that is taking her to Vivianne is that of Tom's door closing. She knows she has closed it for the last time. It occurs to her that she has only one more door to close, this cab door, before she must confront Vivi and the fact of Laszlo's suicide.

The door is ajar, the room in shade. Natalie sees Vivianne sitting quietly in a chair gazing out of the window. She is very still, so still she gives the impression that the slightest movement will cause her to shatter. When she turns her head to acknowledge Natalie's arrival, Natalie can hear the splintering. The tears that start in Vivi's eyes are shards of broken glass which pierce both Vivi's sockets and her own.

"Help me," Vivi says.

Natalie cradles her. It's not enough. Will anything ever be? Laszlo's suicide is not an acceptable alternative. It leaves the two of them without a grip on life just when they thought they were getting a handhold secure enough to risk pulling up on. When it becomes as painful to be together as it is to be apart, that is, when being this close only makes them feel Laszlo's absence all the more, Natalie steps back.

"I can't go to the morgue," Vivi tells her.

"You don't have to. Gregory and I will take care of it."

"Well," Vivi sighs. "At least part of the work is already done. I suppose the guest list for the wedding will do for the funeral," she says in a small tight voice, a voice even less refractive than her person.

"Yes," Natalie says.

"He wanted to be cremated, you know."

"I didn't know. We never talked about things like that."

"Yes. We should do what he wanted. I remember arguing with him about it. Cremation." She shudders. "He was quite stubborn. Natalie, I don't know what I'm going to do."

Natalie tries to find words to comfort her. She herself

feels strangely calm. She thinks of Hermine's roommate, Mrs. Miller, and Mrs. Miller's nurse, Wilhelmina. "Prayer is the only thing which help, Missus, . . . and God be the only proper teacher." She doesn't know any prayers. She does know a poem,

> We will all die, & the evidence
> is: Nothing after that.
> Honey, we don't rejoin.
> The thing meanwhile, I suppose, is to be courageous &
>   kind.

But she can't recite it aloud.

Vivi is weeping. "I can't get out of my mind the picture of him squeezed into the window. Do you know, I can feel myself falling with him? Natalie, I'm so frightened."

"I want you to come home with me now," Natalie says. "I'll pack a few things for you." What strikes her as she rummages in Vivi's closet is that Vivi has no clothes suitable for a funeral or a period of mourning. If this is true, then, conversely, her own wardrobe is appropriate for nothing else. Has her whole life been a period of mourning? She feels like laughing at this discovery. Laughter, now? She remembers that once when she questioned Tom in connection with a minor Indian miniature which showed two men chuckling at the Spectre of Death, he quoted John Cage to her: "Talking about death, we begin laughing."

She closes the suitcase, takes Vivi by the hand. One short easy flight will take them to the sidewalk yet Vivi clings to her like a toddler. Each step requires an unspoken coaxing. It is a perilous descent for them both.

Gregory insists on going to the morgue alone. When Natalie protests he forbids her to accompany him. He goes for his coat. She follows. "Forbid?" she asks. "Forbid?" She is laughing again. It takes an effort of will to stop. "First of all, *I* am going. If you want to come along, fine. In fact, I would appreciate your being there with me. Secondly, neither of us is leaving until the boys get home from school. Vivi can't be left alone."

Gregory surrenders. Grief is too formidable a weapon. He throws his coat over a chair and sits down to wait.

Vivianne is resting. Natalie gave her a Valium. Not until the pill was in her hand and she was recapping the bottle marked Vitamin C did she and Gregory realize the implication. The smile which passed between them was enough of an acknowledgment—more than an acknowledgment, another bond.

They are a solemn little group. Natalie has one child on either side of her. Gregory sits opposite. "We have some very hard news," Natalie tells them. They look at her expectantly. "Uncle Laszlo died this morning."

They sit quietly, absorbing the information. They don't say anything, don't ask any questions. They don't seem particularly shocked or even surprised. They do look embarrassed and self-conscious but this is all. Natalie pushes herself on. What she must say next takes away her breath. "He died by jumping out of a window in Grandma Hermine's old apartment."

The old apartment. She can understand why he went there to die. It was appropriate. She can accept that. But when she thinks of the loneliness that drove him there she wants to die herself.

The boys gasp. This information makes them gasp. "We have to remember that that's the way he wanted it," she tells them. "He couldn't live anymore and he did something about it. Now," she says and blots her eyes, blows her nose noisily to cover her gulping sobs, "Daddy and I are going out to make some arrangements for the funeral but Vivi is upstairs resting. I want you both to take good care of her while we're gone."

The boys stare at the ceiling as if they could see Vivi through the plaster. The fear on their faces dissuades her from continuing. "Never mind," she says. "I'll go alone and Dad can stay here with you."

"No," Stephan says, grabbing her hand. "You stay. Don't you go. Let Daddy go."

"Why?"

"I don't know why. I don't want to see Vivi without you here."

Adam doesn't have to voice his agreement. It's there in his eyes. Laszlo's death seems to be less frightening to them than Vivi's grief. Natalie looks at Gregory. He picks his coat off the chair and puts it on. "It shouldn't take too long," he tells them, giving each one a long tender kiss. "I'll be back very soon."

They approach the wall-length human filing cabinet in silence. The man at Gregory's side stops to check the slip of paper in his hand. He crooks a finger for Gregory to follow, leads him to the middle of the wall, pulls open a drawer, gestures for Gregory to look. Gregory obeys. He looks. He's not sure he can stay on his feet. No one warned him. Why not? He wants to punch the sadistic mime next to him for not speaking, for not preparing him. His anger gives him enough strength to remain standing.

"Yes," he says. "That is Mr. Várády."

It is Laszlo's body strapped to the sideless slab of a drawer. He is glad Natalie couldn't come. This is a sight not easily forgotten. Laszlo must have gone head first. Easier for him to forget, though, than the unseen, unblemished body of his own father, a small break in the neck his only injury. But because he didn't have the courage to check on things in the coffin he is stuck with the absurd fantasy that, below ground all these long years, his father is still strapped to his airplane seat and, what's worse, will be forever.

Now he needs to sit down. His escort leads him to a chair. He finishes answering the questions from there. "About fifty-eight. Uncle-in-law, wife's uncle. No, no wife but a fiancée." Saying this, he wonders how Vivi is feeling. She looked so—he always has trouble finding words to describe her—so frail and broken, leaning on Natalie's arm like an elderly convalescent. He is sorry for her, can hardly believe she once upset him so. "Yes, an American citizen, born in Hungary." Gregory signs the paper that is put in front of him. He is free to go.

By the time he gets home, Natalie has everything under control. Dinner is cooking, the boys bathing, Vivi sleeping. Natalie has a gift for transforming chaos.

"Thank you for going," she says. "I'm not sure I could have managed it. Was it awful?"

"Yes," he says, "terrible."

"As terrible as your mother?" she asks, weeping already.

"Yes. And like my father too, if I had had the sense to look."

"Oh, God," she sobs, weeping for his old, unsettled loss and her newest and darkest one.

They cry, standing a few feet apart in the shadowy foyer. Natalie puts out her hand. Gregory takes it, kisses it hard.

"I love you," she whispers.

"It's going to be all right," he says. "I promise you."

"Yes," she sighs. "It will pass."

CHAPTER

22

"DON'T YOU THINK LASZLO WOULD OBJECT TO A MEMO-rial service?" Gregory asks.

"He'll have his cremation," Natalie answers.

This much she is willing to do for him. The service, she argues, standing firm, is for the remnant of his family, for Vivi, for his friends. Gregory knows there are many friends. They will fill the seats and jam the aisles of the chapel. There will not be a priest. Natalie is planning to conduct the service. This is chief among Gregory's objections. He thinks it's crazy for a member of the family to conduct the service, particularly under the circumstances.

But Natalie has had her own way and so here he is watching numbly as she rises from his side in the first row, as she ascends the podium, as she opens a slim volume. She looks out over the congregation. She is calm. There is a theatrical hush. Even grief has its hush. He has no idea what she is going to do. She refused to discuss it with any-one. He is terrified for her. The whole thing is so unor-thodox, so out of character. He prays that this is not the beginning of another siege of depression and anxiety which will once again place her beyond his reach. This is his prayer for today. Natalie has a different one.

"Dreams drain the spirit if we dream too long."

Natalie states this simply and quietly. Sighs of confirma-tion ripple through the congregation. Behind him Gregory can hear sounds of unrestrained crying. Next to him Vivi is focused on Natalie with a terrible dumb intensity in her eyes.

"There isn't much more that can be said on a day like today. One line is enough to pierce the heart if it is a true line. The line belongs to the poet, Theodore Roethke, and now it belongs to all of us who loved Laszlo. I hope that any of you who want to talk about Laszlo will come up here and join me now."

There is a moment when no one moves, when no one breathes. Then, throughout the chapel, people begin to rise. Many speak. Many begin but cannot continue. When each one finishes he or she crosses to the far side of the podium and takes Natalie's hand. There are people paying tribute to Laszlo whom Gregory has never seen before or even heard of. He is marveling at this when Adam nudges him and whispers, "Dad, aren't you going to get up and say something?" He can't answer. He can't get up. Finally, he says to his son, "Mommy spoke for me too." She did. It's true. She spoke for everyone. Somehow she has managed what is unmanageable.

Natalie listens to Laszlo's friends. What each one is postulating in his or her own way is that Laszlo had a livable life. Then why should he have given it up? Under their tears she can hear this angry question over and over. Where was Laszlo's courage, they are asking one another. They are deeply scandalized by his suicide, by his cowardice. They feel he owes them something. If he were among them now they would take him by the lapels and shake him. They would kill him if he were not already dead. Indeed, they would wish him alive again merely to kill him for doing this to them. What Natalie understands by this is that suicide, of all life's lonely acts, the loneliest, is not a private matter, as she had thought. Society has its stake even if God does not. If a friend dies naturally, that is, not by his own hand, his friends grieve but they also feel lucky. Some even feel superior. They, after all, are still around. But if that same friend should take his own life, watch out! He threatens everyone, for if some no longer share the belief that life is worth mastering, if, in fact, some flaunt their disbelief to the extent of using it as a platform from which to jump (why not pills? they will ask her later), then what is felt by those left behind is a sense neither of luck nor superiority but of heightened danger. Laszlo's suicide had endangered them all. They are trying,

these friends of Laszlo's, but suicide is a hard thing to forgive a man, as hard as treason was in the days when men
still believed in their countries. And, as for the pills, a man
might be forgiven those because his intention could be
open to doubt, that is, if one needed to doubt the intent.

Natalie would agree with Laszlo that under some conditions life might not be worth living. She has experienced
these conditions but only for short periods, periods too
brief to permit the suspicion to harden into a certainty.
Her greatest grief is that Laszlo's did harden. She can still
hear him saying that everyone he had ever loved except for
her was dead. She supposes, and with a sigh, that when
she goes over his life, and it's inevitable that she will, she
will turn up all the other clues he left lying around—he
was always careless—but which she even more carelessly
didn't notice at the time. Ah, even so, she thinks, as the
mourners file by, a suicide is never NOT a surprise. If one
tries it and doesn't succeed, one is dismissed as a fraud. If
the fraud should finally succeed one day, well! When anyone actually does it, the living are always struck dumb
with surprise. Who among the consenters to life can ever
imagine such a thing?

Now Laszlo has joined all those he loved. His ashes are
buried in the family plot which Gregory bought for them
when Hermine died. Though she couldn't say exactly why,
the fact of his ashes being buried gives her back some of
the comfort that the fact of his cremation took away. There
are some other things which give her comfort and about
which, if asked, she could say exactly why: Her children.
Her husband. Vivi. Certain parts of Hermine's diaries, certain memories of Hermine. Certain poems. Certain of her
bedside readings, those which speculate on the nature and
existence of God, and a certain small newspaper article
dealing with the nature and naming of pulsars which just
may be what has helped her to make sense of everything
else.

CHAPTER

23

At the end of September, Natalie opens her first class with this statement: "All translation is an attempt to accomplish what is impossible."

Concerning this as well as other attempts at the impossible, what keeps us going is the aspiration. We live in hope of redemption for our imperfect selves. She doesn't express this last thought aloud but an inward smile reaches her lips. There are a few dozen faces looking into hers. On some she sees her own smile mirrored. This is encouraging. She continues her opening remarks.

"I believe translation to be a necessary art even if by necessity it is unsatisfactory. There is a small school which maintains that translation is death to understanding, that language grows inseparably with thought and to alter one is to kill the other. The often translated Cervantes had a low opinion of our work. Don Quixote compares translation to the wrong side of a tapestry. Though the figures do appear and we can catch their likeness, they are nonetheless partially obscured by the crossing of the diagonal threads."

There are more smiles. A few faces look eager. My God, she's the expert! Those faces out there are looking to her for enlightenment. It makes her want to laugh. Now she knows for sure that there are no experts.

"As I'm certain all of you know already, it's not usually too difficult to get hold of the literal meaning of a word or a sentence. It's the real meaning, the soul of the word or phrase or thought, that must be uncovered or what one

221

winds up with is jargon, a kind of *lingua franca,* and not literature. I'm not sure that the art of translation can be taught at all. My hope is that it can be implied and that those of you who get the implication will be saved a lot of time."

Natalie has the impression that many of the heads are bobbing up and down. Nods of agreement?

"Just one or two more thoughts. There are some personal fringe benefits for the translator though they are most assuredly not monetary."

Laughter. Can it be that she is developing a sense of humor?

"Through the act of translating, we learn or relearn or uncover for ourselves the real meaning of words we have been using or misusing all our lives. And, for those of us interested in language, this is a wonderful bonus. Finally, let me pass along to you the words of an obscure late-nineteenth-century translater: 'The choice of words in translation is what the selection of color is in a painting.' Now, obscure is the significant word here. Never mind the quotation. In much of contemporary painting, color has ceased to be the point. Fashions change."

There is real laughter, deep and generous.

"Obscure in two senses," she continues when the room quiets down. "First, the obvious meaning of being inconspicuous, of being not noticeable. This profession is a guarantee of obscurity. We are noticed only when we don't do our work gracefully. Second, obscure in the sense that the work of translation is toward an infinite goal and, as in the pursuit of all infinite goals, much along the way is veiled or hidden, as on the wrong side of a tapestry.

"So much for my general remarks," she says. "Next week we'll take up tenses." There are a few good-natured groans. Natalie smiles. "Look at it this way," she suggests. "Tense is a category of verbal inflection found in some languages which enables human beings to make time distinctions. I know it's difficult to generate real enthusiasm for something as impersonal as tense but where would we be without it? Tense is the great enabler of our language. The past tense permits us to remember. The present one allows us to exist in the moment. Then there is the future tense. In a way it is the most important one of all because it enables us to dream."

The burst of applause which follows brings Natalie to her feet. "The Russians do this," she says and, blushing, applauds them in return.

When the last student leaves, she exhales deeply. Her shoulders drop a few inches. On impulse she looks down at her hand, the hand she burned last Thanksgiving when Gregory and the boys were in Florida, when Laszlo and Vivi were in the country, when she was with Tom. Almost a year now, and the year and the burn gone without a trace. Correction. There are several traces, important ones. Vivi's baby will be born soon. Her own boys, poised in a new and necessary stage, are eager to teach her how to think, how to behave. Their advice is usually quite sound. This, Gregory says, shouldn't surprise her. It does. Gregory has survived his crisis and remains in substance what he was before—although recently, much to Natalie's joy, some unlikely ripples of ambiguity have begun to make their way across the surface of his precise mind. As for herself, though she is as aware as ever of the nearness of death, she no longer has a quarrel with it nor will she as long as it doesn't prevent her discovering what it is that is required of her; what it is she requires of herself. As long as it doesn't prevent her earning her way from one moment to the next. For this, she thinks as she waits for the elevator at the center of a crowd of students, this, after all the loss, the pain, the fear and the moments of clear, bright, sufficient joy, is what she is at last doing, and what she must go on trying to do.

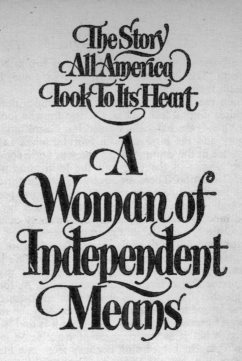

The Story
All America
Took To Its Heart

A Woman of Independent Means

A Novel by
**Elizabeth
Forsythe
Hailey**

THE SPLENDID
NATIONAL BESTSELLER

"Nothing about it is ordinary . . . irresistible."
Los Angeles Times

"Bares the soul of an independent American housewife . . .
a woman to respect . . . a writer to remember."
John Barkham Reviews

AVON $2.50